a sweet hockey romcom

Perfectly WEDDED

Grace Worthington

Perfectly Wedded by Grace Worthington

Copyright © 2024 by Grace Worthington

All rights reserved.

ISBN: 979-8-9887709-4-7

Published by Poets & Saints Publishing

Character design: Alt 19 Creative

This novel is a work of fiction. Characters are the product of the author's imagination or are used fictitiously.

Visit graceworthington.com for a free romcom novella and bonus scenes!

To every girl who's dreamed of finding someone who will promise them forever—and keep that promise.

Note for Readers

In *Perfectly Wedded*, you'll get to see Vale and Sloan's story, but you might be curious about Brax and Jaz, who are already married in this book.

Their love story unfolds in the previous book in another series, *The Roommate Remodel*. While you don't need to read *The Roommate Remodel* first to enjoy *Perfectly Wedded*, it might give you a deeper understanding of their journey and how they fell in love.

Each of my books can be enjoyed as a standalone, but if you'd like to explore Brax and Jaz's story next, it features:

🤍A protective hero

🤍Accidental Roommates

🤍Second chance romance

🤍Introduces the Carolina Crushers Hockey Team

You can find it on Amazon.

Happy reading!

—Grace

ONE

Sloan

I wake to the most impossible dream. A strong hand wrapped around my waist, connected to an arm sculpted by years of working out, all roped tendons and chiseled ridges of muscle. Then another sensation: warmth, followed by the heady scent of cinnamon.

I know that smell. It's my favorite scent in the world. *Him.*

I force my eyes open, struggling to remember last night. I went to the ice-skating gala before heading back to my hotel room. Someone was with me.

I blink against the dim light filtering through the curtains, and the reality hits—Vale is next to me. *In my bed.*

My phone buzzes on the nightstand, jolting me back to reality. I grab it quickly, trying not to wake him.

JAZ

What's going on? Is Vale with you in Vegas?!

I glance at Vale, still asleep, his arm draped over me. My fingers fumble over the screen.

SLOAN

He's just helping me out, no big deal.

I try to wriggle out from under his grasp, but the weight of his arm keeps me pinned down, like he's not letting me go. I blink, hoping I'm just imagining things.

Yep, still there.

I've landed a hockey player in my bed. And not just any hockey player—my good friend. Which means things just got seriously complicated.

Problem two? I can't remember what happened last night. Ever since the car accident, my memory has gaps—*a brief amnesia*, my doctor calls it. I struggle to recall specifics until something triggers the memory like a landslide. But without that trigger, I'm left with nothing but what's in front of me. And what's in front of me is my very single friend who I've had a crush on since he started renting a room in the house I own with my sister.

A sliver of sunlight sneaks through the curtains of my swanky Vegas hotel room. Vale had insisted on separate rooms—he even paid for them—just to make sure I wouldn't back out of the fancy skating gala. Since my car accident, Vale's been my self-appointed bodyguard. He's not just good-looking—*Kevin Costner has nothing on him*—but he also has stellar reflexes when I faint, which, unfortunately, happens more often than I'd like since the accident.

When I showed up with him at the gala, people couldn't stop gawking at the hottest hockey player in the industry standing next to me. Too bad everything after that moment is a blank spot in my mind, like someone took a giant eraser and just wiped it clean.

When Vale wakes up, I can't let on that I don't know what happened between us. Maybe if I escape this hotel room and head back to the ballroom where the gala was held, something will trigger the memory.

Carefully, I inch toward the edge of the bed, sliding out from under him. The phone buzzes again, louder this time, and Vale stirs. I dive to silence it.

JAZ

> Seriously? You never take him to your skating events. Vale rarely asks for time off this close to hockey season. Something's up.

My mind spins, still foggy, and I wince as I trip over my stiletto on the floor. My memory's a mess, and I wish I could say it was because I partied hard last night. But I didn't even have a drop of alcohol.

So how in the hockey did we end up in the same bed?

I'd never risk crossing the line with my friend, no matter how long I have to carry this Olympic-sized torch for him. Telling Vale how I really feel would only jeopardize everything we have.

My gaze lands on his bare shoulders, so unfairly muscular and tanned, it's a crying shame all that beauty goes to waste. Vale hasn't dated anyone seriously since he moved to Sully's Beach to play for the Carolina Crushers. We've been friends ever since, but he's never shown an interest in being more than that, which is why I can't let this little crush of mine ever become a "thing." It's too risky.

SLOAN

> Nothing's up. Honestly, Jaz, my memory's a little fuzzy this morning.

JAZ

> What do you mean, fuzzy? Are you okay?

I sigh, guilt bubbling up.

SLOAN

> No, just the usual . . . you know, since the accident. I'll fill you in later.

JAZ

> Does Brax know Vale is in Vegas?

My stomach knots. I forgot about problem three—Vale's

brother is my sister's husband. This problem of mine has now become a family affair.

SLOAN

How should I know? We'll talk when I get home. Must get coffee first.

JAZ

I can't wait that long!!!

My phone buzzes in my hand repeatedly. Jaz is trying to call me.

I grab my stilettos and sling them over my shoulder before glancing down at my black nightie. I can't wear this out. But I also can't stay and risk waking up Vale with the noise. And my sister's in no mood to let me off the hook.

Besides, this is Vegas, and no one will bat an eye if I wear a nightgown like a dress. Anything goes in this town, and I mean *anything*.

I tiptoe across the suite, grabbing my wallet on the way out.

A sleepy voice breaks the silence. "Where are you going?"

I wheel around to face Vale, my face flaring with heat.

He's sitting up in bed, the sharp outlines of his bare muscles reminding me that he's more gorgeous than any man should be. His long waves are mussed up just enough to be sexy. Everything in me begs to crawl back into bed next to him, but if I did, I'd probably be electrocuted by all that hotness.

"I'm just heading out for a walk," I say, linking my hands behind my back.

"In your nightgown?" he asks with a frown.

I'm so busted.

I glance down at my sleepwear and paste on a smile that feels as fake as the Vegas strip. "Couldn't it pass for a dress?"

He looks it over, and something heats in his gaze before his eyes snap shut, like a wet blanket over a flame. "I can't let you go out like that."

"Vale, it's Vegas. No one will bat an eye." I motion at the door with my thumb. "I was grabbing coffee. You want some?"

"Let me make you a cup," he says, springing out of bed toward the fancy coffeemaker.

For the first time, I see that he's wearing clothes—joggers that show off his narrow waist and hips. I swear the man could look good in a plastic shopping bag. I let out a puff of air, relieved that he isn't wearing less. Because if he were, I'd die right here on the spot.

I hold up my hand to stop him. "No offense, but I want a latte."

"Then I'll go with you," he says.

"I was hoping to go alone."

Vale's lips tighten, but he doesn't argue.

I hate letting him down, but right now, I need to leave and sort through my memory of last night. For some reason, Vale felt *obligated* to sleep next to me and I want to know why.

Because that's what I am to him: *an obligation.* Nothing more.

He frowns, then nods. "Here. Take some money." He plucks a twenty from his wallet and tosses it on the table.

"No, thank you," I say firmly, spinning on my heel. "I can pay for my own."

He catches my arm at the door, places the bill into my hand, and closes my fist around it.

"Sloan, take it," he urges, then grabs his suit coat hanging from the back of a chair. His eyes graze across the strap of my nightgown before his face flicks to mine. "And my coat, to cover you up." He slides it around my shoulders, his fingers grazing my skin like a hot match.

I let out a nervous laugh. "Why should I? It's not like we're on a date."

He looks at me, puzzled. "You're right. We're *not* on a date. But I think I'm allowed to be a little protective. After all, I am your husband."

My heart skips a beat. *Did he just say husband?* I wheel around, sure I misheard him. A panicky laugh escapes my lips, because this is hysterical. Vale and I couldn't be married, because I would remember *that*.

"Wait—what did you say?" I stammer. "Because I thought I heard you say *husband*."

He looks at me, dead serious. "I did. Which means I'm paying for my wife's coffee."

My wife.

The words knock the breath out of me as memories flood in from last night.

A bubblegum-pink Vegas chapel.

A kiss fumbled at the altar.

The memories slam into me as my stomach rolls.

I accidentally married my best friend last night.

TWO

Vale

THE NIGHT BEFORE

"My personal Kevin Costner," Sloan says as we walk across the ballroom of the skating gala. "Can I call you that for the weekend? How about Kev, for short?"

"Only in Vegas," I say. "But please don't introduce me as your bodyguard."

She tilts her head, a smile playing on her full pink lips. "Then how should I introduce you tonight?"

"That's up to you, but if you call me 'Kev,' I might have to start calling you 'Whitney'—for *The Bodyguard* vibes, obviously."

She laughs and her smile is as mesmerizing as the silver sparkly gown she wears, clinging to her body in all the right ways. I can't stop staring at her tonight, and it hits me—if I make the NHL, I'll have to leave this behind. Leave *her* behind. The thought gnaws at me, but right now, she has no idea how stunning she looks, or how hard it is for me to stay focused on anything else. But I can't let myself want her that way—not when we're only just friends.

"Has anyone told you that you look amazing tonight?" I ask.

She slides a hand across the waist of her gown. "In this old thing? I wear it to clean the house all the time."

I laugh. "I'd like to see that when we get home. So what's first on the agenda? Dancing? Food? Dodging that idiot ex of yours?"

"Definitely the last one," she says glancing around.

So far, we haven't seen Anthony, and I want it to stay that way. I never thought Sloan would accept my offer of accompanying her to Vegas last-minute. She's ridiculously stubborn about being independent, even though her coaching income is a sliver of my hockey pay.

"I know how awkward this event must be for you." She glances toward the crowd before her gaze lands on the buffet table, which looks like it's about to collapse under the weight of an enormous feast.

"This isn't about me," I say. "You've worked your butt off since the accident to go back to coaching. Tonight is all about *you.*"

Sloan grins. "Well, right now, this girl needs food, and that buffet is calling my name."

"Lead the way, and I'll make sure no one cuts in line. Perks of having your own personal bodyguard."

"Oh, by the way, I got a call from my doctor's office before I came downstairs," she says as we move along the buffet. "They have a new medicine for me, and they want me to start on it when I return from Vegas."

"That's great, Sloan," I say, then notice the hesitation on her face. "Why don't you look happy about this?"

"Apparently, the first experimental treatment only has a temporary effect. The doctor said I'll need to be on this new drug for a year or two, to let my brain heal. Unfortunately, my insurance doesn't cover it. It's too new of a drug, and the pills are outrageously expensive." She pauses, then looks away. "So I told them no."

I shake my head. "That's unacceptable, Sloan. You *have* to get these drugs."

She shrugs. "I can't. They said they would keep petitioning my insurance to cover the drug. So maybe sometime in the future it will get approved, but until then . . . I wait." She moves ahead in line, like this conversation is over.

"No, you can't wait on something as important as your health. If you need to be on it for two years, you should start now."

"Vale," she says, stopping and turning toward me. "I can't even afford it for a month, much less two years."

I wanted tonight to feel like a celebration, and now the mood has been dampened by one phone call. My mind shuffles through doctors I know, people who could pull strings, but I come up empty.

"Maybe another option will appear," I say as we find a table in the corner.

A tiny crease forms between her brows. "Do you have a fairy godmother I could borrow? Because the doctor said if I don't start on this soon, the chances of this relapse continuing long-term increase dramatically."

A long-term relapse would be a devastating blow. When my brother and I first rented rooms at their place, she spent half the day in bed because of her injury. Then the depression hit. The last thing I want is her falling back into that black hole.

"This new drug is the answer," I say. "There's no other choice."

"I know, but my coaching salary will never cover it. I'll have to quit my job and find a new one." She sets down her fork, like she's suddenly lost her appetite. "I'm not like you, Vale. I don't move for a job opportunity. Sully's Beach, South Carolina is my home."

Home. I've never known what that is since I've spent my whole career moving around for hockey. All my life, I've wanted one thing—to play in the NHL. And it's within reach now, closer than ever. But the thought of moving away from Sully's Beach and leaving Sloan behind? I'm not ready for it.

"The last thing I want is for this news to ruin your evening," I say. "We'll figure it out, even if it means I pay for the medicine."

She scoffs. "I wouldn't let you do that for me. I could never pay you back."

"Consider it a loan from a friend."

She frowns. "That's the type of thing that ruins friendships. And I won't sacrifice our friendship for money." She gives me a pointed look, her eyes locking with mine, and for a second, I can't look away.

"Sloan, if I make it to the NHL, you wouldn't need to pay me back."

"It was one thing to let the team do their fundraiser for me, but it's another to borrow from you personally. Even if you make the NHL—which you will—I'd be eaten alive with guilt."

I put down my fork and look at her. "It's better than you getting another job. You love being a college skating coach more than anything."

She shrugs and her strap slips a little. "I do. But I'll be okay, no matter what happens."

I reach out to adjust the strap of her gown, my fingers brushing against her bare skin for just a second. "Okay is not good enough." Her eyes flick to mine, and for a beat, the world narrows to just us. Those eyes look like trouble—time to back off. Sloan is my friend. *Only* my friend.

I drop my gaze as she picks at her food. "The only way I could get a new insurance plan is if I changed jobs or married, and neither of those things are going to happen—unless you know any princes I could marry?" Her eyes flick over my shoulder and she suddenly goes rigid. Then she slides off her barstool to cower behind me.

"What are you doing?" I ask, turning to face her. As I spin around, my knees brush against hers, sending a jolt through me.

"Anthony just walked into the room with his new girlfriend," she whispers.

I turn and glance over my shoulder. A man with a sharp-cut jaw and bleached-blond hair strides across the floor, holding the hand of a woman who looks at least a decade younger. As he moves through the room, he greets everyone, like he's the unofficial mayor of Vegas. Then his eyes scan the room and stop on us.

"Um, Sloan?" I murmur.

"What?"

"He's headed this way. What do you want me to do?"

"I don't know. Pretend we're talking?"

I glance over my shoulder. "It's not stopping him."

"Got any other ideas?"

"Other than punch him in the face?" I ask.

She points at me. "Under no circumstances can you do that," she warns. "Even if that's the girl he cheated on me with."

"Wait, he cheated on you?" I growl as my fingers curl into fists.

"It happened right after the accident. He said it was because he was lonely and sad."

I grip my fork like a weapon. "You know what will make him sad? If I shove this in his eyeball."

Sloan puts her hand on mine. "Lower the fork, Kevin Costner. I need you to stay civil."

"After what he did?" I ask. "He did not deserve you. Do you want me to make sure he doesn't get to you? Because I know how to play defense."

"I'm not a hockey puck, Vale," she says.

"You're not, but you are mine to take care of this weekend. And I'll do anything to keep that man away from you, even if I have to pretend to be your boyfriend."

The truth is, I'd do it for real in a heartbeat, but I can't let her know that.

Her eyes widen. "You wouldn't," she dares.

I smile wickedly. "Just watch me."

THREE

Sloan

I let those words sink in . . . and then I panic. *Vale is pretending to be my boyfriend?* How am I supposed to keep it together when just looking at him does funny things to me?

Anthony saunters to our table while I decide whether to cry or throw up or launch myself onto Vale's lap.

"If it isn't Sloan Summers, the comeback kid," Anthony says with his usual thick Southern drawl. This might sound like a compliment, but coming from Anthony, it's meant as a childish jab.

"Hello, Anthony," I deadpan. "Did you come to show off your new girlfriend, or do you just enjoy being a nuisance?"

Anthony laughs that stupid chuckle of his. "I'm glad to see you still have your sense of humor."

Another jab. As if my brain injury has taken away everything else. "Yes, I still have my humor, the one thing I conveniently kept after my accident. Unfortunately, I lost the filter over my mouth, so you might want to leave before I accidentally blurt out what I think about you."

Anthony's smile freezes. For a second, he looks nervous.

From his barstool, Vale loops his arm around my waist. My whole body zings in response, and I struggle to keep my expression neutral. My heart's knocking against my rib cage, but I can't let him know that. I'm supposed to look like this is *completely normal*—like his touch doesn't affect me at all.

Vale shoots me a proud smile. "That's my girl."

My girl. I love how those two words make me feel like I'm all his. But I can't get used to Vale treating me this way. Not when it's only an act for tonight.

Anthony motions toward his girlfriend. "Have you met Demetria yet?" The raven-haired beauty sidles up to him in a black dress so tight, it might as well be a second skin. With her green eyes, she looks like a feral cat.

"Yes, I know the woman you cheated on me with," I say with a tight smile.

Anthony clears his throat.

Vale stands, easily towering over my ex. "I'm Vale MacPherson."

"You look familiar," Anthony says, studying Vale, before shaking his hand.

"He's a hockey player," I gush, turning toward Anthony with a smug grin. "A media darling. Women line up for him." I throw an exaggerated smile Vale's way, making it seem like I'm wildly in love. His hand tightens at my waist, pulling me closer, and I lean into him, maybe a little too eagerly.

"There's only one woman I care about." Vale's eyes cut slowly to mine. "Guess that's what happens when you're in love."

I nearly choke on my drink. *Love?* Like that wouldn't totally ruin our friendship.

Anthony clears his throat. "You're dating?"

"We are," Vale says, his thumb making slow circles on the curve of my waist, driving me crazy.

"She didn't force you to attend tonight?"

"Force? Um, *no.* Have you seen how hot she is?" Vale's eyes trail down my body, leaving scorch marks in their tracks. Even though I know it's all for Anthony's sake, my skin is burning up. Vale pulls me into his chest so that my back is pressed into his granite-cut abs, and my sad sap of a heart rockets against my ribs. "We're celebrating tonight."

"No better place to celebrate than Vegas," Anthony says. "What's the occasion?"

Vale's fingers brush my waist—torturously slow, like he knows exactly what he's doing to me. "We're celebrating her full recovery . . . a weekend away for *us*." This might be for Anthony's benefit, but it's working so well, my heart feels like it could launch me to the moon.

Vale stares down Anthony as he circles his thumb along my waist. "Do you remember when she was laid up for months? Oh wait, you wouldn't remember, because you were *gone*."

I have to bite my cheek to keep from laughing—and inwardly, I'm pumping both fists. Gutsy move, insulting my ex.

Irritation flickers across Anthony's face before he straightens his shoulders. "Have you heard our good news?"

"That Demetria won her last competition?" I grab my water, trying to hide my disgust over the fact that he's her coach, even though it's unprofessional for coaches to date their clients.

"No," Anthony says. "Demetria and I just got engaged."

For a moment, my knees go weak, like I've been gut-punched. *Engaged?*

When we were together, Anthony always told me he would be a bachelor for life, even though I stupidly thought that I could change his mind. I'm not in love with Anthony, and I don't want him back. But it's still devastating.

Vale gently pulls me closer, as if to remind me he's here. "How coincidental," he says, filling in the awkward silence. "Because we also have news."

My face snaps toward Vale. Is he referring to my health relapse or that I'm back to working at my underpaid coaching gig? Because both of those pale in comparison to Anthony's announcement. "Uh, Vale, we don't have any news."

He gives me a confident smirk, and I know he's up to something. "We don't have to hide it, sweetie. Everyone's going to find out eventually."

Sweetie? I almost bust out laughing. Vale has never called anyone *sweetie* before or any other pet name.

"Find out what?" Anthony asks, looking from Vale to me. I sip my water and avoid Demetria's glare.

Vale spins toward Anthony. "Sloan and I are engaged too," he announces as if it's the most natural thing in the world.

The words hit like a bomb, and I choke on my drink, spraying it everywhere, while trying to smile and nod like this isn't a total shock.

"Oh, I'm so sorry," I stammer, fumbling for my napkin, and offering it to Demetria to wipe away the mess. There's no way I'm going to touch the cleavage real estate falling out of that dress. *It's like an entire state.*

"My fiancée gets choked up whenever I tell people," Vale remarks, patting me on the back. "It's just so emotional for her. Isn't it, *sweet cheeks?*" He tweaks my face, and I give him a glare that warns him to never call me that again.

"Of course, my little *Fruit Loop,*" I say sweetly.

Vale lifts an eyebrow. *That's the best you could come up with?*

"I didn't even know you were dating anyone," Anthony says.

"Well, it just happened *so fast,*" I say, thinking on my feet. "And we really aren't telling people yet." I hide my left hand behind Vale's back since my ringless finger would be a dead giveaway.

"I see," Anthony says, studying me. "Well, if you'll excuse us, we have more people to talk to tonight." He saunters off, Demetria tagging behind.

Now that the show is over, I step away from Vale, even though I liked his hands all over me. I hold up my fist for a quick bump, just to make it clear we're back in the friend zone. *No harm done. Just over here scrubbing that memory from my mind!* "That. Was. Perfection."

Vale hesitates for a second, his brows knitting together before his fist meets mine. "Whatever it takes, right?"

"Thank you, Vale—my adorable *Lucky Charm*," I add, pinching his cheek, just like he did to me earlier.

Vale grimaces. "Are you going to keep calling me cereal names?"

I laugh. "You don't like them?"

"Couldn't you call me stud-muffin? Or hot stuff?"

I laugh. "*Please*, those are so basic. You deserve something with more flair."

He shrugs. "I'm kind of a basic guy."

"Not to me," I say, shaking my head. "And definitely not with those abs."

Vale smirks. "You noticed my abs, huh?"

"Um, hello? It's hard not to notice when they're practically begging for attention." I say. "I might need to splash some cold water on my neck after that. Could you hang out here for a minute while I head to the restroom?"

"Sure, but if I find any leftover cheesecake, I'm not sharing."

"You better leave some of that cheesecake for me," I say, glancing back at him with a smile. As I head toward the ladies' room, a few women make eye contact with me.

"Congratulations on the news," one woman says.

"Oh?" I wonder if she has me confused for someone else.

"Your future husband is gorgeous," she adds with a sheepish smile.

"He's not . . ." Then I stop myself. That's when I realize why she's congratulating me. I quickly text Vale from the ladies' room.

SLOAN

Word about our engagement has leaked, Cap'n Crunch.

VALE

I just had a woman tell me she's sad I'm no longer "on the market." Like this is a meat market and I'm a side of beef.

SLOAN

You are pretty smokin' hot.

VALE

That's Cap'n Hottie Pants to you. 😊

I feel a zip of nervousness spider down me. How am I going to face everyone now that they think I'm engaged to Vale? For hockey fans, Vale is a freaking rock star. Not only is he a highly regarded public figure, but a sex symbol. Nobody's going to believe we're engaged.

When I return to the gala, I spot Vale across the room, talking to a beautiful woman I've never seen before. Other ladies walk by him and openly stare, and it's no wonder. Even in his tux he gives off smoldering vibes, with his beard and dark hair grazing his collar.

I watch from behind the chocolate fountain, my eyes locked on Vale. I hate the twist of jealousy inside me. He's not even mine. But as I watch her hand brush his arm, I can't help the knot forming in my stomach.

Vale wheels around, then strides over. "Were you standing there the whole time?"

"Watching you talk to that gorgeous woman? Yes," I admit. It kills me that I'm even feeling jealous right now. I know he's just faking his attraction to me tonight, but I want Vale all to myself.

"She doesn't hold a candle to you," he murmurs, making something spiral inside me. Then he cuts into a piece of cinnamon creme brûlée and holds up his fork for me. "Try this. It'll make you feel better."

He watches as I nearly melt from how good it is. "Are you using dessert to distract me?" I say, lifting a brow.

"Is it working?"

"Like a charm. But I'm still not letting you off the hook."

Vale offers me another bite and seems amused by how much I like it. "You think I'd ever want someone like her? Then you really don't know me."

I stop, mid-bite. "You're just saying that." That's the thing about Vale. He's always thinking of how he can cheer me up.

He holds up his fork. "I only speak the truth, my little *Cinnamon Toast Crunch*."

I laugh. "Only you could make a cereal sound remotely sexy."

"It's one of my many talents—besides playing a role in your Kevin Costner fantasy."

The music kicks up as couples flood the dance floor. Vale holds out his hand, and my pulse speeds up.

"Since we're supposed to be practically falling all over each other, would you care to dance with me?" he asks.

Is this a good idea? Probably not. But right now, my decision-making skills are on vacation—somewhere far, far away. I nod and he intertwines his fingers with mine while I try to ignore the way my skin tingles.

My goodness, his hands are massively huge. How will any other man's hands compare now that I've touched Vale's?

He pulls me close on the dance floor, and it's everything I can do to keep up the act. We move in sync, his body warm and solid against mine, and for a moment, I forget we're pretending— everything about this feels too natural, too right. When the song ends, I step backward, feeling the tension rise between us, unsure of where to put my hands or what to say. Without missing a beat, Vale takes my hand, his thumb brushing over mine.

Vale strides confidently across the room, completely unfazed by the attention he's getting tonight. He's used to charming the socks off people, and he easily slips into the role of becoming my hype team as we make our way through the crush of people.

"Have you met my beautiful fiancée, Sloan?" he says to a

stranger. The pride in his voice almost sounds believable. "She's the best college skating coach in the country."

I whisper under my breath. "*Vale.* You're embarrassing me."

"What? It's true," he whispers with that smile that makes me wish this night would never end. Vale's completely lovely and charming, and he's already perfected the role of playing my fiancé.

"What do you want to do after this?" he asks, handing me a glass of water.

"I'll probably head to bed," I say, taking a sip, cooling the heat in my body.

Vale's smile drops. "You're in the city that never sleeps, and you're planning to go to bed?"

"What's wrong with that?" I shrug. "I'm normally in my pajamas by this time, like an eighty-year-old lady."

He frowns, while holding back a smirk. "At your age, you should definitely stay out until at least midnight."

"I don't even know if I remember how to have fun."

"Then it's settled," he says, taking my cup and setting it down. "Tonight, you're going to see the real Vegas with me. And I guarantee to give you the time of your life."

FOUR

Vale

"Vegas is the city of love!" our driver, Tony, proclaims to us as we sit in the back of the rented limo.

"I thought that was Paris," I mumble to Sloan, who's entranced by the blinding lights of the city.

"With the number of wedding chapels we have, I'm *sure* it's Vegas," Tony says with the confidence of a man who makes his money from tourists' tips. In other words, *he's blowing smoke.*

We pass extraordinary hotels, more casinos than I can count, and a few wedding chapels. Everything is dazzlingly bright, and my brain can't fathom the fact that I'm in Vegas with Sloan.

As Tony weaves through traffic, Sloan's leg brushes against mine, and heat floods the spot where our legs meet, spreading through me like wildfire.

"Sorry," she mumbles as she scoots away.

As soon as Tony turns the corner, it happens again, and this time, my hand lands on her knee, holding it down. Her eyes cut to where my palm rests, but she doesn't pull away. "What are you doing, Vale?" she whispers.

Honestly? *I'm not sure.* But this feels right.

"If we're engaged," I say, nodding toward our driver. "Shouldn't we act like it?"

She swallows and looks out the window, trying to hide the flush on her cheeks.

Tony asks if we want to explore the city on foot while he gets gas. He lets us out at the corner, and points us toward a strip of tourist traps.

We pass by a wedding chapel with a pink sign from the 1950s that blinks, "Little Pink Chapel of Love." A couple stumbles out the chapel doors, their cheeks radiant, their eyes hungry for each other. The bride is wearing a satiny pink dress that matches the sign, complete with a ribbon across her chest that says *Just Married!* The groom drinks her in. He can't keep his eyes—or his hands—off her.

They stop on the sidewalk and he sweeps her into his arms, kissing her intensely.

The bride's eyes fly open. "We're in the way," she squeaks to her groom.

"Don't stop for us," Sloan says with a cheeky grin. "You deserve to hog the sidewalk."

She steps away from her husband long enough to hold up a sparkly diamond. "My boyfriend and I came to Las Vegas on a whim and decided to get married! We weren't even thinking about tying the knot before, but then we saw this chapel and thought, *why not?*"

I glance at Sloan and raise my eyebrows. "How long have you been together?"

"Two months," the groom replies with a lovesick smile.

"Two months?" Sloan gasps. "Were you friends before that?"

"Nope!" the bride says proudly. "We were set up on a blind date. My family won't believe this!" She squeals as the groom lifts her in his arms and kisses her again.

Sloan laughs. "Well, if that's not a whirlwind romance, I don't know what is! Good luck!"

We leave them to their celebrating as we head away from the chapel. Sloan keeps her eyes on the ground, like she's thinking about something. "Can you imagine getting married after only two months?"

"I guess if you know someone's right for you, why wouldn't you?" I look at her for a beat before looking away.

"I've known you for a couple years, and that's not enough time to know for sure. But *two months*? That's *nothing* in comparison," she says. "What if one of them gets sick or is in an accident? How can a two-month relationship survive that?"

I frown, thinking about Sloan's situation. I'm not married to her, and I'd be willing to give my right arm to make her better. "That's why you need to get on that medicine, no matter what it takes."

"Well, it's going to take about ten thousand dollars a month, so maybe if I sell my kidney illegally on the internet, I could afford it." She looks up at me with a tired smile, and I want so badly to fix everything, to brush her cheek and tell her it's going to be alright. This is really wearing her down. Exhaustion lines her eyes, and I can see the worry behind her smile.

That's when an idea hits me. *Marrying Sloan could be the solution.* A temporary arrangement until she's better. The clock is ticking on her health, and I can't stand the thought of her getting worse. If she doesn't get this treatment, she'll lose everything she's fought for—and I can't watch that happen.

"You know, there's another option," I begin, glancing back at the chapel. "It doesn't even require you to give up a kidney."

"What's that?" she asks.

I sink my hands into my pockets and avoid her gaze. If I look at her now, I know I'll chicken out. "Well, you just need insurance, right? What if you could get it? You wouldn't need ten thousand a month then."

"Yeah, well, my insurance doesn't cover it, so that's a closed door."

"Unless . . ." I stop, then turn to her. ". . .you got married."

A laugh bursts from her lips. "That's funny, since I'm not

even dating anyone. But I guess it could happen." She points to the pair outside the chapel. "That couple has only been dating two months."

"Exactly," I say. "What if you married someone you've known almost two years?" It's a crazy idea but I have to try.

Her smile drops off her face and her eyes widen. "Are you suggesting . . ."

I nod.

She gasps and shakes her head. "No, Vale! I could never agree to that. You can't even say that out loud. *Absolutely* not."

I step closer to her and touch her arm. "Sloan, you know I'd do anything for you. Let me do this."

I've always been her friend, but right now, standing this close to her, I feel something that scares me—something I've tried to push aside for too long. I'd have to stuff these feelings away, and pretend it's just for her sake, but deep down, I'd know the truth.

She springs back, like my hand is burning her. "This is ridiculous. We're not even dating!"

"I know *that*," I say. "I'm not asking you to be in love with me. This is a way I can provide for you—*as a friend*. I have good insurance, better than yours. If we get married, you would have access to it and could get the medicine you need. You told me the doctor says you'll have to be on it for a year or two. That's not even that long."

As I say the words, my heart hammers in my chest. I'm putting everything on the line, not just our friendship, but this fragile balance we've built. I know there's a chance she'll walk away—that she'll say no and everything will fall apart. But I have to try. I have to make her see that this could solve everything for her.

She shakes her head. "I couldn't let you do that for me, Vale."

"Why not?"

"Because you might miss out on someone else," she argues.

"Who? I'm not even dating anyone."

"I don't know . . . the woman of your dreams?!"

I drag a hand over my face. "Sloan. Who says I'm going to meet the woman of my dreams in the next year?"

She shrugs. "It's just a possibility. But I can't let you take that chance."

"What if I want to? What if I don't care about anyone else?" I'm being stubborn, and she knows it.

"Well, I won't let you not care!" she shoots back. "You might be my friend, but I will not marry you for your insurance. The answer is *no*. I'll find another way." The panic flares in her eyes as she wheels away from me.

I get it. This *is* crazy. But what terrifies me more than anything is the thought of her saying no. If she doesn't take the medicine, and her symptoms get worse—then she'll fall back into that black hole of depression and sickness.

She bolts down the sidewalk, trying to avoid me.

I follow, catching up before she can turn down an alley. I take her shoulders, forcing her to a stop. "Sloan, there is no other way. If we get married here, I can take care of you."

She finally meets my gaze, her chest heaving from the sprint. "How are we going to explain this to Jaz and Brax? How about your teammates? You don't think they'll see through our little charade right away?"

"Not if we come up with a story. We'll tell them we realized we were in love and decided to go for it, just like that other couple."

"They'll *never* believe us," she says, shaking her head. "Not out of the blue like this."

"They will if we make it *look* believable," I say. "Sloan, you can't let your doubts stop you. I'd never forgive myself if something happened to you and I didn't do everything I could to help." I hate that I'm pushing her like this, but this is too important to give up on.

She studies me for a moment and something breaks in her expression. "I don't know if I can do it, Vale. I'm a terrible liar," she says, her voice wavering. "Why do you think I won't play poker with you?"

I chuckle. "This isn't poker, Sloan."

"Easy for you to say," she says, slapping me on the chest. "You played your part tonight like a pro."

"That's because it was *you*." I catch myself and quickly add, "You're my friend. It's easy to step into whatever role you need." That's only partially true. It wasn't easy because we're friends—it's easy because being close to her feels right in a way I can't explain.

"What happens when I don't need the drug anymore? Then what—we just end it?"

I hold her gaze, my throat tightening. "We don't have to figure that out now," I say, my voice quieter. "We'll deal with it when we get there. Right now, all I care about is making sure you're okay." I hesitate, feeling the weight of my words.

She frowns. "But what if I have to take the medicine for four or five years? You'd be stuck with me and that could ruin our friendship for good. The last thing I want is for you to resent me for forcing you into a marriage that's unhappy."

I place my hands on her arms, locking eyes with her. "I could *never* resent you, Sloan. If I have to stay with you longer, I will. We're already living together, and our friendship hasn't suffered yet." I pause, offering a small smile. "Besides, you're a lot easier to live with than Leo."

She bites back a grin. "Leo wouldn't be easy for anyone to live with."

"I know you think you'll be holding me back, but I'm not looking for another woman." My voice is firm. I have to convince her that my offer of marriage doesn't come with strings attached. When it comes to her, I'm all in.

"Why would you do this for me?" she asks, searching my face.

"Because I refuse to stand by and watch you get sick again. I've seen how far you've come, and I can't watch that happen again."

"No," she finally blurts, shaking her head and stepping back. "I can't let you do this." She turns to go, but I grab her arm before she can run again.

"Sloan," I urge. "For once in your life, I need you to remember the person you were before the accident. The one who took risks. The girl who lived life to the fullest. You told me once you wanted to be her again, and now is your chance. Take a risk on *that girl*."

Her jaw clenches, and I know she feels it too: she wants to find that girl again.

She hesitates, and I feel the walls she built slowly crumble, her arguments against this turning to dust. I don't want this to ruin our friendship. But what other choice do I have? If I do nothing, Sloan will relapse and we'll all lose her.

Say yes, say yes, my heart beats like a drum. But I know better than to push her into a decision. Just because I want Sloan—the most generous, beautiful woman I know—doesn't mean I can make her marry me. She has to choose this, choose *us*, on her own.

"Okay. Let me get this straight," she says. "As long as this is only a temporary fix—a marital contract with an end date—then *maybe* I'll consider it."

"Is that a yes?" I ask, trying not to show my excitement yet. If I act too eager, I'll scare her off.

"If I say yes—*and that's a big if*—there are a few things we still have to discuss," she says.

"If this is about who changes the toilet paper roll, I think we can share that job," I say, keeping a straight face.

"No," she says with a smile, then holds up her left hand. "But you'd better put a ring on it."

I grin and point behind us. "I saw a guy on the street corner selling fake engagement rings."

She laughs. "The one with the light-up headbands?"

"A one-stop shop for all your Vegas needs," I add.

"I don't need a real ring," she says. "It's not even a *real* marriage."

"Real enough to get you the insurance you need," I say, my gaze on hers. "There's no turning back after we do this."

The finality of it settles between us.

She hesitates, then finally nods. "I'll do it, on one condition," she begins. "If at any point either of us wants out, we can walk away."

FIVE

Sloan

"The Little Pink Chapel of Love isn't as cute as the charming sign," I whisper to Vale in the lobby which is the size of a small closet. The floor is sticky, and I'm afraid if I sit down, the chair might give me a fungal infection.

Instead of white roses, I'm holding a bouquet of tacky-looking fake carnations in bubblegum pink. But the saddest part is that the only two witnesses are strangers—the officiant and his wife, who run the chapel. Reverend Clarence—who I'm slightly doubtful is an actual reverend—looks like he could fall asleep at any moment, while his white-haired wife, Eunice, can barely hear a word we say. No wonder 1950s organ music is blaring through the speakers.

They've managed the Little Pink Chapel for over fifty years, and I'm sure they're planning on dying here, more than likely in the middle of someone's ceremony. I just hope it isn't ours.

"I'm sorry about the ring," Vale whispers again as he glances at my hand.

"You can't even tell it's not real." I hold up my left hand so that the cubic zirconium stone glitters in the brassy yellow light.

He holds my hands, rubbing his thumb over the stone. "We'll

get you a new ring as soon as possible. This is only for the ceremony."

Vale glances at Clarence, who stands at the front of the chapel with his eyes closed, looking like he's ready to topple over.

"Do you think he'll wake up for the vows?" Vale asks.

"Does it matter? No one will hear us over that thundering organ anyway." I nod toward the speaker hidden behind a spray of fake lilies.

Eunice waves Vale toward his spot at the front. Then she switches the music to the wedding march as the speakers pop violently, waking Clarence from his nap.

I walk down the aisle, a knot of confusion tangling inside me. This isn't a real chapel, and we're not really in love. Vale's reasons sounded so convincing on the street, but now that I'm about to go through with this ridiculous plan, doubt washes over me—the same sort of regret you feel when undergoing a dental procedure.

This isn't what I thought my dream wedding would look like. As a little girl, I always imagined getting married outside under a lovely pergola in Granny's backyard, accompanied by a string quartet, and surrounded by an explosion of flowers. What I got instead is an outdated chapel with peeling paint, music that's making my ears bleed, and garish plastic flowers in neon colors that look like they were purchased from the dollar store.

Sure, marrying my best friend is a dream come true, but the circumstances feel all wrong. He didn't ask me out of love, and I said yes like it was a business deal. I couldn't even admit to him that I *really* wanted to date him, much less marry him. Which means, eventually, I'll have to let him go. And I don't know how I'll survive that.

When I reach the front, Vale takes my hands and smiles. He's so unfairly handsome, it almost hurts. It makes me wish we were getting married for the right reasons—out of love instead of necessity.

Reverend Clarence repeats the marriage script like he's done this in his sleep (probably because he has), and when we reach the vows, every instinct screams at me to run, to bolt down the aisle and escape this mad plan to save us from making this terrible decision. But just as the urge to flee peaks, Vale's grip on my hands tightens, like he's trying to reassure me that this is the only way, even though my voice wavers and my chest aches. How am I supposed to mean these promises when I'm hiding the truth from everyone who matters, especially Vale?

Before I can dwell too long on the words I've just recited, Clarence's voice breaks through my thoughts as he says, "You may kiss the bride."

Panic shoots through me like I've just been told to jump out of a plane without a parachute.

We never talked about the wedding kiss. Did I miss that part of the fake wedding manual? I glance at Vale, who's scanning my face like he's trying to figure out if I want to be kissed.

Eunice calls from the back, "Go on, honey."

I lean forward, hoping to get this over with as quickly as possible. But as I move, Vale shifts slightly, and I suddenly realize I'm on a collision course with his chin. I adjust in time, while Vale dips his head, and somehow—by sheer luck—our lips barely meet.

The second they touch, a spark shoots through me, like two crossed wires finally finding a connection. It's awkward and definitely not the stuff of fairy tales . . . *but it's Vale.* His kiss makes my heart do a little somersault, leaving me feeling like warm honey.

I lean into him, wanting more, but then realize my mistake. I can't want *this*.

Vale pulls away slowly, his eyes heavy on me with questions, but I'm still caught in the moment, the connection fizzing in my chest like a sparkler shooting tiny stars. Maybe he was doing this for my sake, but holy cow did it feel real.

Eunice turns on the wedding march—ruining the moment— and throws a single handful of rice at us right before she drapes a

Just Married sash across my chest. The whole ceremony is ten minutes long and quicker than a fast-food meal.

As we step outside, Tony, our driver, gives us a thumbs up. "The city of love strikes again. I can see it all over your faces."

Is he talking about *my* face? Are my feelings for Vale that obvious?

I shoot a nervous glance at my new husband, who seems unfazed by Tony's comment. "Speaking of the city of love, can we finish our tour now?"

We pile into the car, and Tony parades us around Vegas with the windows down. For a fleeting moment, it all feels like a delicious dream. *I can't actually be Vale's wife—this can't be real.* But that's the thing about Vegas. It's a lot of flashy lights and beautiful facades, and just like our marriage, it's all for show.

When we reach the hotel, still reeling from our wedding, we step into the elevator in silence. I stay pressed against one wall, Vale on the opposite side, keeping his distance. The air between us feels thick, weighted with the unspoken tension of *husband and wife,* even though I can hardly call our marital arrangement anything more than a business contract. I pretend to be distracted by the ceiling, the floor—anything but him. Every time our eyes meet, my pulse quickens, and my heart bucks as if it's forgotten this marriage is just pretend.

"Is there anything else you want to do tonight?" Vale asks from across the elevator, his voice low, eyes snagging mine. There's something heavy in the question, a weight that makes my chest tighten.

My head scrambles, grasping for anything as I fiddle with my ring. "You mean other than go to bed?"

Vale raises an eyebrow.

I quickly backtrack, my face flushing with heat. "I mean, just sleeping . . . I'm so tired!" Then I give a big fake yawn just to make my point.

A teasing grin spreads across his face. "Oh really? I wasn't aware that bed was on the agenda."

"Well, it is now." I can't wait to return to my room, where sleep will drown out my embarrassment and the spinning thoughts of what this new life with Vale really means—or what it *doesn't* mean.

Just then, the doors of the elevator slide open, and Anthony and Demetria appear on the other side. For one awkward second, we just stare at each other, and I can't believe our bad luck.

"We meet again," Anthony says, draping a lazy arm around Demetria's shoulders.

Their eyes drop to the sash draped across my body, and I suddenly realize I forgot to take it off.

"You got married tonight?" Demetria says, her face flashing with jealousy.

"Sure did," Vale answers smoothly, then shifts closer to me, his arm slipping around my waist as if it's the most natural thing in the world. "When you're crazy about each other, why wait?" His dark eyes cut to me as his fingers graze the top of my hip, warming the ice in my blood.

This is how husbands and wives are supposed to act, right? The warmth of his touch sends electricity through me, and I try to act like it's not causing my heart to flutter like a trapped hummingbird.

They step inside, and the elevator doors close, sealing us in together.

Anthony glares at Vale. "I thought you were joking when you said you were engaged."

Vale's lips press into a firm line. "I don't joke about things like marriage." Which is ironic, since our entire ceremony was a joke.

The elevator dings for our floor, and Vale's fingers intertwine with mine as we walk out together.

"Good luck," Anthony says. "Most Vegas marriages last as long as the wedding ceremony." As the elevator doors slide shut, the last thing I see is his smug grin.

I storm forward to give him a piece of my mind, but Vale pulls me back. "Forget him. He's not worth your time. We need to head back to our room before we run into anyone else." Vale pulls me down the hall, avoiding eye contact.

"Wait. Did you say *our* room?" I ask, stumbling on the carpet as he catches my elbow. His hand remains on my arm like it's permanently attached.

"If anyone sees us go into separate rooms, they'll suspect something." His jaw clenches as his eyes dart down the hallway. "I'm sorry, Sloan, but this is the only way. I hate that we have to sneak around, but running into Anthony made me realize that we're not safe letting down our guard, even for a moment."

As soon as the hotel door clicks shut behind us, my chest tightens as the weight of it all hits me like a ton of bricks. Anthony knows we're married, and none of our family or friends have the faintest idea. He could literally ruin everything with a single word.

I toss the cheap flowers into the trash with a frustrated sigh and sink into the nearest couch, my head in my hands. "What are we going to do? He could tell anyone and our secret's out."

"He won't tell." Vale leans against the door, his posture tense, as if he's not sure whether he should come in or stay where he is. Even though he rents a room in my house, it feels strange to have him in my hotel room like this. My brain knows we're pretending, but my body feels every inch of the tension.

I shift uncomfortably, hyper-aware of the space between us, or rather, the lack of it. Vale's presence makes me feel like a tightly wound cord, the tension in my belly coiling tighter with every second that passes.

"You know what this means, right? I'm staying here," Vale finally says, his tone casual.

My face snaps up. "Here? As in, this room?" My eyes dart around, scanning for any rogue underwear in plain view.

"Would you rather stay in my room?" he teases, raising an eyebrow.

"No," I say. "I guess you should, uh, get your flannel pajamas and toothbrush, then. You know, for our *sleepover.*"

Vale's lips curl into an amused grin. "Who said I wear grandpa pajamas?"

I sit up straighter on the couch, heat creeping up my neck. "I assume you wear *something*?" The idea of Vale sleeping in something less never crossed my mind, but now it's all I can think about. It's going to be a long night if he does.

"Don't worry, I wear something," he says. "But if you're concerned, I can always wear a shirt tonight. Wouldn't want to make you *too* uncomfortable." His eyes flash with mischief, clearly enjoying how flustered I've become.

My cheeks are melting off my face like hot lava. "Oh, please. I'm not worried about that. Just make sure whatever you wear covers the essentials." I cross my arms, pretending to be calm, even though the thought of Vale shirtless is doing dangerous things to my imagination. "What do you want to do?" I ask, moving to the bed and grabbing the remote. "Watch something on TV?" Anything to distract my overactive imagination.

"Never thought I'd hear that on my wedding night," he says with a low chuckle.

"Do you have a better suggestion?"

"A few," he says, taking off his suit jacket and unbuttoning the top button of his shirt. "But you wouldn't be interested."

"Try me." My eyes land on the space of his skin where the shirt opens, taunting me. I've never been interested in seeing a man unbutton his shirt . . . until now. Vale is the only guy who could make me feel this way about one open button.

He notices my eyes lingering on his neck and his lips curve on one side. "They all involve going out. Maybe a casino or a show?"

"Oh," I say, feeling deflated. Vale wasn't suggesting a date with me alone. Why would he? We're not a real couple. If we went out, we could blend into the crowd and forget that we're actually married.

"Are you hungry? We could order food." I toss my stilettos next to the bed and root through my luggage, tossing clothes on the floor until I find my nightgown at the bottom.

As soon as I unfold the black silky fabric, Vale's eyes lock on it, lingering just a second too long before he quickly glances away. His jaw tightens, and I catch the subtle shift in his posture, like he's fighting the urge to look again.

Of all the nightgowns I could have packed, why did I bring this one? Oh, right—because I foolishly assumed no one would ever see me in it.

"I'm still full from earlier," he says, his eyes fixed on a blank wall to his right, like it's the most fascinating thing in the room. He's clearly trying not to look at me—or my nightgown. Is he embarrassed by the thought of seeing me in it? I haven't been working out much since the accident, and my body's softer now, not like the fit girls he's probably used to.

"You don't have to avoid looking at my nightgown, you know. It's not going to bite. Unless you're embarrassed or something."

"Me, embarrassed? Nah, just trying to give you space." He leans back casually, crossing his arms like it's no big deal. It almost seems like he's trying a little too hard.

"We're just sharing a room . . . as friends." *No big deal, right?* I rub my forehead, a familiar throb of pain behind my eyelids, most likely from a headache. "You know, I'm not feeling great. I think I'll head to bed instead."

"Are you okay?" he asks, frowning.

"I'm fine, Vale," I say, heading for the bathroom, cutting off any further questions. The last thing I want is to burden him with my problems. I'll just take some medicine that'll knock me out, and he'll never know the difference.

"Are you sure? You suddenly look . . . ." His voice trails off, concern creeping in.

"Yes," I snap, not meaning to, but I can't help it. "Just tired."

He hesitates, his eyes searching mine for a moment longer. "Okay," he says finally, his voice softening. "I'll just grab my toothbrush and clothes from the other room." Before I can say another word, he's out the door like I've just come down with food poisoning.

I sigh, slumping against the bathroom counter. Maybe he's already regretting his decision to marry me, but there's no turning back now. We have to play the part of the perfectly wedded couple, no matter how miserable I feel. Because as much as I want Vale, as much as I long for something real with him, I know I'll never truly have him as my husband.

SIX

Sloan

What happens in Vegas stays in Vegas—unless, of course, you get married and have to drag your Vegas decision home with you. That's exactly how it feels when I'm caught sneaking out of our hotel room after waking up next to Vale. Suddenly, I'm frozen, like a deer caught in the headlights of an oncoming car.

Of all the things to happen in the "marriage capital of the world," getting caught by my husband trying to escape was not part of the plan.

"Forgive me, I'm operating on zero caffeine right now," I say, before turning back to Vale. "But, seriously, why were you sleeping next to me?"

He raises his hands, his voice soft. "Just to be clear, nothing happened. But I was worried about you last night. You weren't feeling good, and I wanted to stay close, to make sure you were okay." He pauses for a beat, studying my face. "Are you?"

I wave him off, pulling his coat tighter around me like some kind of shield protecting me from making any more terrible decisions. "I'm fine. Just a little groggy from the headache."

I can't admit that I forgot about our wedding last night. He'd freak out. My temporary memory lapses really know how to pick the worst moments. If Vale knew, he'd feel responsible, like this entire situation is somehow his fault—even though we both signed up for this insanity.

He gives me a look like he's not buying it, but lets it slide. "You want to get coffee and then go shopping?" He pulls on a shirt that stretches across his chest in that annoyingly perfect way, showing off muscles that should be illegal. My eyes linger a little too long, tracing the hard lines of his abs disappearing just above the waistband of his joggers.

Before I can stop myself, Vale's voice cuts in with a smirk. "Eyes up here." He taps his face, his lips curling into a teasing smile. He's clearly enjoying this way too much.

My face burns like I've been caught red-handed, and—*okay, fine*—I totally have. "Well, maybe if you wore a proper shirt, I wouldn't be ambushed by all of . . . *that*." I gesture vaguely at his chest, forcing my eyes back to his face. "And shopping for what? I don't need anything."

"For starters, I need some flannel pajamas, so I don't *ambush* you," he says with a smirk. "And you need a ring. It's the only way we're going to pull off this marriage when we return to Sully's Beach." Vale takes out his phone, tapping away as he searches for jewelry stores.

I blink. "You don't have to buy me a ring, Vale. Seriously."

He scoffs. "You are not wearing *that* ring. And lucky for us, Tiffany's is close by."

My jaw practically hits the floor. "What? Vale, no! You don't have to spend that kind of money on something that isn't real."

For a second, his lips tighten. Did I just imply that our marriage is a complete farce? Well, okay, technically it is, but it's not like I'm trying to be cruel.

"You're not changing my mind about this. You deserve more than costume jewelry from a charlatan on the street corner." Then he grabs my hand and holds it up for us both to see. "No wife of mine will wear *that* ring."

I yank my hand away, feeling the heat creep up my neck. "No one would even know."

"*I* would know," he says under his breath in a low, growly voice that sends a shiver down my spine. "If we're returning to Sully's Beach as a married couple, then you'll wear a ring that's up to my standard." He levels his gaze at me. "My wife only deserves the best."

Hearing those words sends a tremor through my body, the kind that's unsettling and oddly thrilling. Of all the things he could call me, *my wife* will always be my kryptonite, the one thing that'll make me crumble every time. But I can't let myself get too comfortable, not when I know that someday, I'll have to let him go.

I force out a laugh, trying to shake off the effect of his words. "Vale, come on. People in Sully's Beach are going to have a field day with this. You know that, right?" I can already picture the way the team is going to take this news. And then there's the whole family complication. "It's not just about us. Your brother is married to my sister. If this goes south, the fallout is going to ripple through both our families."

Vale stares at me. "You think I haven't realized that? That's why we're not going to let it go south. We'll make it work."

"You say it like it's simple—like you can just make things go according to plan." I sigh, rubbing my temples where there's still a mild ache from last night's migraine. "Our lives are already tangled enough. This marriage just took things from 'mildly complicated' to 'full-blown family soap opera.' If something goes wrong, it's not just us. It's everyone—Brax, Jaz, your sister and mom. We're practically one big, dysfunctional family now."

He steps closer, his tone softening. "Sloan, I get that this isn't easy. But we'll figure it out. I wouldn't have suggested it if I didn't think we could pull it off."

I give him a smile that says I don't believe him. "Yeah, but that's the thing about me, Vale. I always manage to overcomplicate things." I point at the ring again. "Like buying a ring. But Tiffany's? *Really?*"

He grins, shaking his head. "You deserve it. And if this marriage is happening, we might as well make it look good."

I cross my arms. "You really don't do anything halfway, do you?"

He smirks. "Nope. Especially when it comes to you."

———

When I see the sign for Tiffany & Co., my heart does a flip. I never imagined I would be browsing for rings at an outrageously fancy jewelry store, let alone buying an engagement ring.

Two days ago, I would have screamed into a pillow at this news. Who doesn't want a gigantic rock from an iconic jewelry store? But now I'm scared to death that Vale will drop so much money on a ring that means nothing.

"Are you sure this is a good idea?" I whisper, halting outside the door.

"Why wouldn't it be?"

"For starters, I don't belong at a store like this."

"Hey, at least I convinced you to ditch the nightgown," he says with a smirk.

Vale insisted I change before we left, so now I'm in a cute sundress, feeling a little more presentable but still out of place. Vale grabs my hand, giving it a gentle squeeze. "Let's go inside and look—just for fun."

He leads me inside, his touch making my heart flutter. When I shoot a sidelong glance at him, he gives me an easy smile, clearly unaffected by the moment, while I'm silently reminding myself to keep him in the friend zone.

A man dressed in an immaculate suit approaches us. "Welcome to Tiffany & Co. My name is Edward. Are you looking for something special today?"

"We'd like to look at some engagement rings, Edward," Vale says, then turns to me. "Unless you'd like something other than a diamond?"

My heart skips a beat, but Vale's smile is the only thing keeping me from running out the door. If I'm this nervous faking our marriage in front of a stranger, how am I going to act when I have to put on a show for our friends and family?

"No, a *small* diamond is fine," I say, trying to steady the nerves bouncing around my body.

The salesman doesn't seem to notice I'm not someone who belongs here. He's enamored with Vale, who's used to turning on the dazzle whenever he goes out in public.

Edward leads us to a glittering display of diamonds behind a glass case. They're all enormous and probably have price tags that would make me throw up.

My eyes zip over the jewelry case. These are clearly out of our price range. I clear my throat. "Uh, where are the ones on clearance?" I spin in a circle, trying to locate a giant yellow clearance sign.

Edward laughs. "We don't have any on sale."

"Sloan," Vale says, arching an eyebrow. "I'm not here to get you the cheapest ring. I want you to pick a ring you like."

I lean closer to Vale with a frozen smile and whisper, "Have you looked at the prices? They're ridiculously expensive."

Vale shakes his head. "I'm not worried about the cost. I want you to be happy."

The words prick something inside me. *He wants me to be happy?* No one's ever said that to me before—probably because I'm always so busy making sure everyone else is okay.

Even though he's giving me free rein in this store, I choose the smallest diamond, which is still a huge rock by a normal person's standards. Jaz is going to scream when she sees this. It's even bigger than the ring Brax picked for her.

Edward pulls it from the display case and holds it out for me.

I'm so nervous about dropping it, my hands shake, and I fold them together so no one will notice.

"That'll work," I say, refusing to touch it. Maybe it's because I'm afraid it'll disappear once I hold it, and I'll discover this whole fairy-tale marriage was just a dream after all.

"Don't you want to see how it looks on?" Edward asks.

Vale takes the ring for me. "Don't worry, Sloan, it's not going to bite," he says with a wry smile, echoing my own words from last night.

I can't help but grin as I hold up my hand. "Okay, fine."

He removes the fake ring that I was perfectly happy with and slides the enormous diamond in its place, the heat of his touch traveling up my arm.

I wiggle my fingers so the light catches on the stone. Something twists in my stomach—a gut-wrenching feeling that makes me lightheaded. Here I am, married to a gorgeous man who promised me any ring I want. Most women would kill to be in my shoes, but the weight of it all feels suffocating. I don't want to use Vale for his money. Marrying him for his insurance was bad enough.

"What do you think?" he asks.

"It's beautiful," I begin, admiring the gem glittering in the light. "But . . ."

"You don't like it?" His brows knit together.

"We have so many others to choose from," Edward says. "Try another one." He pulls out two more rings that are even bigger than the one on my finger.

Vale takes off the ring I'm wearing and slides on the next one, a square diamond with two diamonds on each side.

I move my fingers and the diamonds wink back at me in the light. A few days ago I couldn't have even imagined this.

"You don't look pleased," Edward says.

"It's not the ring's fault," I say, trying to figure out why these rings feel all wrong for me. "I just don't think they work for me.

I'm not into big rocks. Do you have anything more . . . modest?" It almost feels wrong to say those words in this store.

"I want you to be happy with your choice," Vale says taking the ring off and handing it to the man.

But that's just it—how could I be happy with something I'm going to return later?

Edward holds up another ring for me.

I pull my hands away like he's offered me a live snake. I can't have any emotional attachment to this ring or that will make giving it back all the harder. I turn and head toward the door.

Vale trails after me and stops me before I can leave. "Is there something wrong?" His eyes search my face.

"It's not the store," I begin, stumbling over my thoughts. "I always imagined holding out for something different."

"Which would be?"

"I don't have a clue." I drop my head in my hands. "I am the world's worst bride," I moan, trying to force myself not to feel anything about this insignificant piece of jewelry.

It's just a ring! It's not forever!

But in my heart, I know I'm lying. It's more than a piece of jewelry. I thought when I'd get a ring like this, it would be *until death do us part*.

"Sorry," I mumble, finally meeting Vale's concerned gaze. "I usually don't get emotionally attached to things, but a ring is symbolic. The whole *'circle never ends'* thing." I make air quotes with my fingers.

"Don't apologize for feeling that way," he says. "We don't have to buy a ring here. As long as you have one before we return to South Carolina."

"We can't choose one later? Maybe a few months down the road?" I know I'm just delaying the inevitable by kicking the can down the road for Future Sloan to deal with.

"I'm not trying to pressure you," Vale says softly. "But what will your sister say if we return without a proper ring?"

I cringe. "She won't believe we're married?"

Vale nods. Returning with a fake diamond isn't an option if we're going to pull this off. "Could we look somewhere else?"

"This place isn't good enough for you?" He grins.

"The problem is it's *too* good. I'm a simple girl. I don't need a huge rock to impress people."

"Then it's settled. Instead of a ring, let's do something fun, like get coffee." Vale knows me too well. We thank Edward and then head outside, where the sunny day is almost blinding.

The guilt I felt in the store hasn't subsided completely, but at least it's not eating me alive. I tell myself this ring is a business decision, not an emotional one. I'll accept the first tiny diamond I can find.

As Vale scrolls through his phone, searching for jewelry stores, we head down the street for coffee. I sip my iced caramel latte, savoring the sweetness, but my mind can't stay still. The city's flashing lights and chaotic energy pull me in at every turn. Vegas is like a giant funhouse, full of mirrors and lights, and I'm completely mesmerized, barely noticing where I'm walking.

Suddenly, Vale grabs my hand, gently steering me out of the way of a lamppost I almost walk into. He knows how easily distracted I get, and Vegas isn't helping with that. Part of it is my ADHD, sure, but the other part is him—his touch, circling through me like a slot machine on the verge of hitting the jackpot.

We pass by a pawn shop, and a glittering object in the window draws my attention. I stop to press my hand against the glass. Next to a gold necklace sits an antique velvet ring box. Inside, a small diamond winks in the bright sunlight. When I study it, I realize it's not one diamond, but seven small diamonds in a circular shape with a center diamond in the middle. The setting looks like a flower, even though they hardly compare to the ridiculously huge diamonds we saw at Tiffany's. But I prefer this version.

"I've never seen a ring like this before," I say.

Vale looks at the ring, then me. "Are you sure about this?"

His hazel eyes catch the sunlight, and I have to remind myself: *Don't get attached. Not to the ring, and definitely not to Vale.*

"I know I'm not your real wife, but I think this is the one."

He holds my gaze and gives my hand another gentle squeeze. "You are my real wife, Sloan." His voice is soft, but serious. "And I'll never be ashamed to tell anyone that."

SEVEN

Sloan

"We need to come up with a game plan," Vale says after we've bought the ring. "Of how to make this look convincing so everyone believes us."

"It's kind of a hard job, don't you think?" I wave a hand toward his ridiculously muscular body as we stroll along the sidewalk. "I'm just a normal girl, and you're walking around looking like . . . *this*. No one is going to believe I'm married to you."

Vale grins, clearly amused. "Hey, don't sell yourself short. You're more than keeping up. For the record, you make a hot wife."

My body heats, even though I know he's just trying to boost my confidence before we head back.

"But it's going to get harder to keep the secret when we arrive home," he says, turning serious. "They know us better."

I stare at him. "You mean, I can't tell my sister everything?"

He shakes his head. "If you tell Jaz, then Brax has to know too. At that point, it'll be hard to keep it from Leo and Tate, since they live with us."

I raise my eyebrows and speak slowly, the reality slowly settling in. "So you're saying . . . I have to keep it from *everyone*?"

He stops on the sidewalk and faces me. "I don't see how else we can make it work. When one person knows, there's more risk of them giving away our secret. The only thing we can share is that we're married."

I sigh. My sister can read me like a book, and the thought of trying to pull this off around her makes my stomach churn. This could go very badly, *very* quickly. "Jaz already knows you're here with me, and she's been bugging me nonstop, fishing for details. Then she dropped a hint that she expects me to spill the rest. I'm putting her off by not replying."

"How did she respond to that?"

"Oh, she's practically bouncing off the walls. She can't wait to hear more. Which means . . ."

". . .my brother knows," Vale finishes for me.

What I don't tell Vale is that she sent me a GIF of someone getting married, followed by a string of question marks. The pressure to tell her something real is already mounting, and I'm not even home yet.

The thought of keeping the truth away from the people I love makes me sick. Jaz can't stand when people hide the truth from her, even if I have good reason to keep it from her.

"Hey," Vale says, sensing my worry, "it's gonna be all right. You know that, right?" His eyes cut to me, and he squeezes my hand.

"It just doesn't feel right, lying to everyone."

"Telling people we got married isn't a lie, because we *are* married. But if they start asking why, that's where things get complicated. And if the truth comes out, we risk more than just your insurance—there's a lot at stake."

His jaw tightens, and it hits me for the first time just how much Vale is risking. This isn't just about me. He's putting his reputation—and maybe even his future—on the line for me. If this news gets out, it could keep him from moving up to the NHL.

"What do we have to do?" I ask.

"Once we tell everyone we're married, then comes part two of our plan. And that's convincing everyone we're in love."

"Won't they assume as much after I show them the ring?"

"Yes and no," Vale says, steering me around a tour group waiting to board their bus. "Since we're going to blindside everyone with this news, we need to come up with an epic insta-love story. Something believable." He smirks, then adds, "And we'll definitely need some ground rules for our relationship."

"Rules?" I ask.

Vale weaves through a line of people waiting outside one of the live shows. "See those two over there?" He nods toward a couple practically tangled together, looking like they're seconds away from ripping each other's clothes off.

I nearly drop my cup. "Wait, are you suggesting we—?"

"No!" he cuts in quickly. "But there's no doubt how they feel about each other. That's the kind of vibe newlyweds have."

"There's no way I can pull that off," I insist.

"Have you ever been in love?"

Two faces float across my mind. "Regretfully, twice. Anthony was one."

"How did you act together?"

"We were nearly inseparable," I admit, before it dawns on me what Vale is doing—he's trying to map out how we should behave in front of others. I quickly add, "Just for the record, I wish I hadn't spent so much time with him. And I never made a fool of myself."

"I'm not asking you to take it that far, but we need to be as convincing as possible. Especially around the people we live with. That's rule one. Be together as much as possible. Which won't be hard since I'm living in your house."

"That doesn't seem impossible. We already spend plenty of time together as friends." I shrug, trying to keep it light. "Anthony was always holding my hand, really affectionate."

Vale's head turns sharply, his eyes flicking to mine like he's trying to read my thoughts.

I quickly add, "But you don't have to do that. We can keep it . . . casual."

"No, they'll expect more than something casual," Vale replies, like we're discussing a job offer rather than a marriage. "I don't want to pressure you, but if we didn't behave like that, people might not believe us. The question is, how do you feel about that?" He studies me for a beat.

"Touching . . . in public?" Already I can feel the heat crawling up my neck. With him holding my hand to guide me through Vegas, it would be no different than right now. But there's something about giving him permission that feels entirely different. Like I'm opening up the floodgates to some very dangerous feelings.

I shrug. "Whatever it takes, right?"

"Okay, so that's rule two. Touch each other as often as possible." He hesitates for a second. "Just promise me if it makes you uncomfortable, you'll tell me?"

I nod and paste on what I hope is an easy smile, even though it feels like there's a weight on my chest.

"Now it's your turn," I say, trying to switch the focus. "How did you behave around the girls you dated?"

Vale lifts an eyebrow. "You want to get into dangerous territory?"

I hesitate. "That bad, huh?"

"I've mainly dated for fun, not love. Hockey comes first, and most of the girls were more in love with the *idea* of dating a hockey player. But if given the chance, they'd be all over me."

"I bet you hated that." I shoot him a look.

Vale laughs. "But for a married couple? I don't think it's out of place."

"Really?" I say, feeling my internal temperature rising ten degrees. Is Vale suggesting I need to throw myself at him? Because I'm sure I could do that quite easily. It's the aftereffects I'm worried about. Once I kiss Vale, I can't go back to being his friend. *Ever.* "You'll have to give me strict instructions on what you mean by too much. Because I can be . . ." I hesitate.

Vale stops, his eyes glancing toward my mouth, lingering there. "Be what?"

"Too impulsive," I finish.

I know it's not a character flaw, just my way of taking action. Maybe in the case of pulling off this charade, it will be a useful trait.

His gaze hovers on my lips for a moment before shifting to meet my eyes. Then, almost abruptly, he starts walking again. "Brax and Jaz can hardly keep their hands off each other. And they're kissing all the time . . ." He gives me a sidelong glance. "I don't mean we should do the same. But there's something about their relationship you can't fake."

I wonder if we're in over our heads in the fake relationship department. My sister knows me better than anyone. If anyone could guess this is a charade, it would be her. Part of me just wants to confess, but I also know too much is on the line.

"I don't know if I can do it, Vale. What if we fail?"

Vale shakes his head. "We won't fail. It's not an option as long as we make rule three the most important."

"And that is?"

"Make it believable. Whatever it takes."

I feel like I just swallowed a balloon. Rule three ups the risks a million degrees. But if Vale wants me to act like his wife, then I'll need to. *Whatever it takes.*

"Okay, but what does that mean exactly?" I ask, nervously.

"Well, there's a fourth rule that keeps rule three in check so we don't go too far."

Something prickles down my spine as Vale hesitates.

"Rule four should be no sex." His eyes cut to mine before they flick away. "Just so we don't get confused."

I nod, while my face feels like it's been shoved into a toaster. Of course Vale is referring to me. He knows I'll get emotionally attached if we go that far. "Agreed," I say, trying to pretend it's not a big deal. "Once we tell everyone we're married, there's no turning back," I add, more to myself than Vale.

Until now, our decision to marry felt like a Vegas dream, something we could shake off once we left.

"Sorry to break the news, Sloan, but you're already married. That ship has sailed. Now we just need to decide how to tell everyone." I see it in Vale's eyes—he's trying to protect me from messing up by establishing ground rules. "But we don't have to decide anything else now. I think we should celebrate at some over-the-top restaurant."

"Every restaurant on this street is over-the-top. It's Vegas."

My phone suddenly buzzes in my purse. I study the screen. It's a message from Jaz with a news link.

JAZ

IS THIS REAL?

The article's headline reads: "Hockey star elopes with girlfriend." I click the link and my stomach drops. It's about us.

"Are you in the mood for steak or seafood?" Vale asks, still looking at the map on his phone.

"Vale," I say in an urgent voice, my eyes glued to the screen. The article is short but reveals that Vale and I eloped in Vegas.

"My name isn't the answer to this question," he replies. "Your options are steak or seafood. Unless you want Mexican?"

I shove the phone in his face. "Look at this."

Two lines form between his brow. "Somebody leaked our news to the media?"

"Not just somebody. Anthony, most likely." I cross my arms. "And now my sister knows. She's going to be furious." I can barely breathe.

"Which means Brax knows. Not to mention the rest of the team."

Suddenly, Vale's phone buzzes in his pocket.

He glances at the screen. "It's the general manager from the team. Looks like our secret is out."

"What are we going to do?" I nearly yell, dragging my hand through my hair. This was not how I wanted everyone to find out.

Vale turns to face me, grabbing my shoulders so I'll look at him. "I think it's best if we head home early."

"Right into the line of fire?"

"Yes," he says, nodding. "We need to do what we can to control the story. We'll talk to our families and team first, and then face the press." He turns to head back to the hotel, and I grab his arm.

"Whoa, slow down, partner," I say in my best fake country accent. "Did you say *press*? Because I don't do media stuff."

"You do now. But I'll take care of how to spin this during our press conference. You don't have to say a word."

"Wait—what conference?" I feel lightheaded, like I'm about to be sick.

"An interview with all the major media outlets," he says. "And you'll appear by my side . . . as my wife."

EIGHT

Sloan

"You got married in Vegas?!?" These are the first words out of Jaz's mouth when we arrive home.

After texting her a brief note that said, *I'll explain everything when I get home,* she sent five more messages, three GIFs, and six phone calls.

She's not mad, *exactly,* but she's also not happy that I sent my reply right before our plane took off. I waited until the last possible second, knowing she'd be furious.

Growing up, we always promised we'd be each other's maid of honor. Now I just broke that promise. Not only did I break it, but I didn't even invite my sister to my wedding. I'm the worst sister in the world.

I worry my lip, and glance at Brax who stands behind her with his arms crossed. I feel like I'm being interrogated by the secret service.

"I know it happened fast, but we both realized we were in love," I say casually, just like Vale and I rehearsed on the plane trip home. I glance over my shoulder at Vale. He gives me a smile that says, *You're doing great.*

Jaz tilts her head, propping a hand on her hip. "You say it like you just got groceries or something."

"For the record, it wasn't planned. Kind of like my grocery trips."

Jaz shakes her head. "This isn't like shopping at Trader Joe's. It's marriage. A serious commitment."

"I know," I say. "I was kidding about the grocery comment."

We couldn't be more different when it comes to organizing our lives. Jaz color-codes her to-do lists while I go to the store with no list and buy whatever looks promising. We're opposites in so many ways. She's the planner who takes care of everyone, while I'm the spontaneous one who keeps things interesting and fun. It kills me to keep the truth from her, but I know she wants me to be well again as much as I do.

"I can't believe you didn't text me right away. How did it happen?" Jaz presses, not moving from her stance in the middle of the entry hall. She doesn't want me hiding in my room until she gets the full story.

I look at the floor. "Well . . ." It's one thing to pull this off to a stranger, but telling your sister a story that's only half true feels downright criminal.

Vale touches my elbow. "You want to tell her or me?"

"Sure. You tell the story so much better anyway," I say, giving him a grateful look.

Vale wraps an arm around my waist, tucking me into his side. "When I moved in, Sloan was still recovering, and I knew it wasn't the right time to start a relationship. But when we were at the skating gala, we realized our feelings for each other were mutual, so we decided to go for it." Vale pulls me even closer to his body. I know we made up the rules for this game, but he's really playing into rule number two.

Brax and Jaz don't say anything for a moment, and my stomach feels like it's going to lose the lunch we were served on the plane.

Jaz's lips curve into a smile. "I knew it!" She claps her hands. "I knew you liked him, but I had no idea it was that serious!"

"You knew?" I ask. If it was that obvious to Jaz, then . . . does Vale know, too? My stomach twists at the thought.

Brax finally cracks a wide smile. "Congratulations, you two. This is the best news I've heard in months."

"Really? Then why did you look so mad?" I ask. "Like you wanted to break your brother's neck."

"Oh, that was because Jaz told me to look that way. In case Vale talked you into this and now you're regretting it."

I glance at my sister. "You were going to let Brax do that?"

"I'm just protecting you," she says. "To be sure you hadn't made an impulsive decision in a moment of weakness."

If she suspects that our marriage is based on my impulsive nature, what will she say when Vale and I break it off . . . that she's not surprised?

"We should definitely celebrate," Jaz says. "Throw a big party with the entire hockey team and our families. What do you say?"

"I don't know if we need a big party," I say. "We're already married."

"Of course you do. And I won't take no for an answer." She pulls me into a hug.

I lift my eyebrows. "Is that really necessary?"

She steps back and gives me one of her looks. "Yes, it's necessary. Otherwise you'll always regret not celebrating."

"But that's the whole point of eloping. So you don't have to."

"Sloan," she says. "Let me throw you a party since I couldn't be at the actual wedding. I need to do this."

The note in her voice is unmistakable. She feels hurt she wasn't there. She's not asking—it's something she wants to do as my sister.

"Okay," I say, already feeling weird about it. She doesn't know we're not really in love, that I don't deserve this.

"Well, I'm feeling pretty tired," Vale says. "And we have a press conference early in the morning, so I'll just head to bed."

Jaz looks between us. "That's another question you need to figure out. Whose bedroom are you using?"

I freeze, glancing at Vale. We hadn't even discussed this tiny yet monumental detail. Obviously, everyone expects us to share a room—it would be weird if we didn't. But the thought of actually doing it sends my mind spinning. Do we head upstairs to Vale's room, right next to the other hockey players? Or stay in my bedroom next to Jaz and Brax's room? I swallow hard, my pulse quickening.

Vale clears his throat, flashing a quick smile. "Your room's cozier," he says, trying to cut through the tension.

"Cozy it is, then," I say, giving a half-hearted shrug and heading toward my room.

Once we reach the bedroom, Vale shuts the door behind us and lets out a relieved sigh. "I think that went well."

I sit on the bed and kick my shoes off. "That depends on how you define *well*."

"What do you mean?" Vale asks.

"I feel terrible not telling my sister the whole truth. I know we agreed to only tell her what was needed. But I left out so much." I look up at him. "Do you really think this is the only way?"

"What's the alternative?" Vale asks. "We tell them, and the news gets out, and insurance refuses to cover your medicine? That's not an option. No way." Vale crosses his arms. "I don't want them to have to keep the secret. It's too risky."

"Which is why I hate that I dragged you into this mess."

"It's not a mess," Vale says, sitting next to me on the bed. "It's marriage."

My stomach flips. Will I ever get used to him saying words like "married" and "wife" when there's no truth behind them?

"If it helps," Vale continues, "I can sleep on the floor. That way it won't be . . . *weird*."

I bite my lip. It seems wrong to ask him to sacrifice good sleep just so we can pull off this charade. But I'm not ready to have him next to me in bed either. There's so much that could go wrong.

"You don't have to do that," I weakly protest.

But I know the truth. He absolutely *does* have to sleep on the floor if I ever plan on sleeping again. Because having Vale next to me all night? *Game over.* I'll die of insomnia.

"It's okay," he says. "When I said I'd do this, I meant it. Hard floor and everything."

"Maybe we can take it in stages," I suggest. "Eventually we'll share a bed, just like a sleepover."

Vale shakes his head, a soft smile playing on his lips. "I can't ever think of sleeping next to you as a sleepover, Sloan."

The way he looks at me makes me feel like caramel over too much heat. His gaze holds mine just long enough for alarm bells to go off in my head.

"Well, time for bed!" I chirp, flying off the bed and hurrying across the room.

I root through my dresser to find the most modest pajamas I own, a pair of lightweight cotton pants and a Carolina Crushers T-shirt. Then I head to the bathroom before Vale sees the flush across my face.

Anytime Vale gets that look in his eyes, it makes me want to run *far* away. Not because he's done anything wrong. But it feels dangerous, like he's the forbidden fruit and I'm a starving woman.

From the bathroom, I hear Jaz's laughter float through the house.

I peek out the door and catch Brax and Jaz in the kitchen, his lips brushing her cheek in what's meant to be a private moment. Their connection is so effortless, so natural, it stirs something inside me—a longing for that kind of intimacy, the kind I wish I had with Vale. It makes me wonder if I can really pretend to be married to Vale without actually getting my heart crushed. *Who am I kidding?* I can't pretend to care for him, then switch it off when this is over. I'm not built that way.

As I tiptoe across the hall, looking over at Brax and Jaz, I run face-first into a very solid object. *Vale's chest.*

I give a muffled *oof* before taking a dazed step away from him.

"Sorry, babe," he says, loud enough for Brax and Jaz to turn our way.

"Babe?" I mouth to him. That's almost as bad as *sweet cheeks*.

His eyes swing to his brother, as he tucks a hand around my side, trying to lean into rule two again. His fingers find the hem of my T-shirt, and the bare spot of skin peeking out where the shirt rides up a little. His fingers rub circles on that spot, flooding me with heat, while he's totally oblivious to how he's torturing me.

"I hope I didn't hurt you." I lightly tap his chest where I head-butted him just a moment ago. I can feel the curved ridges of muscle underneath his soft henley shirt.

"You couldn't hurt me," Vale says, glancing down at my hand on his chest. I can't tell if he feels as awkward as I do, but I make a point not to move it, remembering rule two.

"Look at you two," Jaz croons. "Whenever I run into Brax, I always make sure to give him a kiss. It's tradition for us."

"Is that why you kiss so much?" Vale says to his brother.

"We don't need a reason," Brax says.

Vale takes my hand, the one splayed across his chest and lightly sweeps his lips over the tips of my fingers. An electrical current shoots from my fingers through my arm, and I'm left wondering how much longer I can pretend this doesn't affect me.

"Just a warning—Tate and Leo hate it when we show any kind of affection around them," Jaz says. "But we understand what it's like to be newlyweds. So don't feel like you have to hold back for us."

"Hold back? Oh, we won't," Vale says, tugging me so close, my body might as well be attached to his hip. His hand travels up my back, lightly brushing my spine. "Now if you'll excuse us, we need to head to bed. Don't we, *babe?*"

A laugh escapes my lips. "Sure do, my little *Honey Smacks*." I look up at Vale and smile. It feels good to get even.

With a fire in his eyes, he leans forward and kisses my cheek, right next to my earlobe, and I swear my knees almost buckle.

Then he gives me a sexy half-smile before whispering, "That's for calling me *Honey Smacks*."

NINE

Vale

My back aches as I roll over, desperately trying to find a comfortable position on this miserable floor. I wasn't supposed to wake up for another hour, but between the ache in my spine and the looming press conference, sleep feels impossible.

I rub the palm of my hand into my eyes and peek across the room. Sloan is sleeping on her stomach, one arm hanging off the mattress, her hair a tangled mess. She'd kill me if she knew I was staring, but I can't help it. I drink her in—her brown hair splayed across her pillow, the neck of her T-shirt falling off one shoulder, her pink lips slightly open. It's not just her looks that pull me in— it's everything about her. The way she makes people feel seen and special, the way her laugh lights up a room, and how she throws herself into everything with her whole heart. That's what makes her one of my favorite people in the world. And it's exactly why I'm terrified of messing this up—because losing her would mean losing the best thing that's ever happened to me.

The whole world will be watching us today, ready to pick apart every word, searching for cracks in our story. It's one thing if I slip up and ruin my reputation, but risking Sloan's future? That's a whole different thing.

Which means I've got one job today: convince everyone that

I'm madly in love with Sloan and that includes my friends and teammates. If anyone's going to see through this, it's them.

I sneak through the room, when Sloan suddenly stirs and lifts her head from the pillow.

"Why are you up so early?" she asks sleepily, propping up on her elbow. Her hair falls over one eye, and she pulls the sheet up to her neck, like she's trying to cover her body even though I've already seen her in a much skimpier nightgown.

"I couldn't sleep," I whisper.

"It was the floor, wasn't it?" Her eyes graze over my bare chest before a pink flush warms her cheeks. Judging by the way she's avoiding looking directly at my chest, I've already failed my first test—making her feel comfortable with us sharing a room. If we can't fix this, it's going to be a very long two years.

"I'm heading out for an early morning workout," I say.

I head to the kitchen, where the morning light has cast a gray, sleepy hue over everything, and grab the orange juice from the fridge. As I tip it to my lips, Brax steps into the kitchen.

"What are you doing?" he asks, flicking on the light.

"What does it look like? Drinking some juice. You should warn a man before you give him a heart attack."

"You know the house rules," he says, ripping the juice from my hands. "No drinking from the container."

I point at the container. "I bought that juice."

Brax shakes his head. "Doesn't matter. Leo drank from it while you were gone, and I gave him the same warning."

"Seriously? Gross." I wipe my lips with the back of my hand. "Why didn't you tell me?"

"I could ask you the same question," he says, crossing the kitchen to grab two glasses, handing me one. "You went to Vegas and got married without telling anyone."

Brax turns toward the pantry and takes out a package of bagels.

"Listen, Brax. It wasn't intentional. Things just happened fast."

He whips around. "Too fast to call your brother? I understand why you didn't tell the team. Leo's got a big mouth, and Rourke would give you grief. But I'm family. I should know before it's all over social media. When a reporter called the house, I told him no way were you married. I felt like smacking you for putting me in that position."

"A reporter called you?" I ask, setting down my glass. "I didn't mean for you to find out that way. We were waiting to tell you in person. Figured that'd be better than just a call or text."

"I know that," he mumbles, then checks over his shoulder. "But this is my sister-in-law you married. It complicates things because she's family."

"You don't think I took that into account?" I say. "You don't think this is complicated for us too?"

He sets down his breakfast and leans against the counter, locking eyes with me. "She's not like your other girlfriends, Vale. You were never serious with them—ditching them the moment you got bored. But Sloan? She's family now." His voice drops lower as he points at me, eyes sharp. "If you dare hurt her . . ."

"I'm not going to hurt her," I promise. "She's my wife, Brax. Not like the other girls I've dated. Why are you even questioning me?"

He takes a step toward me, getting in my face. "You know the divorce rate? It's fifty percent. Guess how many married couples are in this house?" He waits a beat to make his point. "It's you or me, Vale, and it sure isn't going to be me. So if anything happens and you break up this family, you'll have me to answer to. Understand?"

I clench my jaw and nod, even though I know I'm totally screwed. Sloan thinks this marriage is a temporary arrangement, and I promised her an out when she wanted it. Even if that's never been my plan, I wouldn't force her to stay married to me if she didn't want to. Wouldn't Brax understand that?

I swallow hard. "Heard you loud and clear."

The gravity of his warning sinks like a rock in my stomach. I turn away from him and stare into the open fridge, even though I've lost my appetite. If I divorce Sloan, I'll lose my brother too.

He runs his fingers through his hair. "Jaz is worried sick. She's been nauseous ever since she found out her sister eloped. She just wants Sloan to be happy. That's why I'm warning you now. Don't screw this up."

I whirl around. "I said I won't, and I meant it. I'm not going to hurt her."

Footsteps echo down the stairs, and we both turn back to making our breakfasts.

"Hey, Vale," Leo says, strolling into the kitchen, oblivious to the tension in the room. "Sorry I missed you coming home last night." He opens the fridge door and smirks. "I can't handle all this newlywed bliss. I was afraid it might rub off on me."

"Which newlywed are you talking about?" Brax asks.

"The same one who got the press all riled up," Leo says, taking my juice and drinking it from the bottle.

"That's my juice." I tear the bottle away from him and glance at Brax. "Did you tell him about Vegas?"

Leo shakes his head. "He didn't have to. It's all over the news." Then he gives me a slap on the back. "You sly dog. Never expected you'd get hitched in Sin City with Sloan. Sounds like something *I'd* do." He laughs and grabs my juice bottle, holding it in the air. "Cheers to the happy couple." Then he downs the last sip.

I narrow my eyes. "Are you trying to be a jerk this morning? Or did I forget how annoying you were while I was gone?"

Leo tosses the bottle in the trash, unfazed. "Looks like somebody woke up on the wrong side of the bed. Didn't sleep well last night or did your wife keep you up?"

"Wouldn't you like to know," I say smugly. There's no way Leo can find out I slept on the floor. "Just stop putting your mouth on my juice bottle."

He gives me an aggravating smirk. "I'm sure if it were Sloan's lips, you wouldn't mind at all."

I take a step toward Leo. "Don't talk about my wife ever again."

"Guys," Brax warns, coming between us. "Knock it off."

"What's going on now?" Tate strolls into the kitchen, looking between us.

"Do you live under a rock or something? I swear you've got your head in a book too much," Leo grumbles.

"At least I know *how* to read," Tate fires back.

"Vale and Sloan got hitched in Vegas," Brax says, beating me to the punch.

Tate nods and grabs a cereal bowl. "I heard. It was all over the news."

"Does anyone not know yet?" I say. "Or can I assume the whole team has heard by now?"

"Oh, they know," Leo says. "You can thank the internet for that. I'm sure our owner, Mr. Marco, wasn't pleased to find out that way."

"Someone in Vegas leaked it," I reply, trying to ignore the gnawing feeling in my stomach. The press conference is going to be brutal today. Protecting Sloan from the onslaught of questions is my number one priority. "If anyone tries to get information, send them to me. Leo, you especially."

"I'm not the one you need to worry about. Your girl, on the other hand, isn't used to the press. Have you prepared her for this?"

I cross the kitchen in a few quick strides, closing the distance between us. "She's not my *girl*, she's my wife. And you'll refer to her as my wife from now on."

Just then, Sloan enters the kitchen, and her eyes cut to me. "What did you say about me?"

"Uh, nothing," I say with a shrug. I give her a quick kiss on the cheek and notice her stiffen under my touch. "Just guy stuff."

"Looks like *your wife* has you wrapped around her finger, Vale-boy," Leo says with a smirk as he leaves the kitchen.

"He makes me want to punch things," I mutter under my breath.

Brax tips his chin at me. "Join the club."

Sloan grabs an apple, while I pour a bowl of cereal. "Do you mind if I use the bathroom first after I work out? I want to look nice for the press conference today."

"It's all yours."

"But what about your hair and beard?" Brax says, grinning at me. "Don't you need an hour to make yourself camera-ready?"

"Shut up, Brax," I say. "My wife gets first priority now."

"Thanks, honey." She smiles, then reaches up to tousle my hair before leaving.

Brax lifts an eyebrow. "You let her mess up your hair? *Wow.* Never thought I'd see the day. Sloan has you whipped into shape."

"She does not," I mumble, fixing my hair.

"Sure looks like she does," Tate says. "How's that going to affect your focus during games?"

"It won't," I grumble. "I'm still the same player. Marriage won't change me on the ice."

"You'd be surprised." Brax leans in close. "Do you think about her all the time? Want to be near her? Can't stop replaying your time with her alone?"

Tate holds up a hand. "Stop right there. We get the idea."

I shrug. "I won't let it affect my game."

But I don't admit the full truth: that my thoughts stray to her all the time. Ever since we got married, she's on a constant loop in my head. Like how stunning she looked in that silver gown. And that nightgown? I can't even let my mind go there without getting completely flustered. How am I supposed to keep this up for an entire year while pretending I feel nothing for her but brotherly love?

"Take it from me," Brax says, tearing off a piece of his bagel. "She's going to be a distraction during games."

"Guys, I'm telling you. I don't have a problem with focus."

Sloan jogs back into the kitchen, her ponytail swinging behind her.

"I forgot my water," she chirps, grabbing her bottle.

She's changed into a pair of workout shorts and a cropped T-shirt that skims the waistline. I can't help but appreciate her gorgeous curves as she brushes by me. When she wiggles her fingers to say goodbye, I give her a wink—just for show, of course—while reaching for my juice glass. I'm so focused on Sloan, I accidentally knock it over, spilling juice across the counter.

"You're right," Brax adds, smirking. "You don't have a problem with focus at all."

TEN

Vale

"It's all an easy sell," I tell Sloan, before entering the media room for our press conference at the ice arena. "As long as we don't say too much, they'll buy our story."

She bites her lip as her brows knit together. "That's the problem. I'm afraid of saying the wrong thing." She's changed into a pair of dress slacks with a cropped blazer and tank, trying to balance the look of being a professional hockey player's wife with her new status as influencer.

"Are you sure I have to be here?" she asks.

"It looks better if you are. More believable," I remind her. "Just leave the answers to me."

As we make our way through the administrative offices, I greet everyone with a casual nod while trying to avoid their questioning looks. I grab Sloan's hand and steamroll past everyone so we don't get sidetracked, even though I can feel the tension around us. Everyone is wondering the same thing. *How did this happen?*

We'll deal with the Crushers' staff later. Right now we have to face down the lions.

When we finally reach the media room, Lauren Williamson, our new PR person, is already waiting for us. She's dressed to kill in a red leather jacket with matching heels, her dark hair pulled back into a slick topknot. Lauren has the confidence of a cougar even though her bubbly personality makes her everyone's favorite PR person. Her ability to woo people is astounding, and she can spin any news with rainbows and glitter, no matter how bad it is. And by rainbows and glitter, I mean she's an epic wordsmith and master spin doctor. But underneath that razzle-dazzle is a relentlessly tough chic who refuses to back down when the media pressures us.

She gives me an easy smile, even though I know what we're about to face will be anything but easy. "You ready for this? If not, I have a sheet to brief you on talking points." She holds out a paper color-coded with bullet points.

"So what you're saying is you're slacking off again," I remark with a smile.

She shrugs. "You know me. I can't do things halfway. Not in a man's world." She doesn't mean it as a criticism. We all know the hockey industry is rife with men. It's hard for women like Lauren and Jaz to be taken seriously.

I look over her talking points. Her answers are vague, yet professional, just like I've planned. *Yes, we eloped. No, we weren't drunk. Of course we're in love. No, it isn't for professional gain.* There isn't anything on here I haven't prepared for, and this gives me a boost of confidence that I can handle the press without Sloan saying a word. "Looks good. Thanks, Lauren."

Sloan glances from the paper to Lauren. "Do you really think they'll ask if our marriage is real?"

Lauren nods. "Expect it. They're already convinced there's dirt on you both unless you prove them otherwise. That's the press's job—to smell if something's off and dig it up."

"Whatever happened to innocent until proven guilty?" Sloan says.

"It's the opposite with the media. That's where I come in," she says with a reassuring smile.

I squeeze Sloan's hand gently to remind her I've got this. "You don't need to worry about it. I'm used to handling the press."

Sloan fidgets as we wait outside in the hall, listening to the journalists gather in the room.

Team owner Rafael Marco appears in the hall and stops in front of us. "Congratulations, Mr. and Mrs. MacPherson." He shakes our hands before turning to me. "Can I talk to you before you face the firing squad?" He offers us his trademark mystery grin, and I can't tell if he's joking or serious.

"I'm all ears," I reply.

He levels his gaze at me. "I hope that whatever you say today will represent the team well. We're rebuilding our reputation after the fallout with past leadership. So I hope this is the only press conference we'll need about this particular issue. We don't want any more trouble."

"Of course. And we won't give you any," I say. As long as our marital arrangement stays secret.

"Good," he says with a nod. "I just wanted to be clear."

His words feel like a vague attempt at a warning. Almost like he doesn't fully believe we're in love either.

When we enter the media room, Sloan and I take seats at the front behind a table. Behind us, a curtain with the team logo for the Carolina Crushers provides the perfect framing for the camera. The room is packed with reporters and photographers who quiet as soon as we sit down.

I look over at Sloan, who is now bouncing her knee nervously under the table. Since the Crushers tablecloth covers our legs, I place my hand on her knee without anyone seeing it. Immediately, her knee stops moving and she gives me a quick glance.

I keep my hand there through the first five questions, squeezing her knee every time it starts bouncing again. The questions are all ones I'm prepared for: *Are you really married? Why did you get married in Vegas? Was this a decision you made while under the influence? Why didn't you wait?*

Then a reporter stands who I don't recognize. He turns to Sloan and totally ignores eye contact with me. "Mrs. MacPherson, I've heard you haven't been well since your accident and that you've experienced a relapse with your brain injury. How did your health play into the decision to marry Vale?"

Sloan's whole body tenses and her knee starts bouncing again. We hadn't practiced this question, because so few people knew about Sloan's injury. It seemed like a part of her past, not her future, and we thought we'd covered our trail.

I glance at her, and my heart sinks. Her face is pale, her wide eyes full of fear. She looks absolutely terrified. Both knees are bouncing, so I hook my leg over hers, just to stop her from fidgeting.

"My wife's health is good," I blurt out.

"I didn't address the question to you, Mr. MacPherson," the reporter says. "It's for your wife."

"When it comes to my wife, she is my business," I shoot back.

Sloan's hand finds mine under the table. "It's okay. I can answer."

She swallows, then turns back to the reporter. "My health is good, though not totally back to normal. We have some other options to try, but I have full confidence that I'll return to a normal life. If there's any question about my ability, I've gone back to work and resumed coaching skaters. As far as our decision to marry . . ." She pauses, then glances at me nervously, before turning back. "There was never any question. I've always wanted to spend my life with Vale."

Her answer is like a shot of adrenaline flooding my system, giving me a sliver of hope that we can convince everyone this marriage is real. I know her answer was just for show, but she said it with such conviction, even I almost believed it.

"One more question," Lauren says from the back of the room. "And then Vale needs to head to practice."

A reporter from *The Charleston Times* stands in the front. "Are you taking a honeymoon? And if so, where?"

I shake my head. "No plans for a honeymoon yet. Even if we were, I wouldn't announce it. I don't want any of you showing up to ruin our fun."

The reporters chuckle as Sloan and I leave the room. As soon as we're in the hall, Sloan breathes a sigh of relief.

Lauren hurries down the hall to find us, her face beaming. "Good idea to leave them laughing at the end."

"You've trained me well," I say. "But seriously, I don't want those clowns crashing my honeymoon."

Sloan's eyes catch mine, and my heart leaps. No matter how much I'd love to have her all to myself on a secluded beach, I know she'd never agree to it.

"I need to head to practice," I tell Sloan, trying to erase that honeymoon image from my mind. "Will you be okay until I get home?"

Sloan nods, but I sense this media thing shook her up. "I think I'll stop in and see Jaz before I go."

"I'm headed that way. We could go together," Lauren offers before they head down the hallway.

Brendan approaches me as the journalists file out of the room. With his dark hair and tattooed arms, he's an intimidating figure—exactly the reason he was hired as our conditioning coach

"Good job in there. Even Sloan was a natural. How's the team taking the news about your Vegas wedding?"

"I'm about to find out," I say. "Judging by the reaction of the people I live with, it won't go well."

"Even Jaz and Brax?"

"Well . . ." I hesitate, trying to figure out how much to say.

Brendan leans against the wall, folding his arms. "Let me guess, they're happy, but equally ticked at you for not telling them."

"You know my brother and sister-in-law well."

He chuckles. "Jaz hates not knowing things first. Especially since she's the team's Mother Hen. But I don't blame you for not telling them. You didn't want them talking you out of it."

"Exactly." I nod. There was too much at stake.

Brendan looks down the hall to make sure no one can overhear us. "Some decisions are yours alone to make, no matter the reason."

That sounds strangely accurate, probably because no one ever tells Brendan what to do. "Thanks for understanding."

"Anytime," he says. "I just hope I get the same ending someday."

"You mean eloping so the press will hound you for details?"

"Nah, I'll save that one for you," he jokes, before his face shifts slightly. "I hope the reason you did it is worth it though."

"Isn't love always worth it?" I reply.

Brendan looks at me for a beat. "Love, yeah. It's the only reason. Because if you marry for anything else, it'll come back to bite you. Trust me."

Vale

The rest of the week, I get the sense that my teammates are hiding something. They rib me about wanting to get home after practice and accuse me of being distracted by Sloan. They're merciless with the bedroom jokes (even though the joke's on them), but I've learned not to give any hints. Not even a *whiff* of a hint. Instead, I hurry out of the locker room with one thing on my mind: *Sloan.*

Even if they don't know our secret, there's a piece of the truth in their accusations. I can't get my mind off the hot brunette I married—how she made me laugh over dinner last night and what show we're going to watch as she falls asleep against my shoulder. I can't stop replaying how she looks when she first wakes, her hair fanning across her shoulders, while I ache to touch her.

Sloan is my weakness, and it's starting to affect me even when she's not around.

During shooting drills when Rourke passes me a puck, I fumble it and miss a usual corner shot.

"Your shooting's off today," he complains.

"Bad shot," I mutter.

"Is it the shot, or is the *wifey* affecting your game?" He smirks, and I glower at him.

I hate the word *wifey*. Like Sloan's some kind of joke. Maybe I'm irritable because his joke hits a little too close to home. I skate over to my cocky teammate and use my six-foot-four frame to tower over him. "That's *my wife* to you."

"It was a joke," he replies. "Or have you lost your sense of humor too?" Rourke's a loose cannon and it doesn't take much to set him off, but right now, I don't care.

"I don't joke about Sloan," I growl.

"Whatever. Why are you so cranky anyways?"

"I'm not cranky," I shoot back.

"I think Vegas affected your game," Rourke says. "You've been acting weird ever since you got back."

"I'll show you what's gonna affect your game," I warn, moving toward him. Rourke skates away before I can do anything stupid.

"Idiot," I mutter under my breath.

Maybe it's the pressure of keeping my marriage situation quiet. Or the added pressure from my brother who warned me about breaking things off with Sloan, but I'm not in a good head space.

Leo skates by, then stops in front of me. "You're *both* right. He's an idiot, and you're clearly bothered by something that's affecting your focus. Is it the press? You should just ignore them and move on."

"Easy for you to say. You're not the one in a new article every day," I huff, frustration building in my chest. I can see how it's starting to wear on Sloan. She's been pulling away from me all week—something I need to fix, and fast. I can't stand the distance she's putting between us. Before we were married, everything was so easy, but now things are different between us, more complicated.

"If you're such an expert on PR, what do you suggest?" I ask Leo.

"Leave town so they can't bother you," Leo says.

"Like I can do that. We're in training camp season."

"Seriously, you need to get away so the press storm will cease. You're totally focused on hockey ever since you got back. You need to have more fun. And by fun, I mean with your wife."

I lift an eyebrow. "Because you've been married before . . ."

"No," he says. "But if I ever settle down, I know that much."

Tate circles around me, stopping in front of me. "Today's surprise might help."

"What surprise?" I say, looking around.

Leo closes his eyes and sighs. "Tate, you just blew our cover."

"I'm giving him a hint," Tate says. "For the record, I had nothing to do with what's about to happen."

I lean against my stick. "Tate, I have no clue what you're talking about."

A shrill whistle ends our practice as Coach waves the team over. A few guys shoot looks over their shoulders, and I swear a few of them are smiling.

"We're cutting practice short today," Coach Jenkins announces. "Meet in the conference room in a half hour."

"What is it?" I ask as everyone files off the ice.

Brax smiles. "The team came up with a brilliant idea for you and Sloan."

"Brilliant, huh?" I ask. "You want to tell me what it is?"

"Nope," Leo butts in, then hits my chest with the back of his hand. "I just hope you know your new bride well."

When we reach the conference room, Sloan waits in a chair at the front of the room, her knee in constant motion. As usual, she looks adorable in a pair of faded jeans and an off-the-shoulder sweater. When her eyes catch mine, she gives me a strained look that says, *What are they up to now?*

I shrug and shake my head.

The front of the room is decorated with gold balloons and the obligatory newlywed banner. It all reeks suspiciously of a wedding shower or a practical joke. Given the company, I'd guess the latter.

"You knew about this?" I whisper to Sloan as my eyes scan the room for clues. It all looks so normal. *Too* normal.

"No. Did you?"

"Not until right now."

When Jaz walks in, Sloan waves her down frantically. "What is going on?"

Jaz shoots us an apologetic look. "The team wanted to throw you a shower. I didn't find out until today. They didn't want me warning you beforehand."

Sloan narrows her eyes. "Why would the team throw us a wedding shower?" The cake and punch in the corner are a dead giveaway, but since everyone's being tight-lipped, I know that's not the whole story.

"I don't know, but there are games involved. Highly secretive ones," she says. "Including a game with whipped cream."

Knowing these guys, it could be anything. They're a bunch of grown men with middle-school senses of humor.

Brax and Leo walk in, each carrying a stack of cards.

"Okay, listen up," Brax says to the room of rowdy men. "We're here to celebrate Sloan and Vale today, and we wanted to have some fun."

The hockey team hoots and whistles like a scantily clad girl has just jumped out of a cake.

"Not that kind of fun," Brax warns with a grin. "I meant we're here to have fun celebrating Sloan and Vale, who tied the knot in Vegas recently. We might not know how to pull off your typical wedding shower, so this is our very own Crushers' version, complete with surprises and competitions. Vale, we planned a few games because you're highly competitive. And, Sloan, the sweets are for you, because other than my wife, you're the only sweet one in this room."

"Hey, what about me?" Rourke says, pretending to be offended.

"I said *sweet*, not stupid," Brax says as a few guys chuckle. "As a team, we couldn't ignore what happened in Vegas. You made a lifelong commitment to each other. And we look for *any* excuse to party. Ready for our first game?"

The guys start whistling again, and Brax has to quiet them down before we can begin.

He directs us to sit in two chairs, facing back-to-back, then hands both of us two hockey gloves, one black and one blue.

"What are these for?" I ask, holding them up.

"The Newlywed Game. The black one represents you, Vale. The blue one represents Sloan. We'll ask a question, and you'll raise the glove that corresponds to the person. If your answers match, you get a point. If not, your teammates get a point. If you win, you get a *very* special gift." Then he pauses for a beat. "If you lose, well . . ."

"What?" I frown.

"I can't tell you yet," Brax says, keeping his face guarded. "Just don't lose."

"This should be good," Rourke yells, rubbing his palms together.

Sloan leans toward me and whispers, "How are we going to win this?"

I shake my head. "Hope we get lucky?"

Now that we know there's a punishment if we lose, there's no other option. We have to win.

"Leo's acting as referee to make sure there's no cheating," Brax adds as he shuffles through a stack of cards. "Leo crowd-sourced questions from the team and filtered out the inappropriate ones."

A few guys in the back boo.

Leo looks at us. "You can thank me later."

Brax holds up the first question. "The team wants to know who made the first move in your relationship?"

I can't see Sloan since she's seated behind me, so I have to go with my gut feeling. I shift in my seat, wishing I had an answer. I've never made any intentional moves on Sloan, but if we were dating, I think Sloan would *want* me to make the first move. She's old school like that.

"This shouldn't be that hard," Leo urges. "Hurry up."

I can feel Sloan's arm move, but I can't see which glove she's holding. I pick the black glove representing me, hoping Sloan's choice is the same.

"They both agree," Brax says with a smile. "One point for you."

"Spill the details, Sloan," Lucian, the team captain, says. "We want to hear the story."

Sloan shifts on her seat behind me. "Well, a few months ago, we were at the beach, taking a walk. That's when he held my hand."

"Awwwww," Rourke says in a fake sweet voice. I glower at him while everyone laughs.

We did walk together on the beach several months ago, but I only grabbed her hand when she stumbled over a rock. It wasn't intentional. And it certainly wasn't a "move."

"Next question." Brax flips through the cards. "Who said 'I love you' first?"

"What's with all the firsts?" I ask.

"This is almost like a freebie, it's so easy," Leo says. "Don't tell me you've already forgotten?"

Would Sloan say I love you before me? I don't talk about my feelings openly. *And saying I love you?* I've never said it to any woman I've dated. That's because I don't want to make the same mistake my father did and make promises I can't keep. When I say I love you, it will be to the one woman who is my forever.

"We don't have all day," Leo grumbles. "And your wife has made her decision."

I hold up the black glove again. The whole room breaks into laughter.

Leo clicks his tongue at our error. "Looks like the newlyweds don't agree. Vale, when did you say it?"

"In Vegas, of course." I didn't actually say this in Vegas, but I remember thinking that I *should*. If Sloan was going to become my wife, why *wouldn't* I say it? Her smile lit me up as bright as the city lights. But it didn't feel right to admit something out of obligation.

"Sloan?" Brax asks. "Is that correct?"

"Ah, yes, I forgot," Sloan says with a laugh. "We say I love you so much, I couldn't remember who said it first."

"That means one for the Crushers," Brax adds.

I shoot him a look. "How many questions are there?"

"Best out of five," Leo answers.

Brax flips to another card. "Who initiated the first kiss?"

I shift in my seat. The only kiss we've had is the one at the wedding chapel—a forced kiss that I haven't stopped thinking about. In a hypothetical situation, if I made the first move, I probably initiated the first kiss. I lift my black glove and Jaz gives me an approving smile that tells me we got the point.

"Two points Sloan and Vale," Brax says, before moving along. He flips to the next card and narrows his eyes. "Who fell first?"

I frown. "How are we supposed to answer that?"

"One person had to realize it before the other," Leo says. "Someone *always* falls first."

"It's not that obvious," I say. "Unfair question."

Leo looks at Brax. "Who fell first in your relationship, you or Jaz?"

"I did," Brax says without missing a beat.

"See? Even your brother knows," Leo says, as if this proves his point.

"Thanks, Brax," I mutter, then lift the black glove just to give him an answer. When Sloan makes her choice, the guys erupt into cheers. *Wrong again.*

"Another point for the team," Brax says a little too gleefully. "Last question will determine who wins The Newlywed Game."

It's our last shot. We have to get this one right because I don't want to know what the team has planned for us if it's wrong.

Brax looks at the question, then shakes his head. "I'm not asking this. It crosses the line."

Rourke and Jaxon snicker in the back of the room. Knowing those guys, they probably submitted this question.

"Then I'll ask it," Leo says, plucking the card from his hand. He reads the card, then smirks. "Who was the most nervous on your wedding night?"

The guys howl with laughter. Sloan stiffens behind me as sweat prickles across my back. No matter how you answer, you make someone look bad. And I can't tell them the truth: that we haven't even had a typical wedding night.

I look at Leo. "You're assuming that *someone* was nervous. And even if we were, that's nobody's business."

"I agree." Brax steals the card from Leo and tosses it to the side. "We're not doing that one."

"Well, it was a lot better than the other options I got," Leo says in defense.

Brax sorts through the other cards and pulls one out. "Okay, here's one. And remember, you don't have to give any details. Just answer the question. Who has the biggest secret that they're keeping from their friends?"

I freeze. Even though I know Brax didn't set us up to fail, it feels like he did. Because we've been hiding the biggest secret in front of him this whole time.

I narrow my eyes. "If one of us had a secret, do you think we'd tell you that now?"

"Nobody's asking you to reveal your secrets," Leo clarifies.

I wish I could see Sloan's face right now. Some sign so we could get this question right.

"Cast your vote," Leo says. "Who has a secret?"

Sloan's been so transparent with me about everything that I can't imagine her *not* being honest about other things. If anyone's holding back, it's me.

I finally cast my vote, lifting the black glove.

Leo's mouth curves into a smirk. "Somebody bring out the whipped cream."

TWELVE

Sloan

Vale wheels around, his eyes lifting to the glove I'm holding. "You voted for yourself?" he says with a confused frown, like I did this for him, and not because I'm hiding a secret.

There's a weight pressing against my chest. I shake my head. "Sorry."

"Looks like you're going to enjoy some dessert," Lucian says as Brax carries a tub of whipped cream into the room.

"This is the punishment?" Vale says, glancing between Leo and Brax.

"Who said it was a punishment?" Leo says. "You might actually enjoy this. Tate came up with the rules."

Tate smirks. "You need to feed each other whipped cream."

I glance at the single spoon and shrug. "Easy enough."

Then he holds up a pair of zip ties. "Without your hands."

"How are we supposed to do that?" Vale asks.

"Use any other part of your body," Tate says, zip-tying Vale's hands together before he moves on to me. "And figure it out as a team."

"You couldn't go easy on us, could you?" Vale asks.

"Just be glad I didn't make you do this with your hockey

teammates," he says. "That was somebody's suggestion." He shoots Rourke a dirty look.

"Have fun, you two," Leo says with a wicked smirk.

"So the only rule is that we can't use our hands, but we can use anything else?" I ask, looking toward Tate for confirmation.

"Correct," he says with a nod. "You each have to do it once, which might take multiple tries."

I look at the tub of whipped cream. There's no way to feed Vale easily without my hands. I turn to Vale. "Do you have any good ideas, or should we accept that this will be totally awkward?"

"I've got nothing," he says. "First lesson in marriage: Don't let a bunch of bachelors plan your wedding shower." His mouth curves into a smile.

Vale's third rule is going to bite us in the butt. *Do whatever it takes.*

I study the spoon as the guys make less than helpful suggestions on how to feed Vale without my hands—including suggesting our lips, tongue, ears (seriously?), and elbows.

Nobody sees what's right in front of us—a spoon. "What if I grab the spoon with my mouth, scoop some whipped cream, and then hold it steady for you to take a bite?" I suggest.

Rourke points at us. "You're conspiring. That deserves a penalty."

"Nobody said we couldn't plan our method of attack," Vale grumbles.

"No penalty," Tate agrees. "You can talk through it."

Vale looks at me. "It's worth a try."

I crouch low, grabbing the spoon with my teeth, and then clumsily tilt my head to scoop whipped cream from the tub. At one point, the tub almost slides off the table, but Vale uses his hip to keep it in place.

My idea is still awkward, putting me within inches of Vale's mouth. *Kissing distance.* But without using any part of my lips, this is the only way to avoid direct contact.

"That's cheating," Jaxon says.

"You should have set up more rules," Tate says, taking our side.

His body almost presses against mine. It's not that this should be awkward for a married couple, but considering we haven't even kissed—other than the awkward kiss in the Little Pink Chapel—it feels like forced contact.

Vale leans toward me, and his eyes flick to mine, then down to my lips. For a moment, there's a ripple of something in his gaze, and I nearly drop the spoon.

"Vale!" I mumble.

He reacts with his lightning-fast reflexes, his lips brushing over the spoon before the utensil drops completely, clattering across the floor and settling under a chair.

Vale licks the whipped cream from his lips. "That still counts," he says. He got a half-bite, and we somehow managed to avoid lip contact.

"Maybe," Leo says. "But we aren't helping you get the spoon back for your turn."

Vale glances down at the spoon under a chair.

"You'll never fit under that," I tell him. The legs are too narrow for his shoulders.

"Watch me," he says with a wink. Vale loves a challenge, and nobody is going to tell him he can't do something.

He drops to the ground, his hands awkwardly tied behind his back, and wriggles his body like a snake.

His wide shoulders strain against the chair legs, but the spoon is just out of reach of his mouth.

"I like seeing you on your face," Leo says, crossing his arms. "It's a good look for you."

Vale scoots out from under the chair and glares at Leo. "You're gonna get your butt kicked on the ice later."

Leo laughs. "Not if I'm too fast for you."

Vale eyes the whipped cream. "Got any other ideas?"

"How about using your feet?" Rourke suggests with an eyebrow wiggle.

"Ew. No," I say, frowning. "I don't do feet."

A few of the guys throw out their ideas, which mostly involve things I know Vale wouldn't subject me to.

Vale hesitates, looking for any way to save me from embarrassment. I know the only options left are ones that will make my cheeks flame like I swallowed a torch. I know some girls are good at hiding their feelings, but I'm not one of them. I'm a heart-on-the-sleeve, show-your-emotions kind of girl. If I ever get taken in by the cops for questioning, they won't have to ask me a single question. They'll just look at my face for the answer.

"Trust me on this, okay?" he says.

"What are you . . ." I begin, but Vale doesn't hesitate. He leans forward and presses his cheek into the whipped cream. The side of his face is now snow white, covered with whipped cream. All I have to do is take one bite.

I smile, then lean forward and let my mouth taste the sweetness. When I do, a thrill surges through my body. I can smell Vale's cinnamon scent mixed with the vanilla as the room erupts into cheering.

"Smart," I say, licking the whipped cream from my lips. "I knew there was a reason I married you."

"We make a good team," Vale says to me with a wink. Every time he does that, it's like the knot of tension in my body unravels a little bit.

After we're freed from the zip ties, we cut into the teal-and-gold cake, reminiscent of the Crushers' colors, and I attempt to follow the rules we set up. I stick close to Vale's side, sometimes brushing my hand across his arm, or looping it under his elbow. At one point, Vale wraps his arm around my waist so casually, it makes my heart bounce around in my chest. He might be used to touching women this way, but I'm not. I feel like a total imposter at this marriage thing.

We finish the cake and ice cream, and Jaz motions me toward the front of the room with Vale. "We have one more surprise to present to you both."

She pulls out a large envelope and hands it to us. "The whole team went together on this. Even though the guys like to give you grief, we really do want you to live happily ever after. It's a gift to say how happy we are that you're together. There's no one on earth I trust more than my brother-in-law."

The guilt swells in my chest. I don't have any reason to be nervous, but something ticks inside me, like a time bomb.

Vale looks at me. "Open it," he says quietly.

I tear the flap and reach inside the envelope.

It's a gift certificate for a hotel room in Cancun, Mexico.

I look up as Brax and Jaz beam at us.

"You guys didn't have time for a honeymoon in Vegas, so we wanted to give you a second chance," Brax says. "With the press hounding you about your news, we're sending you away for a break."

"The whole team chipped in for our honeymoon?" Vale says before he looks at me, his eyes wide.

"It was their idea," Jaz says. "We just reserved the rooms."

Vale pulls me into a hug, and a zing of panic rockets through me.

The idea of a honeymoon throws my whole body into a state of chaos.

"Thank you, everyone," I say, choked up. Vale's heartbeat thrums against my ear. "You have no idea how much this means to us."

I glance at Vale. His smile is forced, and his eyes hold the same fear that's pinballing through me.

"We're going on a honeymoon," he says, his gaze meeting mine. There's no way we're getting out of it.

THIRTEEN

Vale

"Do you think my face gave me away?" Sloan asks as soon as we arrive home. Jaz and Brax are still at the arena cleaning up from the party, which means we have a few minutes alone until Leo and Tate arrive.

She drops her purse on the counter and sorts through the mail, avoiding looking directly at me. Maybe this is her way of keeping a safe distance, the silent tug-of-war between the game we're playing and the way my body reacts to her, almost instinctively. It's the gentle pull I constantly want to give in to—the way we're like two magnets drawn together. Every time I'm alone with Sloan, I want to be closer to her.

"I don't think anyone will question tonight's performance," I say, grabbing a cold sports drink from the fridge to cool the fire inside me. Anything to take the edge off.

What they might question is still down the road—when things are over. Something I've shoved to a dark corner of my mind, avoiding thinking about. *The end of us.* The thought of separating from Sloan sends me into a doom spiral. Even if she doesn't feel the same as me, imagining her with another man makes me insanely jealous. I couldn't live in this house, or even this town, and watch her date anyone but me.

She holds up the honeymoon envelope from the team. "What are we going to do about this?"

"We're going to Mexico," I answer.

"Are you seriously suggesting we take this trip?" she says, her eyes wide.

"We can't turn it down," I say. "That would give everyone an immediate tip-off that something is wrong. What man in their right mind would turn down a honeymoon with his wife?"

She bites her lip, thinking it over.

There's so much danger in taking a trip with her. The possibility of us getting too close or her seeing how much I want her, how badly I'm drawn to her, and risking the friendship we have. She has no idea how she turns me into a weak man when I'm alone with her.

"I've noticed you've been distant lately," I say. "Afraid of messing up in front of everyone. There's so much pressure when we're here in Sully's Beach, but if we go on this honeymoon, we're free from that. We don't have to pretend or even sleep in the same room. They reserved a suite, so it would be no different than here. Although personally, I think sharing a room is a perk of being your husband."

A smirk curves her lips. "Even if I snore?"

"Even sexier," I tease.

She swats my backside with a dish towel. "Watch it, Mr. Coco Puffs, or you'll be sleeping on the couch tonight."

"Oooh, I love it when we role-play with our cereal names."

She tips her head back and laughs. "Just not in front of the kids, okay? We'll scar Tate for life."

"Well, Leo's already scarred by living with two sets of newly-weds," I add.

"I didn't think anything bothered that man. Does he even have a heart?"

"If he does, it's probably made of stone," I say. We hear a door slam and the sound of boxes dropping in the hall.

"Hey, lovebirds!" Jaz shouts. "This is your warning that we're home. So if you're in the middle of your 'alone time' . . ."

Sloan's face immediately heats as she stammers, "We're just in the kitchen . . . doing *absolutely* nothing!"

"How disappointing," Jaz says as she enters the room with a sly grin, Brax following.

Sloan lifts an eyebrow. "You should be relieved." She immediately bumps into me, her hip brushing my leg, sending energy through me. She's blissfully ignorant of how tough it is for me to keep my thoughts straight when she's this close.

"And thank you for a fabulous wedding shower and gift," Sloan adds. "Best sister and brother ever." Sloan goes in for a group hug, pulling me into the huddle.

"It was all Jaz's genius," Brax says, admiring his wife. "Except for the games. But that's the only way we could get the team on board. Especially Leo."

"Leo agreed to this?" Sloan asks, arching an eyebrow.

"Who knew, right? Turns out, if you dangle a competition in front of him, even the alpha male softens up," Brax says. "He and Tate headed to Boots and Buckles for line dancing tonight. I think they're feeling left out now that half the house is married."

"Leo and Tate actually agreed on something?" I say.

"Yeah, for about five minutes . . . right before they were ready to murder each other," Brax adds.

Jaz takes her sister by the shoulders. "Please don't worry about a thing while you're gone. I will take care of everything."

"Since you're getting away before the season begins, the timing is perfect," Brax says.

"And before the press finds out," Jaz adds. "As long as nobody from the team squeals."

Just what we need. The press documenting our every move on our honeymoon. Another reason to take this trip now.

I turn to Sloan. "See? Nothing to worry about. Your sister thought of everything." I wrap one arm around Sloan's waist, noticing the way her body seems to fit perfectly into mine.

"My sister always does," she says, pasting on a nervous smile. "What could I want more than a week alone with my husband?"

The tension in her tone is hard to miss. On our last trip, we got married. The next logical step would be . . . *nope, not going there.* We absolutely cannot end up in bed together.

We'll have to enforce separate sleeping spaces and keep space between us at all times.

Heat rises in my chest just thinking about all the ways this could go very, very wrong. Even if she is my wife, I already agreed to rule four. Which means I can't sleep with Sloan, no matter how much I want to.

———

The next day, I wake up early and quietly slip out of the bedroom so I don't disturb Sloan. She went to bed early with a headache—another sign we need to get her on these new meds ASAP. Brax is in the kitchen when I step into the room, the smoky smell of bacon filling the house. I brush by him, grabbing an apple and a protein bar on my way out the door.

Brax looks over his coffee cup at me. "Where are you headed so early?"

"I want to catch Libby in HR before she gets tied up in meetings. Sloan still hasn't been added to the insurance plan."

The bacon sizzles as Brax flips the meat. "Why not take care of it when you return? She has her insurance with the university, right?"

"Yeah, but she wants to start some new meds before we leave."

"The super expensive one?"

"How'd you know?" I say, stopping to study my brother. I didn't think anyone knew about that drug except for us.

"Sloan texted Jaz about it in Vegas. Sounded like she was desperate to get that drug. Good thing the marriage solved that problem so conveniently." He takes another sip of coffee as my stomach turns to lead.

Another reminder why Sloan probably isn't interested in anything more with me. She was desperate to get her problem solved, not hop into a marriage contract with a friend. And now, I can't help but wonder if my brother suspects it too.

I bite into my apple. "I want to take care of things now. Getting her on my insurance plan could make the difference between enjoying our trip and feeling rotten."

"Makes sense." He nods, then takes the bacon from the frying pan and lays it on a paper towel. "How are you dealing with things?" He studies me, and I know that look. He's worried about something.

"Dealing with what?"

"Getting used to being married. Sloan's had her share of setbacks. It's not easy to care for someone with health problems."

I slowly chew my apple, making sure my face is stone. My twin brother can read me like a book, but I need for him to believe I'm happy. That Sloan and I are in love.

"If I can deal with it as her friend, I can definitely deal with it as her husband." As much as I hate what happened to Sloan, her injury opened the door for us meeting. If she hadn't stopped working, Jaz wouldn't have rented out rooms to a bunch of rowdy hockey players.

"I'm just making sure you aren't second-guessing your decision," he says.

"Why would I second-guess anything with Sloan?" I say, slightly defensive.

"Because a lot of people who get married in Vegas do," he says, looking uneasy.

I frown. "Wait. Did Jaz tell you to ask me this?"

Brax turns back to the stove. "Why would you think that?"

"Because as my brother, you never question my decisions." I wait a beat. "She set you up, didn't she?"

Brax finally drags his eyes to me and sighs. "Only because she cares about her sister. Sloan's made rash decisions in the past. She doesn't always think things through. Especially when she's under pressure."

"We didn't take this decision lightly, Brax," I say, leveling my gaze. "Especially Sloan. And if you want to tell Jaz the truth, then tell her I'm fully committed to Sloan's happiness."

If only they knew I was the one who talked Sloan into this decision. She wasn't drunk, reckless, or swept up by some impulsive moment. If anyone had doubts, it was Sloan—and she had every reason to hesitate.

Brax studies me for a second. "I believe you, Vale. It's just that everything happened so fast. Jaz was worried—and rightfully so—that you married her out of pity or something. And that's exactly what she doesn't need right now. She needs someone to love her."

"And I do," I say with more intensity than I mean to. The words reverberate across my body like a struck bell. I haven't admitted my feelings out loud before, even though I've known it for a while. Maybe the cynics say it's not possible, but some connections are like that—instant and overwhelming.

I rub the back of my neck. "Sloan wouldn't have married me if I pitied her. She's not that desperate."

He nods once, slowly. "You're right. And I know you don't rush into big decisions." He slaps my shoulder, but it doesn't help me feel better. There's still a rock sitting on my chest.

He trusts me to tell him everything, and I've kept the full truth from him. We married for convenience, yes, but that's only half of what's bothering me. The truth is that I want Sloan to feel the same about me. If she did, why didn't she date me a year ago when I asked her out? All she said was that she couldn't, and I was left assuming the attraction was one-sided.

"Sloan is the reason I made the decision, Brax. There's nothing I wouldn't do for her."

Just then, footsteps pad down the hall and Jaz appears, her hair pulled into a messy bun.

"Good morning, love," Brax says, his face softening. He pulls her into his arms and gives her a long kiss.

I clear my throat. "Get a room, you two."

"Already have one." Brax smirks, keeping one arm looped around her back. "I'm just showing you how to greet your wife." Then he wraps his other hand around her shoulder and gives her another kiss to finish what he started.

Jealousy squeezes my chest tighter. More than anything, I want that with Sloan—more than playing for the NHL, more than winning the Stanley Cup. I want someone I can spend my life with. I want her.

Just then, Sloan appears in her pajamas. She blinks at her sister and Brax. "Excuse me," she announces. "But some of us just got up, you know."

Jaz laughs as she pulls away from Brax. "You need to take notes."

That's my cue to greet her like a husband. Maybe not quite so affectionately, but rule two definitely applies here.

"Hey, beautiful," I open my arms for Sloan, but she just freezes, like she's afraid I'm about to bite her.

"I'm not exactly huggable right now," she says.

"You're always huggable," I say, closing the gap between us. When my hands find her body, I pull her into my chest and immediately feel her body soften in my arms. One hand finds the hem of her tank top, while the other strokes her spine. I nuzzle my face in her neck, smelling the faint scent of last night's perfume. I want to brush my lips across the soft curve of her neck, to peel back the tiny strap of her tank top and kiss the skin beneath it . . .

Stop. Right. There. I can't let my mind wander—for so many reasons.

Jaz smiles at us in approval. "Before you two hurry off, I wanted to let you know one more thing. How do you feel about renewing your vows?"

"So soon?" Sloan asks, surprised.

"For your friends and family who missed your actual ceremony. Apparently it's your mother-in-law's wish to have something official—something more than just a party," Jaz says with a smile full of secrets.

When I visited Mom last, she told me how much she couldn't wait for me to get married. Ever since my siblings tied the knot, she's worried I'll be the one left alone. My mom sacrificed her entire life for us as a single mom, but she would never wish the same for me.

"But you already threw a party for us," Sloan says.

"That was a wedding shower. What if you could have the wedding you've always dreamed of?"

Sloan shakes her head. "I don't have the money for a wedding like that."

"I don't mean you would pay for it," Jaz says, taking the eggs from the fridge. "I know someone who would be more than happy to give you the wedding of your dreams. Someone who's willing to pay for the entire thing . . . if they get to photograph it."

"Who?" she asks.

"*The Star Report*," she says. "They contacted me at the office and made an offer. They want to do a feature wedding shoot and in return will cover everything. They contacted me because Vale is refusing to talk to the press right now, and they knew I was the only one who would relay the message."

"No," Sloan says. "It's really not necessary."

Jaz puts down the eggs and faces her sister. "This is every bride's dream, you do realize that?"

"I'm not every bride," Sloan insists.

Jaz turns to me. "Ever since we were kids, my sister has planned her dream wedding. She wanted the white dress, the big outdoor wedding, a string quartet playing 'Canon in D.' She might not plan a lot of things, but this was the *one* thing she always dreamed of." Jaz's eyes drill into me. Nothing like pushy in-laws to pressure you into a very public wedding that will be all over the internet. When Jaz asked me the other day if I'd consider a *simple* party, I shrugged and said yes. Apparently, the "simple" part morphed into a sponsored wedding feature paid for by *The Star Report.*

Jaz takes her sister's arm. "Hey, I'm doing this for you. I don't want you to ever feel like you got shorted on your wedding dreams."

"I'm perfectly happy with our Vegas ceremony," Sloan says.

Jaz gives her a look. "You're a terrible liar, Sloan. You've mentioned more than once how Eunice was deaf and Clarence almost fell asleep."

Sloan looks to me for help and I shrug. "She isn't wrong."

"Then it's a done deal," Jaz says with a satisfied smile. "Vale, your mom will be so happy. When I hinted that *The Star Report* wanted to make a deal for a wedding feature, she was nearly frantic with excitement. She wants a repeat of everything. The vows. The kiss. The whole wedding enchilada."

My gut feels tied into knots. This complicates everything.

It was one thing to get married in front of strangers in a shady chapel we weren't even sure was legit. It's another thing to do it in front of our friends and family—and the entire world, who will see the pictures.

But at this point, I don't have a choice. If I refuse, I'll let down my family, and it will give the press even more reason to hound us for Vegas details. Letting *The Star Report* document our wedding will satisfy everyone, even if it makes me the most miserable man ever. Because all I really want is Sloan. I want to wake up to her sweet smile, to trail kisses across her collarbone at night. To hold her hand as we fall asleep, her fingers curling into mine, not letting go.

But the reality is, I can never have her, no matter how good we are at pretending.

FOURTEEN

Vale

I'm able to forget about my honeymoon—or at least push it into the back of my mind—as soon as I enter the staff offices for the Carolina Crushers. Located on the second floor in the Ice House Arena, the office wing smells like freshly printed paper and burned coffee. This morning, there's an inexplicable buzz in the air as the staff ramps up for a new season. It feels like opening a fresh notebook on the first day of school. Everyone is beaming, fueled by copious amounts of caffeine and hope that this is the year we'll make it to the playoffs.

Given my newly married status, I've got two things to do before I can fully concentrate on the season ahead: Get my wife the medicine she needs and get through our honeymoon without ruining our friendship.

Heading toward the HR office, I round the corner and nearly slam into Rafael Marco.

"Excuse me, sir," I say, pivoting so I don't crash into him.

"Vale! You're a man on a mission." He gives me a brilliantly white smile that's a stark contrast to his tanned skin. He spends his summers at his beach house in Puerto Rico, which explains why he looks like a retired millionaire living on a yacht.

"Where are you going in such a hurry?"

I motion toward the HR office. "Meeting with Libby. Need to get our insurance in order before we leave on our honeymoon."

He smirks. "Is that wife of yours cracking the whip now?"

"I'm trying to be more responsible now that I'm married," I say, shifting uncomfortably under the weight of his stare. I quickly shove my hands in my pockets, hoping he won't press further. "You know . . . trying to do the right thing." If anyone would understand that, it's him, right?

He offers a nod of approval before glancing over his shoulder. "Stop by my office after your meeting. I've been wanting to talk to you." Something in his tone shifts, tipping me off that this isn't just a casual man-to-man chat over drinks. This is serious.

I head to Libby's office and peek my head around the door. "You available for a few minutes?"

"Well, if it isn't the happy newlywed!" She stops her work and motions to an empty chair. "Come on in, Vale." It might only be eight in the morning, but already she's chewing her gum, buzzing with energy.

"I'm sorry if the news was a shock," I say, sitting across from her. I rub my hands across my knees. This is so much harder than I imagined it would be.

She waves off my concern. "If it's love, why wait? Your big announcement was like watching a fairy tale come true. I got shivers just reading about it!" She props her chin on her hand and looks at me dreamily. "Was it everything you ever hoped for?"

"Marrying Sloan was definitely a dream come true," I say, even though the circumstances around it were less than ideal.

Libby waits, clearly expecting more details, and I realize that if I give her even a sliver, I'll be the hot topic around the water cooler for the rest of the week. I clear my throat, forcing a smile. "But hey, I'm not here to talk about my wedding. Actually, I need to add Sloan to my insurance plan."

"Of course!" She hits a few buttons on her computer, and the printer roars to life. Then she hands me some forms. "Sign these, and you'll be good to go."

I start signing while Libby taps away at her keyboard, her jaw still working. "I know people are talking about why you got married, but I'm a hopeless romantic. I don't doubt for a second that it's love."

I pause, pen in hand. "What do you mean, *talking*?"

"Oh, I've heard a few people mention it in passing. You know how people are. They can't believe you'd fall in love that fast."

I wonder who she's talking about and what they're saying. "You mean, people here?"

"Well, yes. And a few people around town."

I tap my pen on the desk. "I've had feelings for Sloan since the beginning. Long before Vegas." Admitting it out loud makes me feel better about signing these insurance forms. Our marriage is fully legal, so I'm not committing fraud. Somehow, it just feels like I'm doing something wrong when she phrases it that way.

"I guessed you've been harboring a secret flame for her," she says, her voice low.

"Did one of my teammates talk to you?" I ask.

"I shouldn't give names," she says, looking torn between confessing to me and keeping her secret.

"If it's a teammate who has questions, they can come to me." Then I lean back in my chair. "Like any of them could talk. They pick up women faster than our Vegas wedding ceremony."

She giggles. "Don't worry. I believe you. So does Lauren in PR. Just between you and me, I'm betting you and Sloan stay married for the long haul."

As if there was some doubt?

"Thanks for your vote of confidence," I say, signing the last form, trying to hide the sting of her words. I didn't realize people were already speculating about the longevity of our relationship. If they knew the truth, they might think I'm an idiot for risking my reputation for Sloan's insurance—or worse, think Sloan used me, even though I know she'd rather cut off her right foot than ask me for a favor. Without question, I wanted to marry her. But people will believe what they want. This conversation is proof of that.

I slide the paperwork across her desk.

She looks it over and smiles. "Good luck with everything! Don't worry, eventually people will stop talking."

"You think?"

"They just need time to see that it's real," she says with a shrug. "If it is, you have nothing to worry about."

I force a smile. "Yeah, nothing to worry about." The only thing *real* in this relationship is how I feel. But maybe—*just maybe*—if I showed Sloan how I felt, she might take a risk on something more. Or she could do what she always does when she's scared: shut me out completely. And that's not an option I want to gamble on.

At least I have Libby on my side. But if my teammates start questioning me, it could destroy the trust we've built—and that will definitely affect our performance on the ice.

Trust is earned, not given.

After leaving Libby's office, I head down to Rafael Marco's door. I knock once and the door swings open. My gray-haired agent, Jim King waits on the other side, along with our general operations manager, Zach Collins.

"Jimmy?" I say, astonished he'd drop in without telling me.

"Hey, Vale. Congratulations on your wedding." He shakes my hand a little too forcefully, tipping me off that something's up.

"I didn't think anyone else was in here," I say, taking a step back.

"Oh no," says Rafael. "We were just waiting for you."

Heat prickles up the back of my neck.

I slowly lower myself into a leather chair and rub my palms across my pants. I didn't know there'd be an interrogation squad waiting behind the door.

"This must be serious or else I'm losing my job," I say with a nervous laugh. "Which would also be serious."

Rafael and Jimmy both chuckle. Zach, I notice, does not. My heart jumps a beat.

"Rest assured, you're not losing your job," Rafael says. "You're one of the best forwards we've ever had, along with your brother."

I breathe a sigh of relief, but the oxygen still feels like it's being sucked from the room.

Rafael knits his hands together in the casual way that high-powered bosses do before they bring down the axe. I'm about as comfortable as a lobster over a pot of boiling water. "We just wanted to ask a few questions. Specifically, about your contract with the Crushers."

Questions about my contract? That can't be good. I've never been questioned about my contractual obligations before.

Zach studies his iPad while Jimmy shifts uncomfortably in his seat. Then Zach looks up at me. "Contracts are evaluated and renewed on a yearly basis, and we realize a player's life might change in that time. In your case, you got married."

I clear my throat. "Yes, but that shouldn't affect my contract."

"It doesn't, but we're making exceptions for you by giving you time off for your honeymoon."

I look from Zach to Jimmy. "Is that what this is about? Listen, if you need to take away a paycheck to resolve my unplanned leave, then do it. I don't want to cause trouble."

Jimmy looks at Rafael. "The boss approved your leave without an additional deduction from your pay. You have him to thank for that gift."

I turn to the boss. "Thank you, Mr. Marco."

Zach leans an arm on his leather chair. "Even though some might take offense at getting extra paid vacation time."

"Has anyone complained?" I think through who might grumble about me getting an extra week of vacation. Jaxon or Rourke? "Obviously, I wasn't expecting to get married."

"We realize that," Zach says, shifting his position. "And that's why we brought you in today—to discuss changes." He looks to my agent for help.

Jimmy takes the cue and leans toward me. "We wanted to ask if you and Sloan have discussed a no-movement clause now that you're married?"

"Not yet," I say, realizing it never even crossed my mind. A no-movement clause would keep me from being traded to another team without my consent. It allows a player to remain in one location and is important for married players who want to keep some stability in their families. My brother initiated a no-movement clause after he married Jaz, so it only makes sense that I'd do the same. "But I'm sure she'd feel strongly about not moving away from Sully's Beach."

"Before you do, I have news." Jimmy shifts forward, his eyes glinting. "Our NHL affiliate team has shown an interest in moving you to their team. I was going to mention the possibility of a trade when you returned from Vegas, but then I found out about your marriage and decided to talk with Zach and Rafael on your behalf about your options."

"Tampa is interested in me?" I blurt out, trying not to act like a kid who's about to unwrap his first gift on Christmas morning. "I've wanted to play for them since high school."

"They are *very* interested," Jimmy adds with a quirk of his lips. This is why he's a good agent. He can sell anything. "Except now that you're married, we realized *you* might not be. Sloan's ongoing medical condition throws a monkey wrench into things." He looks at Zach and something passes between the two of them. "There are significant concerns about how that will affect you."

I hold up my hand to interrupt. "Hold on. What does Sloan's injury have to do with my current hockey contract?"

Zach slowly brings his fingertips together. "Should she continue to have health issues, she might need additional care. More hospital stays. Additional travel to Cleveland. We don't want there to be a situation in which you're asking for more time off. We expect you to adhere to the contract—sick wife or not."

So that's what this is about. They're worried about me breaking my contractual obligations because of Sloan's health.

"I won't break my contract," I say firmly. "She's going on a new medication that will hopefully resolve her issues. From what the doctor has said, this new drug should keep her from relapsing anymore."

"And if it doesn't?" Zach asks. "Then what?"

I don't say anything because I haven't thought that far ahead. There never was a question of whether this *wouldn't* work. We went into the marriage determined that when Sloan made a full recovery, we could decide what to do at that point.

"We want you to know that we're on your side," Zach adds.

Ironic, because it doesn't feel like it.

He taps his fingertips together. "But we also want you to know that if you're interested in a no-movement clause, we may need you to make some concessions. Just in case."

I frown. "What kind of concessions?"

"In order to add a no-movement clause to your contract, we'd need to negotiate a lower salary," Jimmy says. "But we might be able to get some performance bonuses instead. And given your talent, you'd probably have no problem meeting those goals."

I shift in my seat. One minute I'm dreaming of playing for Tampa, and the next I'm being asked to renegotiate my salary with the team. This feels like I'm being punished for getting married, even though I know that's not the case. Sloan's health is a liability, and everyone here knows it.

"Whatever it takes to add that no-movement clause, I'll do it."

Jimmy holds up a hand to stop me. "Don't rush into it, Vale. Go on your honeymoon. Talk to your wife about it, and then give me an answer. That's when we'll renegotiate your contract. If you add the no-movement clause, you're turning down Tampa's offer. You realize that?" He levels his gaze at me.

"Of course I do," I say, my voice scraping like a knife across wood.

It's always been my dream to play for the NHL. I'd be a fool to turn them down. But what choice do I have? I made a promise to her. Asking her to uproot her life right now would be unfair and selfish. I can't even consider it.

Zach leans back in his chair and folds his hands together. "Good. Because I wouldn't want you to rush into things. Giving up the NHL this year is a big decision. If your marriage is important, I'm sure there will be no concerns about adding a no-movement clause into your contract, even if this limits your future." His gaze penetrates through me.

Limits my future? In other words, give up my dream. Possibly, for good.

Jimmy nods. "I'm sure you'll make the right decision." He wants me to be sure I know how this affects my career.

A hockey player already has a limited shelf life. Four and a half years, on average. If I give up the next year or two for Sloan, there might never be an opportunity to play for Tampa.

If I knew she wanted to stay with me forever, there would be no question about this decision. I'd sign the new contract in a heartbeat. I'd stay with the Crushers until I retired from the sport.

But if I'm only doing this for Sloan's health, then what will be left for me when the marriage is over?

Nothing. Not Sloan. Possibly not even an NHL career.

I'll be a washed-up hockey player with nothing to fight for.

Which means there's only one thing I can do before I sign my life and NHL dreams away.

Hold on to the one dream that's still possible.

Convince Sloan to really be my wife, in every sense of the word.

FIFTEEN

Sloan

"You ready for this?" Vale asks when I finally get my seat belt buckled in the airplane. The last week has been a blur, like a video clip sped up to triple speed.

Since then, we've added me to Vale's insurance and received the prescription drug shipped overnight delivery in time for our trip. It's been such a rush getting everything done that I can hardly believe we're headed to Cancun as husband and wife.

Well, *sort of.*

By law, we're married. But in our hearts, we're anything but on the same page.

I crack open a book and lean my head against the comfy first-class seat. "Now that we're on the plane, we can finally relax," I say with a sigh. "We don't even have to pretend we're married."

"Yeah," Vale says, not sounding as excited as I'd expected.

"What?" I ask, glancing at him. "I thought you'd be ecstatic about that."

"Yeah, no more pretending we're the perfect happily wedded couple," he says, his voice thick with sarcasm.

"I don't get it. I thought this would be a relief to you."

"Who said I don't enjoy being with you?" he asks, putting on his headphones.

"Even when you're sleeping on the floor?" I raise an eyebrow, giving him a knowing look. "I saw you limping around this morning—your back's practically screaming at you. You can take the bed in the hotel room. My honeymoon gift to you. I'll sleep on the sofa."

He shakes his head. "No wife of mine will do that."

There's a soft flutter inside my chest. How much longer until I grow tired of Vale calling me his wife? *Probably never.*

I pull off his headphones so I can have his full attention. "Why do you do that?"

"Do what?"

"Call me your wife?"

He glances up from his phone. "You are, aren't you?"

"You know what I mean. That's for when we're around people," I say.

He waves his hands at the passengers in first class. "These aren't *people?*"

"You know what I mean," I say, turning back to my book. "You can call me Sloan. Just Sloan. Not *my wife.*"

"What if I like calling you my wife?" He smirks and my heart tumbles, free-falling like a tiny pebble off the edge of the Grand Canyon.

There's something about the way he says it and then grins that makes my pulse hammer. It's dangerous how much I love it. Every time he looks at me like that, I have to fight the urge to climb into his lap, wrap my arms around his neck, and kiss him just like a proper wife would.

I quickly avert my eyes, changing the subject so he doesn't see the heat splotches making their way up my neck. "What do you want to do when we arrive in Cancun?"

He flips to the notes app on his phone, then turns his screen around to show me. "I made a list of fun things we could try."

The list is called, "Things to do in Cancun with my wife." Already, I have a love/hate relationship with this list.

Snorkeling
Jet Skiing
Parasailing
Zip-lining
Scuba diving
Boating
Deep-sea fishing
Putting lotion on Sloan's back

"One of these is not like the other," I say with a laugh. "Nor as challenging."

He lifts an eyebrow. "As your husband, I will not let you burn, and that is a challenge to me. Since no one can reach that spot in the middle of their back, I volunteer as tribute."

The thought of Vale stroking my back, rubbing me down with lotion, makes me feel like my face is melting off. He's offering me the chance to enact the fantasy of every woman in America right now.

I clear my throat, trying to rein in my thoughts, which are running wild like a toddler in a candy store. "I'm warning you, I burn like butter on a hot skillet."

"Challenge accepted," he says, his gaze loosening the last of my defenses. "And I like butter. On everything."

Holy moly, I've got to stop thinking about how much I like butter.

I turn back to his list, avoiding his heated gaze, even though it tips my heart over like a spilled glass. "You, um, actually think I could deep-sea fish or scuba dive?"

"I could teach you," he says. "It would be my pleasure to."

I set my book in my lap. "Vale, I wasn't expecting you'd want to do things with me."

"Why not?" He frowns. "I'm not going to Cancun to be alone, Sloan."

I sigh. "I just don't want you to feel obligated to hang out with me. I'm not exactly a daredevil. I'm more of a sit-by-the-pool-with-a-book-and-pink-lemonade kind of girl. If you stick with me, I'll probably just end up holding you back from all the fun."

"You would never hold me back," he scoffs. "And I want to have fun with you. You're my wife."

There he goes again, calling me his wife! I glance at my book, pretending to read, hiding the way his words barrel though me. He makes me feel like someone he actually *wants* to be with, not just someone he's stuck with on this honeymoon. But no matter how sweet or charming he is, I cannot let myself fall for my best friend. Because that will only make it harder when we end our marriage.

"Uh, Sloan? Is your book good?" he asks.

"Mm-hmm," I mumble, refusing to meet his woodsy eyes that I know will only make things worse.

Without warning, he takes the book from my hands.

"Hey!" I protest, reaching for it.

He flips it around, smirking. "You can't read if it's upside down."

I blink. "Oh . . . right," I say, fighting the flush creeping up my neck. "Well, you don't have to entertain me, Vale. I have a book."

"You won't get much reading done if you don't know which way is up." He lifts an eyebrow.

I shoot him a pointed look. "Listen. This trip might not be all rosy. What if the medicine doesn't work? I don't expect you to babysit me because I'm down with a migraine, like you did in Vegas." I think back to our first night together, waking to Vale's arm locked around me, and the swirl of emotions when I thought something more had happened.

"Okay, then how about a compromise? If you're feeling well, you'll go on one adventure per day with me. We won't do anything too hard or scary, but you'll let me pick the date."

"Date . . . like a *real* date? Wait, did Jaz set you up with this idea?"

He scoffs, pretending to be insulted. "I'm hurt you'd think I couldn't come up with this all on my own, without your sister's help."

"You know Jaz. She *loves* to help." I lean my head back. "She's basically planning my entire wedding while I'm gone." After years of bossing everyone around, she's used to pulling off last-minute events with seventeen color-coded checklists. I'm a fly-by-the-seat-of-my-pants kind of girl. As sisters, we couldn't be more different. "Before I left, she wrote me a note with advice . . ." I immediately stop, but not before Vale notices my abrupt halt.

His face turns to mine. "What kind of advice? Like a list of activities?"

"No." I shake my head quickly, hoping he'll let it go. "It wasn't important." I fold my book into my chest, hiding my evidence. Only two seconds ago, I remembered the note is inside my book, holding my page. It was the only way Jaz could get me to take it.

"It sounds important," he says, studying my unconvincing poker face.

"Definitely not. Where is our flight attendant?" I glance up and down the aisle. "I could really use a drink about now." Or a hole in the floor to jump out of. Even an emergency landing would be better than Vale discovering Jaz's honeymoon advice.

"Your sister loves her to-do lists," he says. "Even the to-do lists she creates after she's done something just so she can cross it off. Knowing Jaz, I'm sure it was full of all kinds of important tasks for your honeymoon."

We both know that Jaz would never give me that kind of list for a vacation. She might have an unhealthy attachment to her color-coded lists, but she's also intuitive enough to know when they're not needed.

I search the front of the plane for the flight attendant, who seems to be hiding. "It was a girls-only list. Private stuff. Not meant for husbands."

"Intriguing," he says with that unfairly persuasive smirk that instantly disarms me. "I'd love to know what kind of private stuff."

"You'll have to pry it from my cold, dead hands, Vale," I warn him with what I hope is my equally persuasive death glare. "Which might actually happen when I go scuba diving and forget how to use my oxygen tank."

He squeezes my hand gently and smiles. "You will not run out of oxygen during scuba lessons. I'll make sure of that."

Maybe, but the way he's sucking oxygen from the plane by giving me that sexy smile is going to be my undoing.

He strokes his thumb along the back of my hand, sending tingles up my arm. "And I'll *gladly* get a lemonade with you pool-side and rub lotion on your back. But I won't leave you sulking in the room. We'll have fun *together*. Remember the list we came up with earlier—the one about how we behave as newlyweds?"

"Yes," I say, my heart skittering across my chest. "But that doesn't count here, right?"

"Those still hold true."

I mentally replay them. *Be together all the time. Touch each other as often as possible. Make it believable, whatever it takes. And never, ever have sex.*

"The last one makes total sense—if we want to stay friends." I give him a quick glance. "But why would the rest apply, when no one's around?" It's not that I don't immediately warm to the idea. It's that I'm terrified of losing myself in this charade—of blurring the lines between what's real and what isn't. It could happen too easily. I could lose myself in this game completely.

"People will be watching. This is a test for us. I think we need to get comfortable with each other." His gaze locks on me. "Get to know each other . . . on a *different* level."

"Like marriage isn't enough of a different level?" I ask, suddenly feeling nervous.

"Sloan, I think we need to date first."

Suddenly he's raised the stakes. Because if he treats me like someone he *actually* cares about—with romantic gestures, kissing, the whole dating kit and caboodle—how am I supposed to stop myself from believing our relationship could be real? *I won't.*

"Will you go out with me tonight?" he asks.

If I say yes, it will shred my emotions like ice in a blender. He'll make me feel like *his*, wrapping himself around my heart in the most splendid ways.

But I'm already committed to this partnership. I can't back out now.

"Okay," I finally say. "Just don't ask me what the list says."

He chuckles. "Deal."

Until now I'd mostly been dreading the idea of enduring this honeymoon alone. But now everything feels like the moment before you jump out of an airplane.

Like this could be the best or worst decision of your life.

———

When we finally reach our hotel, I'm drenched in sweat from the short walk from the shuttle stop.

"I'm off to find a drink," I tell Vale, leaving him in the lobby check-in line to explore the hotel by myself. I discover a cute tiki-style outdoor bar near the pool waterfall and settle on a barstool.

Not a minute after I take my first sip of ice-cold lemonade, my phone dings. It's a text from Vale.

My heart does a weird flip when I read *Vale MacPherson would like to cordially invite you . . .*

Then it has a link, which I click on. My phone opens a virtual invitation that says, *"Dinner overlooking the ocean. We'll watch the sunset while enjoying a delicious meal together. After-dinner activities include: a walk on the beach or a sunset swim, your choice. If you accept this invitation, festivities begin at five sharp."*

I check my watch. It's four p.m., which only gives me an hour.

Before tapping the button that says I agree, I open my book and find the note Jaz gave me.

Across the top it reads, *Advice for Your Honeymoon* and the first thing listed is "Always say yes when he asks you to do something together. Even if it's something out of your comfort zone. And second, never be afraid to say what's on your mind. Even if it's something hard to say, speak up. He'll love you more for it."

Vale can never see this note, but maybe my sister is onto something. I can say yes to his list of date activities, but the idea of being completely honest with him—especially about my feelings—makes my heart gallop like a wild stallion. Risking our friendship is a leap I'm not sure I can take right now.

I tap the button to say yes to Vale's virtual invitation, before tucking the note back into the book.

At least I can tell Jaz I used it now. And maybe it will come in handy later.

Just then, a man strides across the patio toward me, his gaze heavy. My breath catches when our eyes meet, and I realize it's Vale. His mouth quirks into that boyish half-smile that will be my undoing on this trip.

"Hey, beautiful," he says. "Here's your key to our suite. Enjoy." He hands me the key card and turns to go.

"Wait. Where are you going?" I ask.

"I need to run an errand before our date tonight."

"What errand?" I ask, wondering what he's up to.

His smile reaches all the way to his eyes. "Can't tell you. It's a secret." He takes a wisp of my hair and tucks it behind my ear. "You can have the room to yourself while I'm gone. See you at five." Then he wheels around and leaves me with my sweating glass of lemonade and the ghost of his touch.

I know he's just being thoughtful, giving me space so I won't feel awkward about sharing a room with him.

If only he knew that when he leaves me like this, it makes me want him all the more.

SIXTEEN

Vale

"Always keep surprises up your sleeve. It's how you keep your wife guessing," Brax told me before I left for the honeymoon. "Look at this trip as a chance for you and Sloan to really bond."

"Listen, Brax, I appreciate the advice, but why are you so worried about this trip? Isn't the honeymoon the easy part?"

"I just want this to work out for you."

Of course, Brax wants it to work. If we eventually end this marriage, it'll put pressure on the entire family, and I can't be the one who causes a rift. That conversation has been weighing on me ever since we left Sully's Beach. Now that we're here, the pressure feels more real than ever.

With that in mind, I arrange my first surprise: a picnic dinner in a secluded spot, away from the usual tourists. The perfect chance to show Sloan how much she means to me—if I don't screw it up.

As soon as I leave the hotel, I arrange dinner plans and then head to the street market to find Sloan a bouquet from a flower cart—something to let her know I'm thinking about her.

With only a few minutes left to spare, I rush back to our suite and knock.

For a few panicked seconds, there's no response. My mind races, wondering if Sloan is rethinking this whole dating thing. Tonight was supposed to be the start of showing her just how incredible she is. It's the first step in wooing her, in making her see that I want more than just friendship. It might seem crazy that we're doing this whole dating and marriage thing backward, but I've never been a conventional guy—or someone who backs down when there's an obstacle.

Finally, the door swings open, and there's Sloan, looking stunning in a deep teal dress that grazes her knees. Swimsuit straps peek from her shoulders. I soak her up like an old, shriveled sponge—because, let's face it, it's been a long time since I've even tried to date anyone, let alone someone like her.

"I hope this will work?" she says, glancing down at her dress. "Or should I change?"

She must have mistaken my silence for disapproval, when in reality, I was just struck speechless. "Sloan, you look fantastic. Don't change. Please."

Her gaze falls to the bouquet in my hand. "Flowers? You're really pulling out all the stops, huh?" She grins, taking the bouquet and placing it in a glass of water. "So, are you going to tell me where we're headed for our date? Because I've been googling all the local restaurants that overlook the ocean."

My stomach churns nervously. Is she expecting a fancy restaurant? Because that's not what I had in mind for our first date.

"What?" she asks, studying me as we head to the elevator.

"Sloan, I'm not taking you to a restaurant tonight," I say slowly. "If you want to change plans, we can."

"Oh, Vale," she says. "I didn't mean to make it sound like I wanted to change plans. I'm perfectly fine with whatever you've planned." She plays with her new ring while avoiding my gaze.

Something has shifted between us, and I can't put my finger on what. Maybe it's the fact that we're finally alone. Away from the team. Away from the pressure and the press. With all the time in the world to get to know the person we married.

The elevator dings, and the doors slide open. We step inside, the awkwardness hanging between us as I catch her reflection in the polished doors.

"I hope I won't disappoint you, but we're picking up dinner from the chef downstairs and then heading to a surprise location."

"Where?"

"Show me your sister's list and I'll tell you," I say with a smirk.

"Vale," she says. "That's not fair."

"Then I guess you'll have to wait to find out."

We pick up the food and walk out of our hotel as I check my notes for tonight's date. According to the Facebook posts I read in the Honeymoon to Cancun group, the people who told me about this spot claimed it was off the beaten track and incredibly romantic, known by the locals as "Lover's Hideaway."

As we head onto an overgrown trail, we suddenly escape the crowds and cars and are thrust into a thick grove of trees. I'm hoping that trusting a stranger in a Facebook group for a romantic date spot wasn't a stupid idea, or Sloan may not ever trust me again. Suddenly, the lush forest opens up as we reach the summit, and we both stop in our tracks, stunned by the breathtaking view. The sky unfurls before us, a gaping stretch of orange and pinks, like a tropical drink spilled across the horizon. Below us, the waves crash on the shore, the endless ocean rippling like a blue rug.

This is so much more romantic than I even imagined.

I grab the blanket from my backpack and spread it on the ground. "I hope the view makes up for the work it took to get here. Sorry it's not a fancy restaurant."

"Vale. Remember the jewelry store? I don't do fancy." She looks over at me, and I can see her nervousness ebbing away. "This is so much better. So much more *me*."

I smile, and as she sits, I do a silent fist pump behind her back. "I hope you don't mind, but I took the liberty of ordering for us."

I open the lid on her spicy mango shrimp and rice dish, the

smell of coconut, spicy pepper sauce and fragrant cilantro blending together.

Her face lights up. "How'd you know?"

"I'd like to take full credit, but it was a panicked text to your sister that saved me."

She laughs.

I open my carryout box. "And since your sister couldn't decide between that dish and the grilled salmon with pasta, I got both."

Her eyes widen. "You got two meals?"

"I'll eat whatever you don't want. Consider me your personal cabana boy."

She laughs, then picks up her fork. "When my sister and I order amazing dishes, we just eat off each other's plates. Anthony was always strict about the no-sharing rule."

I slide my dish between us. "Your food is my food."

One point—me. Zero points—Anthony.

With a smile, she slides her dish my way, and we fall into a rhythm of picking at each other's entrees. At one point, I even pluck a shrimp with my fork and offer to feed it to her. "For the full cabana boy experience."

She takes it with a laugh, all the worry gone from before. We just needed to get out of the hotel to a place where we could relax, without any pressure about what happens later.

"I'm curious," she says, putting down her fork and studying me as I finish the pasta. "How did your family react to the news when you first told them?"

"You mean harassing me about the fact they weren't invited to my wedding?" I say.

"That well, huh?" she asks with a pained expression.

"My sister was miffed, but Mom wasn't mad. A little disappointed, maybe, but this whole wedding renewal ceremony will make up for it."

"Yeah, about that . . ." Sloan jumps to her feet and immediately starts cleaning up. "Do you think we should just skip it? I mean, we could have a reception and let *The Star Report* cover it, and I can tell everyone we're not interested in renewing our vows."

"Are you nervous about the wedding?" I touch her arm to get her to stop moving. I can see that she's having second thoughts, because whenever she gets nervous, she avoids eye contact and busies herself.

She shakes her head. "It's one thing to have tied the knot in Vegas already. It's another to stand in front of everyone we know and fake our vows."

"Sloan," I take her shoulders gently so she'll look at me. "We can't solve everything right now. We're only on the first day of our honeymoon. I know we're doing everything backward. But maybe this trip is our chance to pretend that the rest of the world doesn't exist for a few days—that it's just us and nothing else."

Her shoulders relax. "You're not nervous about it?"

"The wedding?" I shake my head. "No, because my first goal is to get you to relax this week and forget about everything in our real lives." I turn toward the ocean. "I bet the water feels fantastic. Are you ready to take a swim?"

She looks up at me and cringes. "So soon after dinner?"

"Are you worried about swimming after eating? I think that's an old wives' tale."

"No," she says quietly, looking down. "It's not that. It's just . . . I'm not ready for you to see me in my swimsuit."

I blink, taken aback. "Are you kidding me?" Then I hold up the blanket we used for the picnic. "You could be wearing this, and I'd think you were hot."

She lifts an eyebrow, clearly not convinced. "Well, the blanket might be an improvement. At least it hides everything."

"You don't need to hide a *single* thing," I say.

"I don't believe you. Not when you look around at all the beautiful women on the beach."

I scan the beach. "I don't see any, except for you."

She points at a woman in a bright pink bikini, the size of a few dinner napkins. "How about that girl?"

I shrug, looking back at Sloan. "Maybe you think she looks attractive, but I don't."

She scoffs. "How could you say that?"

I step closer, keeping my eyes locked on hers. "Because she's not *you*."

Sloan's mouth opens, then she shakes her head. "You're not serious, are you?"

"Dead serious." I reach for her hand. "I don't care about anyone else on this beach. Whenever you're ready, Sloan, I'll be here. I'm not going anywhere."

SEVENTEEN

Sloan

Even though Vale's words nearly knock me off my feet, swimming is still out of the question. Part of me was hoping I'd suddenly feel courageous enough to rip off my dress and run into the water like a *Baywatch* lifeguard. Then I remembered I don't look like Pamela Anderson, despite what Vale insists. He's just giving me a confidence boost so I won't be embarrassed to be seen by him in my swimsuit.

But there's something else going on too. Instead of acting like we're married only when people are around, it's like he wants to flirt with me when we're alone too. I almost get the feeling that he enjoys being with me—as more than his friend.

Which leaves me wondering: *Is this still pretend?* How can I believe that when his hand brushes mine as we walk the beach, or when I catch him staring at me like I'm the only one here? It's not like he hasn't seen me a million times. But it's the way he looks at me, his eyes darkening, landing on my lips for a split second too long. And then he asked me to date him, which left my body zinging with fireworks and my heart more confused than ever.

When we get back to the hotel, Vale opens the door to our room and gives me a hesitant smile. We both drop our eyes. The moment feels too weighty. This is the first time we've been alone since we eloped. We're stuck together in a romantic honeymoon suite with a stunning view of the ocean. The whole scene feels like the perfect setup for a night to remember.

If Vale even showed the least bit of interest, I'd fold like a house of cards and jump into his arms. But that would also be a massive mistake. Because if I do, I'll start hoping this could actually work. And logically, I know better. This was never supposed to work, not when our whole relationship is built on a business agreement.

My eyes land on the couch. Vale looks at me, and shakes his head. "I know what you're thinking, and you need to stop."

"What?" I say innocently.

"You feel guilty for taking the bedroom." He settles on the sofa and flips off his sandals. "I've slept on plenty of couches in my lifetime, and a few left me feeling like I needed a tetanus shot afterward. This is not one of them."

"Do you at least want to see the bedroom?"

"And see what I'm missing?" he asks with a smirk. "No, thanks."

"We could take turns sleeping there," I suggest. "To be fair, you earned this suite too."

"It's all yours," he says. "I'll be on my comfy couch, watching a movie." He leans back and links his hands behind his head. "You're welcome to join me."

"Can I wear my pajamas?" I ask.

He lifts an eyebrow. "As long as I can wear mine. And fair warning: they're not flannel pajamas either."

Heaven help me, if that man's pajamas involve boxer briefs, I'm a goner.

"As long as you follow one rule," I say, trying not to let my face show how much seeing Vale in his "pajamas" scares me. Right now, the swimsuit under my dress is so tight, it feels suffocating. "You have to wear more than just underwear."

He bites back a smile. "You thought I'd show up to movie night in my underwear?"

"Well, yeah," I say with an embarrassed shrug. "I saw you a few weeks ago, before Vegas, in the living room . . ." I blurt, then stop myself.

His mouth quirks. "Sloan. Have you been spying on me?"

My cheeks flame. "For the record, I *wasn't* spying. I walked into the kitchen late one night to get water and I thought someone had left the TV on. That's when I saw you doing pushups in your underwear."

"And you didn't say anything?" He folds his arms across his chest.

"Vale. That would make it *look* like I was guilty."

"And were you?"

I scoff. "You need to learn manners."

He narrows his eyes. "*Please.*"

I was totally ogling my husband. Vale was a sight to behold, all muscles and tanned back, along with other assets.

"It's kind of hard *not* to notice," I say in my defense. "Look at you." I wave my hand at his tight T-shirt. The poor cotton is being stretched to near shreds by all that muscle.

"What?" he asks innocently.

"You're very muscle-y."

Vale catches me staring at his chest and grins. "Would you like a repeat performance?" It's so unfair that any man should be this good-looking . . . *ever.*

I put my hands on my hips. "You know, you should be glad I don't walk around in my underwear."

"Maybe you should," he suggests with a cocked eyebrow. "Just to make things even. Every good marriage is based on equality. And it would be very unfair for me not to suffer through the same experience."

I smack him on the arm. "You wish."

He smirks. "I do, actually."

I laugh. "Stop. You're teasing now."

"Who says I am?" The way he asks it, like the truth rather than a question, makes me take a step back. Maybe this is how it feels to go to the edge of a cliff and put your toes over, just to feel the razor-sharp edge of danger.

"I thought we . . ." *were only faking this marriage.*

The words won't come out. They're lodged in my throat, too heavy to say. My eyes drop to the ground. "I should change into my pajamas."

I hurry to my bedroom, leaving Vale on the couch, still reeling from how much I want to give in and step off the edge of the cliff. Why is he making me feel this way?

Because he feels what you feel.

When I swing open the bedroom door, I immediately freeze. My bed is covered in red rose petals, alongside a box of chocolates and a card on the pillow.

I shake my head and back away like it's a live snake. "No," I whisper.

About the time when everything feels like a dream, when I might believe Vale feels the same, reality comes back to smack me in the face. None of this is real. Not Vale's flirting. Not the way he looks at me with longing. Not even this rose-covered bed that practically begs for us to fall into it.

I grab the envelope and rip open the seal, pulling the notecard from inside. In my sister's perfect handwriting, she's written, "Happy honeymoon! Expect more surprises this week."

Surprises . . . what surprises?

"Uh, Vale?" I call. "There's something in our bedroom you need to see." My voice trembles slightly.

"What is it?" He looks around the room. "Looks like someone vomited rose petals all over the bed."

I shove the note at him. "Did you have anything to do with this?"

He reads it, then shakes his head. "No. But it's the honeymoon suite. Jaz probably arranged it beforehand."

"What does she mean by surprises?" I ask. "Did she tell you anything before we left?" My voice sounds accusatory, convinced everyone is scheming against me even though Vale's done nothing to deserve my suspicion. If anyone's to blame for my inner turmoil, it's me. I inconveniently fell for a hot hockey player and then married him. Nobody knows it's a fake marriage, and my own husband doesn't know I'm harboring irrational feelings of desire for him on a daily basis.

The rose petals were just a warning. *Back away from the bed . . . and the hot man next to you.*

Vale touches my arm, gingerly rubbing his thumb over my skin, like a lit match. "If I knew about any surprises, I couldn't hide it, Sloan. When it comes to you, I'm pretty much an open book."

His thumb stops moving, and so does my heart.

So what he said earlier is true?

Don't get too cozy, Sloan. The honeymoon suite is doing weird things to your brain.

I whirl around to face him. "How long do you want to be married, Vale?"

He drops his hand and stares at me. "As long as it takes. I never set a timeline on this marriage."

I straighten my spine, about to rip the Band-Aid off this fake marriage and pretend it doesn't sting. I point between me and him. "This thing between us was only supposed to be temporary. I think this will be easier for everyone if we set an end date now."

A crease deepens between his brows. "You're already worried about the end of our marriage? I thought we'd decide later, based on your health."

I fold my arms across my chest. "My health is unpredictable. I just think it would be in everyone's best interest to have a clear timeline. Just so . . ." I glance around the room. "So we keep expectations in check."

"Expectations about *what?*"

Like he doesn't know. Literally every romance movie that features a bed with rose petals has a couple crashing into it within the next ten seconds. Maybe it's the lack of control I feel right now, but I take a step away from Vale, making it clear we should put space between us. "I don't want either of us getting ideas about what will happen this week."

"Exactly *what* do you think will happen this week?" he says, taking a step toward me, his eyes burning with questions.

I back away, suddenly feeling like this is a game, and I'm about to lose . . . *spectacularly.* It's not that I don't want Vale. The problem is, I do. *Overwhelmingly so.* But I'm afraid of the future, scared to care for him so much, terrified of hurting him and everyone who believes this marriage is real. It's like I'm facing off with a locomotive, barreling toward me full speed.

"I'm not saying anything *will* happen," I say, my voice wavering. "I'm establishing guardrails. So we don't do anything we'll regret." Especially rule number four.

"And what would we regret, Sloan? I want to know," he presses.

The back of my thighs bump against the mattress, and I lose my balance and fall to a sitting position on the bed, scattering rose petals everywhere. It's like I can't get away from the siren call of those stupid roses. Vale stands over me, his gaze dark, and excitement shivers through me.

"We should never be in this bedroom together," I say, my voice low, determined. "And definitely not in bed."

Vale hooks his fingers under the straps of my swimsuit and hauls me to a standing position.

"Then why are you sitting on the bed, looking all lonely and kissable, like you're inviting me to join you?"

Am I that transparent? Apparently so, because I wasn't even trying to look kissable or inviting.

"You should definitely not kiss me," I warn. "Especially not on the lips."

"Because we'll regret this tomorrow?" His voice scrapes like gravel.

He's only a breath away, his fingers still looped under my straps, holding me so close, he can probably feel my heartbeat thumping against this chest.

"Regret it for the rest of our lives," I tell him. "And I wouldn't want to ruin your life."

"So kind of you to think of my future. But you've already ruined me, Sloan."

My stomach drops. *He didn't just say that.* He's not playing fair, and he knows it.

"That's why we need an end date," I remind him. Maybe I'm playing dirty now, but we need to stop this madness before everything in me turns molten and burns down the bedroom.

"Sloan," he warns, his hands sliding across my shoulders, sending a shudder down my body. "I will never give you an end date."

Vale is a man who keeps his promises. *If I force him to give me a date, he'll have to keep it.*

"Even if I ask nicely?" I say, tipping my chin up to him, hoping that if I look kissable again, he'll give in.

"Never," he says, his voice gravel.

I hitch myself toward his lips. "Even if I let you kiss me?"

His thumb trails up my neck to tease the corner of my jaw. "I thought you said it would ruin us."

"You said it already had," I whisper. I kiss the corner of his jaw, and he sucks in a breath.

"I *refuse*," he says in a strangled whisper.

Even if I regret making this tradeoff, it will be easier for us in the end. We won't get emotionally involved. We'll avoid falling into the erroneous belief that this week is something more than it is. His defenses are slowly crashing down. One more push . . . *and the rest will fall.*

"Can I tell you a secret?" My lips barely brush his and his eyes spark, a foretaste of something I know he wants too. My entire body exhales. "I've wanted you to kiss me ever since we got here."

"Sloan," he says, his voice thick. His jaw flexes, and I can tell it's taking every ounce of resistance not to give in. "I want to," he says, dipping his head, leaving a line of kisses along my collarbone.

Tingles flood down my body.

"You don't know how much I want this," he groans. "But not if it means setting an end date to our marriage."

I tip his face to mine. "But I thought we agreed. You just kissed me. That was the deal. A kiss for an end date."

"I never promised not to kiss you other places," he says, one corner of his mouth tipping up.

He tricked me at my own game.

"That's not fair." I put my hands on the sides of his face so he can't get away, can't leave me without giving me what I want.

Is this really about forcing him to give me an end date—or do I want him to kiss me like a husband should?

I lock my gaze on his. "I won't take no for an answer." Then I reach up and finally place my mouth on his. This time he doesn't fight me. His hands slide to my back. As my lips graze over his, a loud rap at the hotel door knocks me back into reality.

"Vale? Sloan?" a woman calls through our door.

"Jaz?!" I say ripping my lips away from Vale's. His hands stay locked around me, reluctant to let this moment go.

"Your sister is here?" he mutters under his breath, scraping a hand across his jaw.

"In Cancun?"

"Unless it's someone impersonating my sister who just happens to know our names." I wiggle out of his arms and rush to the door, barely able to contain my ragged breathing—or the relief flooding my body. *What in the world was I thinking in there?* I was just about to give in to Vale . . . in return for setting an end date to our marriage.

And he refused.

But why?

I don't have time to answer that question, and Vale's face doesn't offer any answers. The dark desire in his eyes is gone, replaced by something that shakes me more: *what almost happened.*

Vale is back to playing the part of my dutiful husband to a tee.

"Are we still following the rules?" he asks, his face unreadable.

I can hardly stand not seeing the same man who was just with me in the bedroom, the one who looked like he wanted to shower me with kisses.

"What rules?" I say breathlessly, my body still flushed from our encounter. I can barely think, let alone remember any silly rules I might have agreed to.

"The ones we created before we came home from Vegas."

"Oh, those rules about touching all the time and making our marriage look believable?" *And no sex. Let's not forget that one.*

"We agreed we'd do whatever it takes," he says. "Is that still the case?"

"Sure, fine. Whatever." I turn back to finish my trek to the door. The tension is so thick in here, I could cut it with a knife.

"Good," he says, nodding. "I just wanted to be sure."

I wheel around to open the door, and then spin back. "Why do you ask?"

My sister pounds harder. "Sloan, what's taking so long?"

"One minute!" I call to her.

He pulls me away from the door, so Jaz won't hear. "Because I *strongly* feel we should keep those rules. Personally, I didn't do a very good job back at the house. I think there may have been some doubts about our relationship."

"Doubts?"

"Yes. So in full disclosure, I plan on making our relationship even more believable."

"More believable?" I say, my voice an octave higher.

"One hundred percent more believable," he says, his eyes sparking, a vivid reminder of what almost happened a minute ago. "I plan on making it so believable, we might not be able to tell the difference between what is real and fake."

"You can't do that," I say, shaking my head, remembering the no-sex rule. But even without that rule, there's still a lot we can do. And Vale's the type to push the boundaries of all those rules.

"I most certainly can. *And will.*"

The air sizzles between us. I want him to make it more believable right now, by finishing what we started in the bedroom. But I hold back, mostly because my sister won't stop knocking.

"Sloan!" Jaz calls.

"Coming!" I say, dragging my hand through my hair. I point to Vale and whisper loudly, "Don't you dare use those rules against me."

"Against you? *Never*," he promises. "But I will use them to fully convince you that you're my wife. Whatever it takes."

Vale

"Surprise!" Jaz screams, holding her arms out and barreling into her sister with a hug.

"What are you doing here?" Sloan asks, trying to smooth her hair and pretend she's not totally shaken by our encounter.

"Crashing your honeymoon," Jaz says, like this is a sufficient and logical answer. Of course family members always show up unannounced at a couple's honeymoon suite with no warning.

Brax steps out from behind her in the hall. "Hey, Vale."

"You're here too?" I gasp. *Impeccable timing.*

"You didn't think I'd let my wife come without me on a beautiful tropical vacation?" Then he chuckles. "You're shocked?"

"Shocked doesn't even begin to describe it," I say slowly, glancing at Sloan, who has a smile that looks drawn on by a preschooler with a Sharpie.

"Did we interrupt?" Jaz asks, then holds up her hands. "Wait. Don't answer that. I don't want to know the answer." She raises her eyebrows as she steps around Sloan. "Nice suite. Can't wait to see ours."

"Wait—what?" Sloan asks.

"We have a suite just like yours," she says, crashing onto the couch I was planning on using as my bed. This feels oddly famil-iar. Just like home, and yet, not.

"You're staying *here?*" Sloan asks.

"Isn't it great? When I booked your trip, I mentioned to Brax how much I'd like to go to Cancun. We hardly had time for a honeymoon since he was in the middle of hockey season, and we only got away for an extended weekend." She makes a sad face, and Brax joins her on the couch.

"I suggested a second honeymoon to Jaz, and she was totally on board. Since they were making an exception for you, the boss had to approve my time off as well," Brax says. "When we checked out the options, your honeymoon package was such a great deal, we booked two. One for you. And one for us." He wraps his arm around Jaz's shoulders and smiles. "A whole week of family bonding time!"

"Lucky us," I mutter.

"All the earlier flights were booked," Jaz says. "But yay us for making it happen!" She puts her arms in the air like a cheerleader, while Sloan shoots me a panicked look of *What are we going to do now?*

Brax looks at me and reads my expression. "Don't worry, we're not going to interrupt or get in the way. If you want to do things together during the day, that's fine. We're not forcing ourselves into your honeymoon."

"So we might see you or we might not. I can live with that." I link my arm around Sloan's waist and rub my thumb over the top of her hip. My hand warms from the feel of her body close to mine. "Because Sloan and I want *a lot* of alone time together."

Her body tenses.

Sloan turns to me. "It would be rude not to spend time with them," she says, sweetly.

"No, it won't," I say. "Brax just told me as much."

I know what her game is. She wants to hide behind her sister and avoid me. She's using this surprise visit to throw a monkey wrench into my plans to woo her.

This was my week to convince her I'm not letting her leave this marriage without a fight. It was our chance to be together, without putting on an act. But that will be nearly impossible now.

That's why I'm desperately hanging on to the rules we agreed to. And not just hanging on to them, but pushing them to their limits. *Whatever it takes.*

"Vale, they're family," she insists. "Of course we'll spend time together. We can't hang out in our room all day."

I arch an eyebrow. "I'd like to prove that theory wrong."

Sloan's eyes widen.

Jaz snort-laughs. "Brax, maybe we should go . . ."

"No!" Sloan grabs her sister's arm. "You want to hang out now? We weren't doing anything important."

"Sloan," I warn wickedly. "We were in the middle of something I'd like to finish."

Sloan's eyes cut to mine.

"Maybe tomorrow," Jaz says with a yawn. "I'm tired from the flight." She stands and heads to the door, glancing at the bedroom. "Did you like the rose petals and chocolates? We asked the concierge to arrange it for you."

"Quite the surprise," Sloan says in a mock cheerful voice, not meeting my eyes and trying to inch away from me.

"Yeah, Sloan couldn't wait to fall into them," I add, not looking at Sloan.

"Vale loves to exaggerate," she explains, then looks back at her sister. "Can we meet up in the morning, bright and early?"

"Oh, I don't know," I say, hooking my hand around her shoulders and pulling her under my arm. "We might be exhausted . . . since we're newlyweds."

Sloan's eyes widen before she looks at me like she wants to stab me with the hotel pen. I lift my eyebrows to remind her of the plan. We need to look like newlyweds who can't keep their hands off each other, not retirees rising at the crack of dawn for free hotel breakfast.

"We might just do breakfast in bed." I give her a wink.

She blinks before looking back at her sister. "I'll text you in the morning."

Brax steps toward the door. "We thought we might go snorkeling tomorrow."

"Oh, really?" Sloan says. "That's exactly what we had planned!"

She's lying through her teeth, since I'm the one who made the list of dates for the week. This is her attempt to get away from any situation that might leave us with too much time on our hands in the bedroom.

"Maybe we could go together?" Jaz suggests.

"I love that idea!" Sloan says. "Let's plan for that all day, and then maybe we can have dinner together afterward?"

"Sounds perfect," Jaz answers, then links her arm through Brax's. She beams up at him. "That airplane seat did a number on my back, and I'm starving. What do you say we order room service and go to bed?"

Brax's lips curl into a wicked grin. "Is that even a question?" They leave, the door slamming with an ominous thud.

So much for having Sloan to myself tomorrow.

Sloan immediately pulls away from my arm before she wheels around. "Did you enjoy embarrassing me in front of my sister?"

"What?" I shrug. "I'm just behaving as obnoxiously as any newlywed couple would." If Sloan considered me her real husband, of course I'd brag about getting up late and spending time alone with her. And I wouldn't feel the least bit guilty about those bragging rights as her husband.

"What they don't know is that I'm sleeping on the couch tonight," I add. "So clearly I'm not winning. Unless you'd rather we tell them the truth?"

Sloan looks at me, stunned. "The truth? Do you know how much that would hurt my sister, knowing she arranged this and it's all a sham? We owe Jaz and Brax this, even if some day we have to break the news that we're ending the marriage and my sister blames me."

"Why would she blame you?" I ask.

"Because, according to my family, I don't stick with things. I'm always on to the next shiny thing in my life, whether it's a new job or a new boyfriend."

I frown. "What do you mean? You're not a quitter."

She sighs. "But I've never stayed in a relationship very long. Not even with Anthony. Even though he left me, I knew long before that he wasn't the right guy for me. In every relationship, I'm always wondering if there's someone better for me. Someone I can never have." She looks at me for a fleeting moment before flopping onto the couch. "Apparently, I'm better at committing to a fake relationship than a real one." She leans her head back against the couch and closes her eyes.

I sit next to her, but this time I don't touch her, even though I want to more than anything. "Sloan, you are the most loyal friend I have."

She gives me a weak smile. "I'm also married to you, so I kinda have to be loyal."

"But you don't have to be my friend. You choose to be. There's a difference," I remind her, holding her gaze. "Just for the record, when you find the man who's right for you, I think you will stay for the long haul."

Her eyes meet mine. "You really think that?"

I nod. "I do."

I want that person to be me, but I can't force her into choosing me. Even though I plan on being as convincing as possible, I have to let her make the final decision. If I push too hard, I might push her away forever. "We said we were going to do this trip the right way. That we'd have fun together and go on dates. Just because Brax and Jaz are here doesn't change things."

"It changes how we act."

But is it an act? Not with me. "I still want us to have a honeymoon we'll never forget."

She looks up at me with her wide eyes, and something in my heart flips.

"Whatever it takes, right?" she murmurs.

Every time she looks at me that way, I feel even more strongly that I can't end this marriage. It kills me to even think about giving her up.

Which is why I won't. I can't. "Whatever it takes," I repeat softly.

She lifts her eyebrows. "So you'll let me off easy? Not embarrass me with our marriage rules?"

"I didn't say that," I tell her, shaking my head. "I'm still planning on following every rule to a tee."

Sloan scoots away from me to the other side of the couch, putting more space between us, more road blocks to kick down.

"But I'm also going to make sure that you're relaxed and comfortable. Starting now." I pat the space next to me. "Scoot over, wife. You need a shoulder massage."

"What?" she asks, pulling her knees up on the couch. "I'm fine."

"Sloan. Your shoulders are so tense, they're almost to your earlobes. Doctor's order."

"You're not a doctor."

"No, but I am your husband." I grab her waist and slide her closer.

"You're forcing me to get a shoulder rub?" she says.

I spin my finger in a circle. "Turn around so your back is toward me."

She sighs. "If you say so, cabana boy."

I grin. "You like calling me that a little too much." She's still in her swimsuit, her teal sundress over top. Her shoulders are mostly bare, her upper back fully exposed for a shoulder rub. I brush her hair over to one side and admire the soft lines of her back, the freckle on one shoulder blade, the way her skin feels like silk. I gently place my hands on her shoulders and start kneading my thumbs into her muscles.

At first, she tenses, but the more I work her muscles, the more she melts in my hands. And the fact she doesn't have to look at me seems to make things easier. Like how it was at home, before we were married, when things were simple for us.

"That feels . . . *gooooood*." Even though I can't see her face, I'm pretty sure her eyes are closed. "You know, you could have a second career as a cabana boy."

"Glad to know I have a job prospect when I retire from hockey," I say with a laugh. I glide my fingers down her spine. Touching her is a pleasure.

"You make a pretty decent husband," she admits. "Most of the time."

"I don't aim for pretty decent, Sloan. I want to be *best ever*." I find another tense spot and slowly knead it. A little moan escapes her lips.

"*Mm-hmm.*"

"Did you just moan?" I half laugh. I'm not sure I've ever heard her make that sound before.

Her body stiffens. "No, I do that all the time! I moan about everything."

My hands go still. "You made a sound like you were experiencing pure bliss."

"Okay, fine, I did that. Happy now? Your magic hands made a weird sound come from my lips. How in the world did you learn to give massages like that?"

"I get a lot of sports massages," I say, working the muscles between her shoulder blades.

"But I'm not a hockey player. You could probably crush me with your hands."

"I don't go as deep, but the technique is the same," I say, using my knuckles to work out a tense spot. "I'd like to get better at it."

"Well, you can practice on me any day," she says, her head tipping back.

"I'm going to remember that," I say. "And hold you to it."

She looks over her shoulder. "By the way, how are we going to hide that you're sleeping in the living room?"

"I'll have to remake the couch every day and hide my things in the bedroom."

She frowns. "But what if they stop by before you've had the chance? There's too much risk of them finding out. We need a better plan."

"Do you have a suggestion?" I ask, working my hands up her neck. Every time I massage a new spot, she seems to turn to putty in my hands.

She pauses, and I can't tell whether it's because she's falling asleep or thinking.

Without turning around, she says, "You could move into the bedroom."

I stop moving, my hands still resting on her shoulders. "I thought you said we shouldn't be in there together. You said *never.*"

"I said that before my sister showed up. If they caught you sleeping on the couch, they'd immediately suspect something was up."

I wait a beat, studying the way her shoulders lift, then drop when she sighs.

"Are you sure about this?" I ask, not pressuring her.

"It's a king-sized bed." She glances over her shoulder. "We can easily fit two people plus plenty of space between us for a pillow wall."

I laugh. "To protect who? Me from you?"

She smacks me with the couch pillow. "No! To keep you from crossing the imaginary line in the middle of the bed."

It seems perfectly reasonable. And a lesson in frustration. But I'm a strong guy, right? I can imagine she's not on the other side of the pillow wall. Not close enough to snake my hand under the covers to hold hers. Not near enough to rest my chin on the soft curve of her neck, taking in the scent of her body.

"I won't hate this part of the charade," I say with a smirk.

"On the other hand, maybe you *should* sleep on the couch tonight," she says, smacking me with the pillow again as she scoots away.

"Oh, no, you don't," I say, grabbing her arm and tugging her toward me. "You can't dangle a king-sized bed in front of me and then take it away. That's not fair."

"All's fair in love and pillow fights," she says between shrieks of laughter, smacking me with a pillow in the chest. She leaps off the couch, grabbing the other pillow, holding them up like shields.

I lift an eyebrow. "Is that a threat? Because in case you didn't notice, they're pillows, not nunchucks. And second, you really don't want to fight me."

She adjusts her stance to something vaguely martial arts-like. "Oh, really, Mr. Hot Stuff? Just try me."

"Oh, I will." I leap forward as she jumps out of the way.

"Not too shabby," I say. "Maybe you should play hockey."

"And show you up?"

"Yeah." I take a few steps toward her. "Then again, maybe I don't need pillows."

I dart forward as she laughs and leaps away from me. She climbs over the couch, jumps on top of the armrest and takes off for the bedroom. I chase her down the hall and finally catch her just before she reaches the door. I duck low, sweeping her off her feet and hauling her over my shoulder in one smooth move.

"Vale, no!" She laughs and kicks against me.

I loop my arms around the back of her knees as she dangles over my shoulder.

"What are you doing?" she says as I carry her upside down into the room.

"Letting you win," I say. I drop her on the bed as flower petals fly everywhere. She's on her back, looking up at me, her chest heaving with every breath.

She looks so kissable right now, but that's exactly what I shouldn't do if I want her to trust me.

I lean over her, placing my hands on either side of her shoulders. "That's what you wanted, right? To win?"

For a fleeting second, something ripples across her face, and her eyes drop to my lips.

I don't want this to go further until I'm sure she can trust me. At this point, she doesn't even trust me enough to sleep next to her without a pillow wall, let alone anything more. The last time she tried to kiss me, it was because she wanted me to set an end date. But I can't kiss her until I know she's not running just to get the end date she thinks she needs—until this thing between us is real, and not just another escape plan.

Let's face it, she only asked me to stay because she's afraid of people finding out about us. It's fear driving her now. And that's not how I want this marriage to go.

I need her to ask me to stay because she wants me here—without question. When she does, it won't be because she's counting down to an end date of her own making.

I turn to go.

"Wait—where are you going?" she asks, frowning.

"Since you're so worried about me sleeping here . . . I won't."

She props herself on her elbows and frowns. "But where will you sleep?"

"On the couch. I'll clean up my stuff before anyone sees it."

"You don't have to do that, Vale," she says, sitting up. "I thought we agreed on this."

"Until you trust me, I'm sleeping somewhere else."

"I do. I just thought . . ." For a second, she looks torn.

I want her to say it, to tell me she wants me here, for real this time. "You thought what?"

"We need to keep up the charade."

Everything crumbles in me. I hate the word *charade*. I hate everything about this stupid arrangement. The more we're together, the less I can do anything about the pent-up desire that feels like a can of soda about to explode. I'm living in a perpetual state of frustration, wanting her but never within reach of actually having her. Just about the time it seems like Sloan reveals a piece of her heart, she emotionally backpedals on me. She's pulling a Houdini, giving me every reason to believe she's invested in this, then disappearing like it was all a perfectly executed magic act.

"Well, I can't keep this up." I grab a pillow off the bed, and head to the door. "I'm not staying in this room until you actually want me in here. Until you ask me to because you're no longer afraid of what might happen between us."

NINETEEN

Sloan

"Are you sure you're okay with us tagging along today?" Jaz asks me in the lobby as the guys arrange for a ride to the snorkeling location. She searches through her backpack for some lip gloss.

"Since we're headed to the same place, we'd see each other there anyway," I say, pretending we had this planned all along.

I take a sip of the hotel coffee. It's bitter and dark, kind of like my mood when Vale left my bedroom last night. I wanted him to stay, but I didn't know how to say it or whether he wanted me too. He puts on a good flirting game, playing by the "rules" we created, but sometimes those rules feel too real. When he walked out, I knew I'd made a mistake because he took a piece of me with him, a piece I don't know how to get back.

Please stay. The words lodged in my throat all night as I slept in that humongous bed alone while Vale crammed onto that tiny couch. So close, but still miles apart.

"I told Brax how you've always rolled with change," she says. "It's kind of your superpower."

"I'm not sure anything could have prepared me for your surprise." I bump her with my arm, so she knows I'm not upset that she and Brax barged into our honeymoon suite last night. "Good thing I roll with the punches."

"See? I knew it'd come in handy someday."

The *it* being my ADHD diagnosis. I received the diagnosis in college, when I was struggling to focus in my classes and my advisor recommended getting tested. When I got the results, it was a surprise to everyone in my family but me. I had the kind that most undiagnosed females have, the typical inattentive type, often labeled as "distracted" and a "daydreamer" by my teachers. It's why I flew under the radar for so long without a diagnosis. I wasn't disruptive—I just couldn't stay focused on a goal and changed my mind too much.

It's probably the reason I was able to rush into marriage with Vale in Vegas so easily. Taking risks isn't hard for me. But sticking with something is another deal entirely. Because when I get scared or bored or start to think things won't work out, I run to the next shiny thing. I get worried people will grow tired of me and I'll be too much for them. And I don't want to wait for them to leave me, so I run first.

But I can't do that to Vale. That's why I want him to set an end date for our marriage, so both of us know it's coming. That way, I won't let myself run away early, and I know Vale will stick around until the end. He's just that way, the type who keeps a promise, no matter how inconvenient. But his refusal to set a date makes me uneasy. I'm afraid he'll wake up one day and decide I'm too much work, or he'll leave me when something better will come along. And I'll be left behind, just like I was with Anthony. It wasn't that Anthony no longer cared. It's that I was a different person after my accident. More needy. Less fun. When he realized that, he started to fade out of my life with excuses about how busy he was. He didn't have it in him to become the person I needed. I was too much for him, so he moved on. They always do.

Jaz takes her phone out and starts shooting video of the lobby.

"What are you doing?" I ask, trying to lean out of her shot.

"I'm creating a honeymoon video for us. Once I edit the

footage, we can watch them on our anniversaries each year. That way, we'll remember this trip for the rest of our lives."

Something catches in my chest that makes it hard for me to breathe.

For the rest of our lives.

I can't tell her there's no future for Vale and me. Once we end our marriage, this video will only be a painful reminder of how much I wanted this to be real.

"The driver is here," Brax calls and waves us over.

We pile into a taxi, with Jaz, Vale, and me crushed together in the back seat, while Brax sits in the front. The air-conditioning only seems to be half-working, and I feel smothered in the middle seat. Since Vale's so gigantic, his legs take up my space too. It shouldn't matter, but it feels like an intimate thing when our knees brush together or the way his thigh presses into mine with every turn. There's no getting away from touching him when we're stuffed together like a burrito in the back seat.

We swerve through busy traffic, and the heat stifles me even more, leaving me lightheaded and dizzy. Brax and Vale talk about their plans for the day while Jaz films them on her phone. I stare out the front window, my hand resting on my unsettled stomach. The bitter coffee isn't sitting right—or maybe it's because Vale's sitting too close.

"Sloan, you want to talk on camera about how you're going to lose the race?" Brax asks.

"What race?" I ask, keeping my eyes glued on the road ahead, willing myself not to throw up.

Vale pats my knee. "The race to reach the snorkeling beach first—we even have bets riding on it."

Like that's going to help my unsettled state.

When we pile out of the taxi at the Jet Ski rental, I hang back on a rickety bench as the guys head inside the tiny building to sign waivers.

Jaz sits next to me. "You seem quiet. You feeling okay?" She studies my face in concern.

"Motion sickness," I groan, closing my eyes.

"You and Vale didn't have a disagreement?"

I lift my head and look at my sister. "Not a fight exactly." I hesitate. I can't tell her what happened, but I can't hide it either. "Over a stupid thing. I'd rather not talk about it."

She looks out at the ocean, watching the Jet Skis in the distance jump the waves. "I know it can be overwhelming at first, especially being married to a professional hockey player. But you're his wife first. No one else gets that title. You get to see him in his weak moments. There's a lot of pressure in the industry not just to perform, but to become a celebrity. The fans play into that —constantly interrupting every moment you have alone. It takes so much trust to marry an athlete. But that's the thing about Vale. I know he'd never do anything to hurt you."

Of course he wouldn't. Because he's too good to everyone he meets. When this relationship goes down, everyone will be blaming me for not sticking with him. That's the part that irks me the most. Vale won't come out of this looking bad. I will.

Brax and Vale walk out of the rental place with life vests hooked over their hands. "You guys ready to ride?" Brax nods toward the Jet Skis parked off the dock.

Jaz stands. "Yes!" She shimmies out of her cover-up with one quick swipe, revealing a pretty floral bikini underneath. Brax gives her a quick wink and then kisses her on the cheek before helping her with a life vest.

Last night, I wasn't ready to let Vale see me in a swimsuit, but I've realized I just need to get over it—like pulling off a Band-Aid. Taking a cue from my sister, I try to slide off my cover-up the same way, but I'm anything but smooth. It's a one-piece dress with an elastic waist that immediately shrinks to miniature size when I try to slide it off. My elbow catches on the elastic, trapping me inside the cover-up while it's halfway over my head. I'm flailing like a fish caught in a net.

"Do you need help there?" Vale asks.

I can barely see him through the gauzy fabric as I wrestle my way out. "I'm good," I say in that way that women do when they're too embarrassed to ask for help. When I get the elastic stuck on my ponytail, I finally give up. "Okay, get me out of here."

He chuckles. "I wondered how long it would take to ask for help."

He tugs the cover-up off me, like a tablecloth off a table. I'm grateful to be free, until I realize Vale's eyes are traveling down my now exposed body. My red tankini isn't too revealing, skimming just above my belly button, but it's enough that I feel self-conscious with him this close, memorizing every curve.

When I bought the suit, Jaz told me it brought out all my best features. Judging by the way his eyes flare, he agrees.

I clear my throat. "Ready?" I say, pretending I'm confident in this suit, even if standing next to his muscular frame makes me feel soft and curvy.

"Yes," he says averting his eyes, before they flick to my face. "What I said before stands."

"What?" I say, putting on a life vest.

"Last night on our picnic, you were comparing yourself to those other girls on the beach." His eyes hold mine. "They've got nothing on you."

He straddles the Jet Ski as a fiery warmth spreads through me.

"Hop on," he says, patting the seat.

I climb onto the Jet Ski behind him, but the seat is so small, I'm practically forced to spoon him. He smells incredible, a mix of cinnamon and coffee that makes it hard to focus on anything else.

"Before we go, let's take a picture. Lean into each other," Jaz instructs, even though I'm practically on Vale's back. "Can you at least look like you're married?"

"What?" I ask, frowning.

"Your hands are so awkward," she notes.

"Oh, sorry," I say, realizing I've been hiding them. I wrap them around his waist. Since Vale hasn't put on his life vest yet, my fingers brush over the tight cut of his abs. Without hesitating, he places a hand on my knee. His touch sends energy spiraling through me, making me wish I could be this close to him all the time. I love the feel of his body next to mine, how solid he is, like nothing could ever hurt me. I steal a quick look at him, and he flashes me this adorable grin that sets my insides on fire.

"Your sister is going to be doing this all day, isn't she?" he mutters under his breath.

"Yes, unfortunately."

"Well, *whatever it takes*, right?" Vale reminds me, squeezing my knee.

If he keeps touching me like that, I don't know how I'm going to survive today.

"Race you there?" Brax asks as Jaz climbs on.

Vale slides on his life vest. "Sure, as long as you . . ." Before he can finish, Brax takes off, a plume of water shooting behind their Jet Ski. " . . .don't cheat," Vale growls in disgust.

We bolt ahead like a rocket, and I have to grip his waist for dear life to keep from falling off.

Vale tails his brother, but Brax is intent to keep the lead, cutting us off and throwing his head back in laughter.

My body tenses, my arms burn. Vale glances over his shoulder, noticing my struggle to hold on, and slows down, keeping a steady pace behind Brax. I can tell he'd love to pull off some daredevil move, but he holds back for my sake, losing the bet.

We reach the snorkeling beach after them, and Brax has the audacity to pump his fist in victory.

"Why were you driving like a grandma?" Brax teases when we cut the engines.

"He did it for me," I answer, then give Vale a grateful look.

"Next race, I'll let you go first, but you'll still lose," Brax says, then jumps into the water. When he surfaces, he drags his hand through his soaking wet hair. "Water feels fantastic. Who's snorkeled before?"

"I haven't," Jaz says. "And I can't wait for you to teach me."

"The pleasure's all mine, princess," Brax says, kissing her lips as he lifts her off the Jet Ski like she weighs nothing.

She slides her body into his arms and their kissing continues in the water, arms and legs wrapped around each other, while we stare at everything but them.

Vale fiddles with something on the Jet Ski as I decide whether to jump ship or wait on Vale's help.

Compared to them, we look like two middle schoolers at their first dance—awkward and ready to go home.

Vale clears his throat, and when they still don't stop kissing, he leaps into the water, landing a cannonball next to his brother.

"Hey!" Brax immediately pulls away and wipes the water from his face.

Vale surfaces with a wicked smile. "Oops, did I do that?"

Brax pushes water at Vale, but he only dodges it and splashes his brother back.

"Stop acting like a bunch of immature boys," Jaz says, even though she knows they can't stop their competitive natures, especially when it's all in fun.

Vale waves to me. "Jump in."

I hesitate, looking at my sister who's hanging on to Brax like he's her personal life preserver. They look so happy together, and a twinge of jealousy twists inside me. That's exactly what I want with Vale.

"You need help getting in?" Vale asks, pulling my gaze back to him. "You can jump in or I can throw you in. Your choice."

"Those are my only two options?"

"Unless you want me to help you down like your sister."

I think of Brax's hands gripping her waist, the way their bodies slid together as one. *Definitely not that option.*

I shake my head and stir one toe in the water before Vale swims over. His brow furrows into a creased line. "How can I help?"

I shake my head. He's always asking this. He's so thoughtful, almost *too* thoughtful, and sometimes it drives me crazy. Every time he offers help, it makes me feel like I should be able to handle things on my own. I need to learn to rely on myself, not always lean on someone else.

He places a hand on my foot to get my attention. "You're only making things worse taking it slow. Jumping in is like leaping off a cliff. Once you start, there's no turning back. It's scary at first, but thrilling once you're in the air."

Normally I'm an all-in kind of gal, rushing into things without thinking, like getting married without considering the consequences. But today, I'm thinking too much. About last night. How I wanted Vale desperately. How I wanted to dive headfirst into love, recklessly, completely, without reservation.

But today, I'm running scared. It's easier to dodge hard things than face them head-on. That's why I couldn't confront Anthony after our relationship fell apart. Part of me couldn't face the truth —that I wasn't enough for him once I had something "wrong" with me. He rejected me, and when someone walks away, I can't let them back in. Same with my dad. He was always looking for something better after Mom died. First with my stepmom. And then when he grew tired of her, he walked away from us too. Because someone better always comes along.

That's what I'm afraid will happen with Vale. He'll find someone better, and when he does, I won't be able to come back from that. I'll be hollow, lost, no longer able to risk everything on someone who might leave me in the end.

"The longer you wait, the less believable this looks," Vale says as Brax and Jaz swim away from us.

Jaz is getting her own private snorkeling lesson, while I'm hesitating on the sidelines. A shriek, then a giggle erupts from Jaz. She glances over and yells, "Come on, you guys! This is so fun!" Then she wraps her arms around Brax's neck and he spins her in the water. They might as well be starring in a commercial for honeymooning in Cancun.

"Are you afraid?" Vale asks, his voice lower.

I scoff. "Hardly."

"Then what is it?" he says, still holding on to the side of the

Jet Ski, like he's not letting it go while I'm on it. "Because you've been a little standoffish. Like a wet cat."

"That's a very unpleasant comparison," I huff, even if it's true. "You mean you don't remember last night?"

He blinks. "Of course I remember last night."

I guess if I'm going to pick off the scab, I might as well do it now. "You left me, Vale. I basically invited you into my bed and you chose the couch over me."

"Wait." He shakes his head once and closes his eyes, pinching the bridge of his nose. "Let me get this straight. You told me I should never sleep in the bedroom. I heard that message loud and clear. Then you got a little frisky in the pillow fight and gave me your bedroom eyes. And you're mad at me for keeping my word?"

I scoff. "I did *not* give you bedroom eyes!"

"You totally did! And then you dropped the bomb of 'keeping up the charade.' Don't you think I wanted to sleep there? Even with the pillow wall between us, it's better than sleeping on a couch. Anything with you is better than alone."

His words feel like a loud drum beating against my chest. *Anything with you is better than alone.*

"Then why did you leave?" I narrow my eyes, still not understanding even though he's already said it.

His face grows serious, almost hurt. "Because you asked me not to."

"But what about the rules? That whole thing about being very convincing?"

"I want to convince *you,* so you'll ask me to stay. But I won't ever force myself into your life. You have to choose me too. You can't say one thing and then run the other direction."

His words feel like small paper cuts across my skin. All this pent-up rejection from my past has me running from anyone who gets too close. Even Vale, who would never willingly hurt me.

"So you wanted to stay?" My voice cracks on the last word, the emotion a lump in my throat.

"More than anything," Vale says, his face softening, his eyes searching my face. "If you asked, I would never leave you."

My heart goes from bruised to soft in a beat. *He wanted to stay.*

Is that why I put up my defenses every time he gets too close?

I know past scars never completely heal. But I want to believe that love can be the one thing that heals us, changes us into something better than we were.

"I see you looking at your sister, wanting what she has," Vale says, his voice a raw scrape. "Just tell me what you need. How I can make things better. How I can be a better husband to you."

There he goes again, tossing out words like *husband,* and making me feel like I'm something to him.

It hurts how much he cares, even if that caring is only limited by the time we're married. But I need this, need *him,* even if it's only for now. I want to stop running every time he scares me, every time I worry he's going to leave. What makes me tremble, more than anything, is the devastating realization that I'm falling off a cliff and can't stop myself. That when this marriage ends, *so will I.*

"I want what they have," I say, looking at my sister as Brax cradles her in the water and nuzzles her ear. "I want to love that way, but I don't want to risk losing you when this ends. Our friendship means too much to me to ever risk that."

"Who said you have to lose anything?" he says, tipping his face up to mine. "You won't lose me if you don't push me away. But you also can't wear a mask around me and pretend it's invisible, like I don't notice you're pretending. *I see you, Sloan.* And I want the real you. Not the you who's hiding. Not the you who's trying to be someone else. I want the Sloan who's not afraid to be herself. Because I can handle the *real* you." He holds my gaze, waiting for me to respond.

I know if I agree, I'm risking everything. Risking rejection. Losing my heart. But I can't stand playing into this charade without letting my heart feel everything, without letting myself fall completely for Vale.

I want to. I already am.

"I agree," I say, then slowly, "And I'm asking . . ." I let out a long breath. "Would you please sleep in my bed tonight? Because I can't stand the thought of you sleeping on the couch . . . by yourself."

His mouth tips up in the corner into a smoldering grin that makes hot fire race through my bones. "Yes, I'll sleep next to your Great Wall of Pillows tonight, and every night after that if you want me there. But with one caveat: As my wife, you'll jump into this water and let me into your world. No more hiding. Because today, I want to be your husband, if you'll let me." He puts out one hand, an invitation to jump. To take a chance, even if it's scary.

I do it before I can even think, knowing that thinking has confused me more than anything today. Leaping off the Jet Ski, I sink into the cold water, the water whooshing into my ears with a roar. I'm washing off all the tangled emotions in my heart, washing myself clean of the past, of all the fears I've buried deep inside.

Vale catches me just like he promised. His hands wrap around my waist, holding me against his hip, our bodies lightly tangled under the water, all the pressure points tingling with pleasure.

This is where I'm meant to be. This is who accepts me, even though I'm "too much."

I tip my head back and laugh while the sun warms my face and my hair drips across my shoulders, sending streams of water down my chest and back.

From afar, my sister yells, "Finally! What took you so long?"

I can only yell back what's true, a feeling of newborn hope blossoming in my chest: "I don't know why I waited so long."

TWENTY

Vale

We swim on the surface of the water for hours, fully immersed in the colorful underwater show. Bright blue fish, sunny yellow ones, zebra-striped, a school of orange clownfish—an entire sea circus putting on a spectacle just for us. A full-on show under the surface of the water, things we wouldn't have seen had we not slid on our goggles and peered into the depths.

In some ways it reminds me of what's happening under the surface of our marriage. If Sloan could see inside me, I think she'd realize how complicated this is for me. How much I want her. The lengths I'd go for her, *if she asked me to.*

But like so much with Sloan, she's too afraid to look beneath the surface, too afraid of what she might find there.

At the end of our time in the water, I notice her looking at me, her mouth quirked into a curious smile.

We're just swimming now, letting the waves push us around, our life vests doing the heavy lifting so we can just float.

"Is my sister looking this way?" she asks.

I glance over, and Jaz's face turns away on cue. "She was."

"If we're being watched, now would be a good time," she suggests.

"For what?"

"I don't know, a hug maybe? Something to prove we're not strangers today." There's an openness in her eyes, an invitation that wasn't there before. We've been swimming next to each other all morning, lost in our underwater world, but now that we're bobbing on the surface, wrapped up in the glorious view and each other, something's changed. *She's* changed.

Maybe she's sun-drunk, that lazy feeling after being at the beach too long, fully relaxed, fingers wrinkled as prunes, her cheeks and shoulders grapefruit pink from the sun. I swim over to her, then unsnap the first buckle on her life vest.

"What are you doing?" she gives a little half-laugh, her eyes flaring with surprise.

"We can't hug with these life vests on. That's like hugging someone while wearing an inflatable sumo suit."

"Vale MacPherson, are you saying I look like a sumo wrestler in my life vest?"

"Not at all. I'm just saying I want nothing between us."

"So you're, what—just taking it off?"

Click. The last buckle pops open. "Yes." I slide off her vest, letting it float in the water beside us. She wraps one arm on it like a flotation device, her legs treading water. "What if I can't swim without this?"

"You think I'd remove your life vest if I couldn't keep you afloat? How little faith in me you have." I unbuckle my life vest, wrestling out of it. "Lifeguard in high school."

She lifts an eyebrow, unconvinced. "That was a hot minute ago."

"It's like riding a bike." I pull her into my arms, slide my hands across her back. Her breath hitches when our bodies lightly collide under the water. A brush of her leg against mine. Her warm breath against my shoulder.

Skin-on-skin close.

"Believe me now?" I whisper against her ear. Her skin erupts into goose bumps across her back.

"The question is whether my sister does."

I spin us enough to see Jaz over Sloan's shoulder. Then I move my lips close to her earlobe again. "She's looking at us again."

"And?" Sloan asks in a ragged whisper.

"She approves," I say, then after a beat, "The question is, do you?"

"You take me to Cancun to go snorkeling and ask me if I approve?" She laughs. "Of course I approve. This entire trip has been amazing."

"No, I meant, *this.*" I stroke my hands along her back, reminding her that she's in my arms. *She's mine.*

She lets out a contented sigh. "*This* is something I could get used to. Maybe even addicted to. Like Nutella."

I laugh. "You're comparing me to Nutella?"

"I've very attached to it, Vale," she says seriously. "Some might say obsessed."

"In that case, I'll be your addiction."

"You could be, if I let myself get carried away." She tugs away from me, then floats on her back, her eyes squinting into the sun.

"Where are you going?" I ask, grabbing her hand, like she's a loose starfish I'm rescuing before it floats off to sea.

"I can't get too comfortable with this," she says.

"Sure you can." I want her to get used to us—to being together this way, feeling this happy and content.

She tips her head up to look at me, her lips curling. "It feels too real." Then she lies back in the water again, her face glowing from the sun. "I don't even know what's real anymore. All I know is I haven't felt this alive for a long time." Then she flips her body over with a splash, and starts kicking for the shore.

After returning to the hotel, Sloan heads to our room to shower off and take a nap while Brax and I finalize plans for tonight. If I'm honest, I get the sense she needs a break from me, from the tension that's crackling under the surface every time we touch.

We're like stretched rubber bands, pulled taut to the point of breaking. One more tug, and we'll snap.

With her wet hair slicked back from her face, her face lightly pink from the sun, she's the most beautiful woman I've ever laid eyes on. She waves goodbye as she slips into the elevator, the doors closing between us. The end of the best date ever. With one exception: the other night when her lips brushed mine in the bedroom and I almost broke down and gave in to her. It would've been so easy to melt into her, to give her everything.

After all, she's my wife, and I want another chance at kissing her. But this time, I want it without a bargaining chip and minus the pressure to set an end date. I refuse to give in to her demands if those demands come with an agenda that involves splitting up. It's my *one thing*, the hill I'll die on. I'm not leaving this marriage. That's my endgame.

Which means I need to show her my hand.

"So, what's your plan for tonight?" I ask Brax as we load into the back of a cab and head away from the hotel.

"It's time for secret date number two. More romantic than snorkeling."

"Which is?" I ask, intrigued.

"A sunset dinner cruise. You think Sloan would like that?"

My thoughts circle back to kissing Sloan, but this time we're on a yacht, her face gently lit by the tangerine sky.

"Earth to Vale." Brax backhands me in the chest.

"Oh, sorry." I shake my head. "Yeah, she'll love it."

We head to the place to book our reservation, and a man wearing a crisp suit takes our information and tells me about the amenities for tonight—live music and dancing, a viewing deck where we can enjoy the sunset, and a menu that includes all the seafood and steak we want.

It's overpriced and ridiculously touristy, but I don't care. For Sloan, I'll do all the schmaltzy guided tours. When I'm with her, the rest of the world grinds to a halt, leaving just us. Maybe I'm enjoying this husband role too much, but I can't let her go, even if she eventually finds someone else. Someone who fits her better than me.

Something cranks hard inside my chest, like an overtightened screw. Am I so selfish that I wouldn't give her up so she could be happy? What kind of man am I to hold on to someone, even if they didn't want me anymore?

An image floats through my memory. My dad leaving right after Christmas, confessing to Mom that he wasn't happy. That the life he'd grown into didn't fit him anymore.

He'd made marriage vows, and then decided they were disposable.

And somehow my mom found the strength to accept this and let him go.

But I'm not her. I'm not sure I could be that strong.

What's worse is how Dad left Mom to fend for herself with three kids. He was supposed to be the one who took care of us, the partner who carried half the load. Instead, he chucked his responsibility, leaving it all behind to find a new life. One that fit better.

I've always resented him for that. Even when I found out he'd died, I'd wished for one last chance for him to say he was sorry, that he had missed out on so much happiness by always looking for something better.

Now here I am, in Mom's shoes, wondering: If Sloan asked me to let her go, would I? Or would I keep her to myself, selfishly wanting her to be mine, even if she chose someone who could make her happier?

My mother and father are not me. But that's the funny thing about families. We never quite leave behind our blood connections, the way the same traits emerge in different circumstances and unfold in a whole new way.

I would never leave Sloan the way Dad left Mom. But could I be selfless when it came to letting her go? If she just left, could I accept it and move on?

Something twists inside me. *Never.*

But I'm not sure I'd get a choice.

You can't force someone to stay in a marriage. It's a decision two people make to stay with each other, no matter how hard it gets.

Marrying a hockey player is anything but easy. We travel nonstop. The industry is highly unstable. I'm not sure Sloan even thinks it's a legitimate long-term career option. Professional players only stay in the NHL for about four and a half years. Barely half a decade. If I turn down the NHL, what then? Will I get another shot?

I haven't thought about what I'll pursue after hockey, but Sloan needs someone who supports her dreams and provides her with stability, in case her health remains uncertain. What can I offer her that another man can't? And if I lose her to someone who makes her happier, what will I become then?

Because a life after her is no life at all. I don't want to imagine the man I'd become without her.

I'm quiet on the drive back to the hotel, suddenly doubting this whole plan to convince Sloan to be my real wife. Whatever the future holds, I won't be my father. I won't walk away. But if she asked me to give her up because I can't offer her what she needs—what then?

That's where I keep getting stuck, the snag in the plan.

I knock softly at the door in case Sloan is sleeping. It opens with a jerk, like she was waiting for me.

"So, what was your little secret trip with Brax all about?" she asks eagerly.

"I can't tell you about it yet. But be ready by six," I say.

She bites back a grin. "Everything is so secretive with you these days."

"It'll be worth the wait. Trust me." I rub the back of my shoulder without thinking.

"Are you hurting?" she asks, concerned.

"An old hockey injury. Sometimes it flares up, but I'm used to living with pain as a professional athlete. It comes with the job."

"Job or not, I don't want you feeling terrible tonight," she says. "Did you know we have our own private hot tub on the deck?" She nods toward the sliding glass doors just outside our room.

To be honest, I've thought about getting in that hot tub with Sloan so many times.

"We could use it together after our date," she says. "If you don't mind sharing."

"Mind?" I say with a spark in my chest. "Why would I ever mind sharing a hot tub with my wife?"

She tilts her head, and I can see the word *wife* pleases her.

"Later tonight. Just you and me," she murmurs.

I forget about my twisted thoughts, the ones about having to let her go if I can't convince her to stay.

She's mine, for now. And hopefully, forever. *If she chooses to stay.*

TWENTY-ONE

Sloan

"Gorgeous," I say when Jaz comes out of the bathroom in her pink dress for tonight's surprise date.

Jaz decided we should get ready together—without the guys—and promptly kicked Vale out of our room. Gloomily, he headed off to find Brax, suit in hand.

"That way, we can surprise them with our stunning transformation from beach bums to glamor girls," Jaz said after shutting the door behind Vale.

For the next hour, we cram into the bathroom, covering the counter in travel tubes of makeup and magical lotions that promise to turn me into a goddess. Jaz forces me into some glittery highlighter to "accentuate my cheekbones" and pulls my hair into a sexy loose updo with a few stray curls that frame my face.

I choose an off-the-shoulder yellow dress that complements my dark hair and finish it off with a pop of lip gloss that smells like vanilla. When we finally come down to the lobby, Vale is talking to Brax, his back toward me.

Brax nudges him, then nods. When Vale spins around, his gaze sweeps over me. Judging by the spark in his eyes, he thoroughly approves.

I stop short of wanting to press myself into a hug, but he does it for me, closing the gap between us. "You look beautiful," he murmurs against my ear, sending shivers down my arm. How is he so good at this? Always making me simultaneously shiver while blood courses through my veins like lava.

I run a finger over the lapel of his suit coat. "You're like a hot mafia man."

He laughs. "Is that a good thing?"

I lift an eyebrow. "I'm highly combustible right now, and you're a lit match in that suit. Way too dangerous to be standing this close to me."

He tugs me closer, slides a hand across my back and whispers, "The feeling is mutual. So let's burn it all down tonight."

My heart leaps. *Yes, let's.*

When we arrive at the dock, Jaz nearly squeals with excitement at our surprise date. We board the enormous boat, where couples lounge on the top deck, fancy drinks in hand, looking like the type of people who have yachts of their own. It's one of those high-end tourist experiences I could never have afforded in a past life, but thanks to Vale, I now have access to.

I twist the skin on my wrist, just to remind myself this is real. This dream life is my life now. Nothing could ruin tonight.

We're handed complimentary drinks as we board and choose a table with an amazing view of the water. As the boat sets sail along the coastline, I lean into Vale's arm, admiring the endless views of water and a sky so big it feels like we could sail to the ends of the earth.

He leans toward me, whispering in my ear. "Does this feel too much like senior prom on a boat?"

I muffle my laughter. "Senior, as in, citizens?"

Many of the guests are double our age plus a few decades, and the women are wearing beaded mother-of-the-bride gowns.

"Now that you mention it"—he looks around—"we are the young bucks on this cruise. Sorry I didn't choose the singles' party boat. That might have been more fun for you."

"Getting hit on by drunken twentysomethings who will call

me the wrong name and slosh their boozy drinks on me somehow doesn't have the same appeal."

Vale's grip tightens around me. "If anyone hits on you tonight, they will lose their teeth."

"Vale," I say biting back a smile, "most of these men don't even have their real teeth."

He laughs and rubs the back of my arm in small circles, something that drives me insanely crazy. It's not until a waiter approaches with king crab legs and jumbo shrimp that he finally stops touching me. We feast on so much food that I lean back in my chair, fully satisfied, the remnants of crab shells and shrimp tails littering my plate. A waiter offers me a bright green key lime macaron, while Vale finishes his tiramisu.

"If I eat any more, I'll be sick," I say, spinning my macaron in my fingers before I turn to Vale. "Do you want to head to the upper deck and puke over the railing?" I give him a cheeky grin.

He throws down his napkin. "There's no one I'd rather lose my dinner with."

Jaz and Brax stay at our table, sharing a tiramisu and promising to join us for dancing later.

When we reach the top deck, a sultry saxophone plays in the corner of the dance floor. I prop my elbows on the ship's railing, admiring the bloom of colors in the sky, like a woman's skirt spread across the horizon, all orange and pink taffeta.

"I love everything about this," I say, feeling better already. Turns out, I just needed fresh air and a short walk.

He slings an arm around my waist, like it's always belonged there. Like it was made to touch me.

I love being here with Vale, adore being his wife.

I should tell him. Share with him exactly how I feel, how I always want it to be this way. *Just us.* He still doesn't know why I turned him down the first time he asked me out, and it's something I've avoided talking about, mainly because it's about me.

"Vale, I've been wanting to tell you something," I begin, the words a lump in my throat, aching to climb out.

"What is it?" he asks, his face turning toward mine.

This is my chance to explain that he wasn't the reason I said no. I was. I couldn't ruin what we had.

"This thing between you and me," I say. "It's been incredible, but . . ."

"But?" he asks, like I'm about to drop some bad news on him.

"Not *but*," I flounder. Wrong choice of words. "I wanted to explain why I said no the first time you asked me out."

There's a tap on the shoulder, probably a waiter with more food. When I turn to say *No, thank you*, I'm met with the last person on earth I'd expect to see.

"Anthony?" I gasp.

Anthony holds a drink in one hand, wearing an immaculate tux. Probably something his rich parents bought him for all his galas.

"I thought that was you," he says, not addressing Vale, a smile playing on his lips. He seems only too happy to intrude on us.

"Why are you in Cancun?" I blurt, wishing this nightmare would just go away. Not him. Not now.

"I could ask you the same thing," he says.

That's when I remember Vale beside me. I grab his hand for support so I don't topple over from the shock. He knits his fingers through mine, as if to say *I'm here for you.* "We're on our honeymoon."

"Oh, right." His brow pinches. "Vegas wasn't enough?"

"I can never have enough of her," Vale says, drawing his shoulders up to his full six-four height. He makes Anthony seem small in comparison. Then he pulls me into his hip, my back pressed to his front, one arm snaking around my waist. "I'll take every opportunity to be alone with *my wife*." He looks down at me, a faint grin that rumbles through me like a volcanic explosion, his words coursing hot through my veins.

"Is Demetria here?" I say, looking over his shoulder, expecting a woman in a black dress to rise from the ocean like a giant tentacled sea monster.

"No, this is a business trip," he says, taking a sip of his drink. Funny . . . so was the gala, and he didn't have a problem with flaunting her there.

"It seems like wherever we go, you keep showing up," Vale says with a tight smile.

"Pure coincidence," Anthony says, motioning toward a group of older men in suits behind him. "I'm wooing some philanthropists who need to be wined and dined before they'll give money to the U.S. Skating Federation. It's just part of the job."

Anthony's eyes skim over the antique ring on my finger. "Is hockey not paying well these days?"

"What?" I balk. "Why would you ask that?"

"I'd expected a rock on your finger, not diamond chips."

He means it as an insult to Vale since Demetria's ring looked like a freaking planet with its own galaxy.

"I picked it out," I say, my anger flaring. "Because I don't like big gaudy diamonds."

Anthony sniffs, unimpressed. "Appropriate for a college skating coach."

Ouch.

When I took the coaching job at the university, Anthony told me he didn't think it was good enough. That I was settling. He wanted me to keep training for skating competitions. To be his "little star," because it made him look good to date a successful athlete. But I was done competing, the stress of it wrecking my mental health, while I battled constant injuries.

When I told him I wasn't returning to skating, he was disappointed not just because I was "settling for something less," but because I couldn't stick it out. He called me unfocused, blamed my diagnosis, even though I was ready for a change and my ADHD had nothing to do with it.

I love teaching college skaters—the thrill of seeing them improve, the relationships built over four years before they launch into the world.

Even if he hadn't cheated on me while I was recovering, I

would have ended it between us. He was always looking for something to fill the hole, the parts of him that were never satisfied, like Dad. And I wasn't good enough for either of them.

Isn't that why Dad never calls or visits, even now? Because there's always someone better. A new work acquaintance who invites him to a lake house. Another girlfriend to take wine tours with. A dopamine hit of meeting someone who's better than the last.

You always date someone like your father. It never really rang true for me, until now, as I realize Anthony and my father are strangely similar, always looking for that person to make them feel more impressive so they'll feel better about themselves.

Anyone who's too much work is left behind. And I've always been too much for people. I talk too much. I flit from one thing to the next. I have big emotions, and I wear them on my sleeve like a preschooler's paint shirt.

But somehow Vale never makes me feel like too much. He never gets that exasperated look Anthony always had when I talked too much. And he's never accused me of quitting or thought me reckless for taking chances. Isn't that why I married him? Because he asked me to take a risk and we took the plunge together?

Anthony drains his glass, changing the subject. "I plan on taking Demetria to the Amalfi Coast for our honeymoon. She *loves* Italy."

He's trying to one-up us, being a total schmuck to Vale on our honeymoon. That's the thing about people who are always comparing themselves to you. They try to make you feel small so that they can feel better about themselves.

"I love this place," I say with a smile so wide, I'm nearly glowing. "Vale took me on my first snorkeling excursion, which was fantastic."

Anthony frowns slightly. He's never liked swimming all that much. He's more the yacht club type, who loves big boats, probably to make up for what he's lacking in other departments.

"I heard from someone you hadn't been feeling well again." He attempts a look of fake concern, but it looks more like he sucked on a lemon. The man is about as compassionate as a rock.

I cross my arms. *Who told him?* We never had many mutual friends. When he left me, I had no one except my sister and the skaters at the university. He kept me emotionally caged so that I depended on him for everything—social interactions, professional connections, even friendships. Losing him meant losing my entire network. And I'll never let a man do that to me again, controlling my community and my friends so I'm invisible. Forcing me to be *less* so he could be more.

Vale would never dream of pushing me down so he could lift himself up. Even though we share friend groups—including the entire hockey team and Crushers' staff—he'd never ask me to give those friendships up if things don't work out.

"Is it true?" he asks again. "You're relapsing?"

"I'm feeling much better, Anthony. Thank you for your *concern.*" We both know he's not concerned about my health. Otherwise, why would he have left me at my worst? People who love you don't abandon you when life gets hard. They stay when nobody else does.

Or in my case, Vale stayed. He brought me cold compresses when my head hurt. He rubbed my forehead when I couldn't sleep. He even attempted to make soup for me even though he didn't know how and the noodles were mush. He asked me, *How can I help you? What can I do?* even if all I needed was someone to listen to me.

It's what made me fall so hard for him. And it's the same reason I turned him down the first time he asked me out. I didn't want to ruin the friendship I had with him.

Which is ironic in hindsight, because my marriage just might.

Anthony turns to Vale. "You look surprisingly different in a suit. Less like a barbaric hockey player."

"I like barbaric hockey players in suits," I say. "And *out of them.*"

Anthony gapes. I grin at Vale. Knowing we've never even had a real kiss, this is just a fantasy. But Anthony doesn't know that.

My ex turns to me, face pinched. "I'm surprised you're still in your hockey era. Never thought you'd date someone like him."

Someone who couldn't be less like Anthony.

Vale stiffens beside me, his hand rubbing over the curve of my waist. He could snap Anthony in half if he wanted to. But he pretends not to be bothered by this slight.

But I'm bothered. Too much.

"You thought this was temporary?" I loop my arms around Vale, almost climbing the man like a tree. Then I tip my face to my husband. "You have no idea how hot this man is. I could never grow tired of him."

Anthony flinches, while Vale's pupils flare. He cups one side of my face, kisses my forehead, his lips lingering there while heat races down my body.

It's enough to make Anthony shift, glance away.

The victory prize of the night.

Vale smiles at me, nuzzles his nose against my cheek. "I hit the lottery when I met Sloan." His fingers knit into mine as the saxophone wails a slow tune. His eyes never leave mine. "Excuse us, but I've been waiting all night to dance with *my wife.*"

Anthony's eyes follow us to the dance floor, glowing from the hanging twinkle lights above us. The sun has sunk below the horizon, casting everything in an orangish, otherworldly glow.

Vale pulls me so close to him, I can feel the warmth of his body through my dress. Through the pressure points where our bodies meet.

For a moment, we don't say anything. He twines his fingers with mine, as his other hand presses against my lower back, like he's letting Anthony know I'm his. We gently sway together to the jazzy cry of the sax, and my body finally exhales.

I'm where I'm meant to be, and I don't want this to ever end. Vale and me together, while the whole world looks on.

"Sorry about that," I finally say. "He can be such a jerk."

"Don't apologize for Anthony being the way he is. He could help himself, but he walked right into that one on his own. When you made that comment about barbaric hockey players, the look on his face was priceless."

"He deserved it after the way he treated you."

"He hasn't liked me since we met in Vegas," Vale says. "I don't take it personally. I'm the one who got the prize." His hand presses me closer, reminding me I'm the prize, our bodies creating pockets of energy and heat.

"Oh, he'd be glad to tell you how relieved he is to be rid of me. He never wanted someone who's broken."

"You are *not* broken," Vale says, offended I would say it.

"He always thought I was," I reply, my body cocooned into him like he's my safe space to admit this. "He saw my ADHD as a liability—saw me as too unfocused and scattered instead of seeing the good parts. The way it helped me take risks. When I had the car accident, he couldn't accept the fact that I might not heal. That this might be the death of my success and reflect poorly on him."

"If anyone is unworthy, it's him," Vale mutters, his hand sliding up my back protectively.

"I know that now," I say with a sigh. "He never supported me in my dreams. Never loved me for who I was. He's probably so relieved to be free of me."

"That's where you're wrong," Vale says. He pulls back just enough to see me with his darkened pupils. "If he's so glad to not be with you, then why is he watching you with me, looking like his last hope just died?"

"What?" I swallow and turn my head toward where Anthony is standing, expecting to see him chatting it up with his rich clients.

Instead, he's leaning against the railing, body turned toward me, his brow furrowed, his hands sunk into his pockets.

"But he has Demetria. He never really wanted me," I say, more as a reminder to myself than Vale. I don't want Anthony back, but I never believed there was a chance. Never believed he *could* want me. From there, I began to believe no one could want me.

"You think she has anything on you?" Vale lets out a low rumble of a laugh. "Right now he feels like the smallest man who ever lived. Because he knows what he lost and he can never get it back."

His words drill through me, send a seismic quake through every part of me.

Vale leans close to my ear. "If you want, we can take it to the next level. Give him the kiss of a lifetime." His lips are so close to mine, I can smell the sugar-sweet tiramisu in his breath, a hint of spice on his lips.

My heart is a drumbeat in my ears, adding to the confusion in my body. I'm not sure if I want to make Anthony regret letting me go, or if this ache is because I want this man next to me.

If none of this is real, the possibility of this kiss shouldn't mean anything. It shouldn't affect me this way.

But it does affect me. Because I want him. All of him.

I don't even think about my decision.

I melt into him and drink in his lips. He responds to me instantly, sliding a hand to my jaw, arching it toward him for a better angle, then consuming my lips.

My body curves into him, wanting to be closer, *closer*. His hand slides into my hair, tangling into it, like he can't get enough, and I respond by knotting my fist into his shirt, pulling him toward me, feeling the heat under his jacket. He bends me backward, almost a dip but not quite, and continues to drag kisses on every inch of my cheek, neck, earlobe.

I don't want to stop. I won't. But I'm nearly breathless. The dance floor is spinning. I feel consumed by him.

When the sax stops playing, everyone claps, and a few people whistle. That's when I realize most of them are smiling at our very intimate public kiss.

Except for Anthony, who's gone.

Heat is still pulsating over every inch of my skin, so I step away from Vale, just enough to catch my breath and stop the dizzy feeling. That's when I realize the boat is swaying, tipping dangerously.

"Is there something wrong with this boat?" I ask, blinking, glancing around, suddenly feeling like the world is madly spinning.

"No, why?" Vale looks at me, his brow furrowing. There's a look of intense concern, then panic as he grabs my arms.

"Sloan, no!"

And then everything goes black.

TWENTY-TWO

Vale

It's only the second time she's fainted on me. The first happened at home, when she overexerted herself cooking dinner for the team. I should've known that today, despite how incredibly exciting it was, would be just as exhausting.

Seeing her idiot ex only made her feel worse, because that's what people who bring you down do. They remind you of all the ways you don't measure up, even though in my world, she is the standard against which I measure all women.

That kiss only made my ache for her worse.

But thinking of kissing her doesn't solve my problem now. Ever since the car accident, overexertion makes her prone to fainting. The doctor said that might never go away, even with medicine. It's something I'll have to expect, to plan for by building in time for rest. I should've given her more breaks, not pushed so hard. Her capacity to jump into things wholeheartedly will have to be curbed until we know what she can handle.

And I'll have to be the bad guy who forces her into bed. Which isn't all bad if I get to be in bed with her.

She lies on her back in the hotel, worrying her lip as I sit on the edge of the mattress, studying her.

"There's nothing wrong with me now. I swear!" she begs. "Let's go out." She tries to get out of bed.

My hand lands on her shoulder, forcing her back down. "Oh, no you don't. You should rest. I'll watch you all night if I have to."

"But I'm fiiiiiine," she whines. "And I hate being treated like an invalid. It was a freak accident. My new medicine is working. I've never felt better!" She swings her legs over the bed, but I catch her ankles and carefully place them back on the bed.

"Nice try, but no. You're stuck here until tomorrow."

She pouts, pushing out her bottom lip. "Not even for a date with you?"

"You're cute, but I'm not giving in to your charms," I say, crossing my arms.

"So I have charms now?" she asks, her face lighting up.

"So many you don't even know about," I assure her. "But don't try to use them against me, Sloanie Baloney. Because the answer is still *no.*"

She frowns before switching tactics. "I'll tell you what I think it was. It wasn't because anything is wrong with me. It's actually *your* fault."

"My fault?" I laugh, putting a hand on my chest. "How am I to blame?"

"It was that kiss," she says, a playful smile curving her lips. "In Regency times, women always swooned over kisses. That's how you know it was good."

"Is that right?" I say, arching an eyebrow. "A compliment *and* a diversion to get me to say yes to going out? Well played, my lady."

"The kiss was *so* good, it took my breath away," she goes on.

"I agree. It was very good. But kissing doesn't cause fainting. In the case of Regency women, it was overly tight corsets restricting their breathing that caused them to faint."

She frowns. "I thought you wouldn't know that."

I tap her nose with my finger. "I know a lot of useless things. I also know that you should rest."

She bites her lip, thinking. "What if we stay here and do something fun?"

"Fun, as in, Sloan stays in bed?"

"No, the hot tub. For your back."

I narrow my eyes. "I'm not sure that's safe for you. Don't hot tubs come with a warning about people fainting?"

Her eyes dance as she pokes me in the arm. "Even if I do, you're a former lifeguard, so you can save me."

I frown. "Not funny."

"Come on! I want to do something fun, and this is a compromise. Just for a short time. You promised we would."

"That was before the dinner cruise," I remind her. "Are you sure you don't feel dizzy anymore?"

She holds up a hand. "Nope. I'll even walk a straight line to prove it. I probably could balance on the edge of the hot tub, I feel so good." She heads toward the sliding door to the patio to prove it.

I grab her arm. "You will most definitely not."

I pull her next to me on the bed and she links an arm through mine. "Then pretty please, let's have a date in the hot tub. What do you say?"

She makes lazy circles on my chest and my heart rockets.

"Fine," I say, sucking air through my teeth. I'm reluctant to leave her alone, but I have to since she needs to change into her swimsuit. "I'll change in the bathroom. But leave the door unlocked, okay? Just as a precaution. I won't come in unless you're unresponsive."

She nods, then stops me at the door. "Vale. Thank you. I'll make sure it's a night to remember." Then she reaches up and gives me a kiss on the cheek, flashing me a flirty smile.

My heart knocks against my chest. Heaven help me, I can't give in to her tonight.

The bedroom door is still closed when I finish changing, and I can hear her rummaging through her suitcase, which means she hasn't fainted yet. I climb into the hot tub, keeping my back to the sliding door.

A few minutes later, the door slides open, and she comes out with a towel wrapped around her. From the look on her face, she's debating whether she wants to drop the towel. I thought I'd made it clear how I feel about her, that her body is utter perfection to me, but apparently I've not made it clear enough.

"Do you need me to leave?" I ask. "Because I don't want you to feel uncomfortable around me. Just for the record, since I've already seen you in a swimsuit and think your body is incredibly perfect, I'm hardly the problem."

Her eyes flick briefly to me with a smile of gratitude before she looks at her bare toes. "The problem isn't you. It's me."

"That sounds strangely like a breakup text."

"It's not. Just old baggage. Anthony was always so critical of my body since I wasn't a size zero. And since my accident, it's only gotten worse. I'm softer. Less in shape. It's not that I care so much —the voice in my head still tells me I'm not good enough. That somehow I'll never be enough."

"Sloan," I say gently, but firmly. "You're so beautiful, and you don't even realize it." I wish she'd believe me. But even more, I wish she'd find the strength to believe it for herself.

She glances down at her towel. "I had no choice but to wear a different suit, since the swimsuit I wore snorkeling is still wet."

"Is it more revealing?"

She nods. "A little."

I cover my eyes. "Is this better?"

"You don't have to do that for me."

"You have ten seconds to talk yourself into it until I drop my hand."

"Vale." She peels my hand away, looks at me over the rim of

the tub. "You don't have to cover your eyes. I need to do this . . . *for me.* If I can't be brave in front of my husband, I'll never have the courage."

The words *my husband* surge through me. In the past, she always used that word like it was part of the charade, but this time feels different. She's starting to believe that our agreement is more than temporary.

She glances at her feet. "I'm trying to accept I have scars, even if they're ugly."

"Wait—what scars?" I ask, suddenly wondering how I don't know about this.

"From the accident." She pulls open her towel just enough for me to see a large scar that cuts across the side of her abdomen. "I stopped wearing this suit because of it. It used to be a favorite and I thought I'd wear it again someday, but I haven't. I only threw it in my bag because I needed an extra. Then I tried it on tonight and saw my scar again and was afraid you'd find me . . ." She pauses. "Repulsive."

"What?" I nearly choke on the word. "I would *never* think that. If you want to know the truth, I find you devastatingly attractive. Whatever worries you have about your body, that's not the way I see you. I think you're more beautiful *with* scars."

She laughs in disbelief.

"Sloan," I whisper. "If you knew the thoughts I have about you . . ." I shake my head, my voice gravelly and low. "You might not ever come near me again."

"Really?" she asks with a furrowed brow.

"Yes, *really.*"

She tilts her head and studies me. "I didn't know you felt . . ." Her voice drops off.

"Attracted to you?" I finish.

She nods.

"Well, you are my wife," I say with a smile.

"Okay, husband," she says, climbing the steps to the hot tub. "Move over and make room for me."

With a quick whoosh, she drops the towel and climbs into the hot tub without hesitating this time. Though I try not to gawk, I get a glimpse of her yellow-and-pink floral two-piece, which makes my heart trip and stumble. She's gorgeous. And she's my wife. *My wife.*

Those words will never grow old to me.

She slides under the water as the bubbles float around her shoulders. Above us, there's a beautiful sky filled with moonlight and stars, and in the distance, music plays from a local club. She scoots closer to me in the hot tub, her arm brushing mine.

"I'm surprised you want to sit next to me," I say. "After everything I admitted."

Part of me wondered whether admitting my attraction would make her run scared the other direction.

"Vale," she says slowly, her shoulders wet with droplets. "As your wife, I want to sit close to you, okay?"

"Okay," I say, looking at her, "but you might have to take my mind off the fact that you're close to me in that gorgeous swimsuit."

"Tell me something I don't know about you," she says, studying me.

"You know everything about me. Everything that's important, at least."

"I don't. The Newlywed Game proved that."

I lean my head on the back of the hot tub. "Okay, let me think. When I was ten, I rode my BMX bike off the roof of our house."

Her eyes widen. "Tell me that didn't end with an ER trip."

I shake my head. "Not for me. But Brax wasn't so fortunate."

She grimaces. "Your poor mom. You've given her so much grief."

"And gray hair," I add. "At least I found a way to make her happy now that I married you. I think she likes you as much as I do. Given you're my favorite person, that's a lot."

Her face turns to mine like she doesn't believe me. "She does?"

"You're so much better than the previous dates I brought home. Most of them weren't serious, but Mom was scared I'd end up with someone who only wanted me because I'm a professional athlete."

Sloan tucks hair over her shoulder. "Well, I married you for your insurance, which isn't any better."

I shake my head. "It's not the same thing. I wanted to marry you more than those other girls."

"You're a good person, Vale," she says. "I feel really lucky to have you in my life."

"I know you mean it as a compliment, but it feels like you're putting me on a pedestal I don't deserve. Or somehow, you think you're not a good person. But you are. Even when you were laid up from your injury, you always found a way to make people feel like they belonged somewhere. You invited the team over for dinner or helped Jaz with one of the hockey team events. It's like you know how to bring people together. That's a gift."

She plays with a strand of loose hair. "That's because I've never felt like I belonged. So I had to create the family I didn't have." She stares into the dark sky. "After Mom died, I lost half of myself. Then Dad remarried, and it seemed like I finally had a shot at a family again. Things were good for a few years, until their marriage fell apart, and Dad just drifted off into the sunset, like a lone cowboy. He never thought about his responsibility to me." She looks at the bubbles in the water, lost in her thoughts. "That's why I like to have people around me. It feels like I'm getting back the thing I've lost. Even coaching makes me feel that way."

"I can tell. Every time you come home from practice, you seem different," I say. "You're not just investing in your skaters to win, but because you care about them as humans. You treat them as equals. That's special." I put my hand on her face and turn it toward me. "You're special."

She shakes her head. "I talk too much. I'm loud and intense

and my emotions are the same. I'm too much for some people. I think that's why my dad never visits, honestly. He wishes I was different. More like him. Less like me." There's a slow ache beneath her words. Like she wishes she could fix the past—or herself. But there are some things you can't change.

"I wouldn't want you to be different," I say, touching her chin so she'll meet my gaze. "I like you the way you are. All your big emotions. Everything you say."

She smiles. "You might not be saying that after we've been married a year."

"Do you want to make a bet on that?" I lift an eyebrow.

She considers this. "No, because you're a very patient man, Vale MacPherson. You just haven't seen the worst yet."

I laugh. "I don't think there is a worst when it comes to you." I sink a little deeper into the water so we're on the same level. "It's your turn to share an embarrassing story."

"About what?"

"I want to know all the dirt on Sloan Summers."

"You won't find any," she says overconfidently. "But you can try."

"Okay, how many guys have you dated?"

She squints at the sky as she thinks. "Not many. Maybe three if you're not counting first dates." She looks at me and pokes me in the arm. "I'm not a famous hockey star like you."

I scoff. "Three?"

"I know, it's hardly any," she says apologizing. "I'm not good at sticking with something, remember? And I'm really picky."

"No, it's not that. It's the number," I say, suddenly feeling protective of her. "That means you dated them longer. You probably even had feelings for them."

"I'm not sure the feelings were mutual. Anthony was the longest at two years. The others were shorter. Maybe a year, if that."

"A year?" I gasp, the jealousy growing in my chest. "That's practically married!"

She frowns. "Definitely not married." She studies me for a moment, her mouth curving into an amused grin. "Wait a minute. Are you . . . *jealous?*"

I shake my head. "No, I'm not jealous. I just can't think about you with anyone else without becoming irrationally angry."

"Vale," she says. "That's what jealousy is."

"I know, and now I'm regretting asking you." I run my fingers through my hair, sighing angrily. "I don't even want another man looking at you ever again."

"That's impossible," she says. "Just because I dated someone doesn't mean I was in love with them. I thought I was with Anthony, but looking back, I realize it never really was. I just wanted it to be something more. And honestly, I felt like I never had a real kiss until today. Not even with Anthony."

Now I'm the one who's confused. I let out a hoarse laugh, rub the back of my neck. "What do you mean you've never had a real kiss?"

"I mean the kind of kiss you remember long after it happens. The kind that makes everything in you feel alive again."

"What about those guys you dated before Anthony?"

She shrugs. "It always felt forced. Like I was playing a part. Doing it because it was expected. Tonight felt different, even though I know it was just to make Anthony jealous."

I level my gaze. "It wasn't just to make him jealous, Sloan."

She frowns. "That was the agreement. You only kissed me because he was there to see it. The problem is, I felt confused, like I wasn't just playing a role anymore. Because when you kiss me like that, I don't want it to be for Anthony, or my sister, or anyone else."

I stare at her in disbelief, my thoughts unraveling like a tangled thread. "I thought you wanted me to kiss you. I thought we were following the *rules.*"

She turns to me, her body facing mine. "We were, but then I realized something had changed. And I know I agreed to this, but things are different now. I don't want you to touch me because of the rules. Or kiss me because someone's there to see it. It's *too real* for me. Which is why I can't kiss you again. Not unless it's for me and no one else."

"There's no one here now," I say, my voice a low rumble. I move closer to her. "This time, it's not for show."

Then I take her face in both my hands and kiss her.

It's swift. Messy. Breathless.

My hands slide down to her back, feeling the curves of her shoulder blades, the ridges of her spine, the dip of her waist.

The water spins and bubbles around us, the heat rising, the sweat prickling down our neck, along the curves of her shoulders.

In a ragged voice I pull away just enough to tell her between kisses, "I've wanted to kiss you every day since I married you. Every time I heard your laughter in the house. Every time you were close to me. Every night you were in bed alone." I drop my head into her damp shoulder, leaving a kiss.

Her hands slide into my wet hair as she brushes my ear with her lips. She pulls back just a little, her breath in my ear. "Then why didn't you?"

I straighten, so I can see her eyes. "I thought you'd only agree if there was a reason. If it was part of the charade."

"Is there a reason now?" she asks, bewildered.

My hands cup her face. "Is it enough that you're the only woman for me?"

She leans forward and answers *yes* with a kiss, her warm mouth on my lips, her body pressed to mine.

Everything feels like *yes* with her. Like it's the way it's supposed to be. Husband and wife, light and heat, while the whole world fades into night. I feel like I've swallowed a torch, my body lit from flame and heat.

We still haven't made it clear what the future holds or how long she wants me in her life as her husband.

I've already made my decision.

She is my endgame. *My wife.*

I pull back, bracing her shoulders. "As much as I want *you*—

and in case it's not clear, I *really* want you right now—there's something else I need to tell you. I want this to be real. *Us,* together, as husband and wife. I told you I'd hold to the marriage rules, but this is not an act." My voice frays. "I'm not good at pretending with you. When I kiss you, I'm doing it because I want you. More than anything, I want to be married to you . . . but I'm also terrible at reading your mind and knowing if you feel the same. If what you want is *us.*"

She takes my wrists, draws circles on the insides with her thumbs. "I know you're what I want. And that I want to take things slow and figure it out. Even if that's hard for me to do."

I blink, recalibrate how this is going to work since my heart is bucking in my chest. "Take it slow. Figure it out," I repeat, wondering if I've pushed too fast, too hard. "Whatever it takes for you not to give up on us."

I slide back, giving her space, but she grasps my wrists. "That's not what I meant." She shakes her head, thumbs circling again. "I have the tendency to panic when things get hard. I run away, make rash decisions. But when it comes to you, everything in me wants to move fast. To lose myself in you. To fall hard and swift and give everything to you. And that scares me because that's what happened with Anthony. When he didn't stay, I didn't know who I was anymore. I want to take things slowly so I don't make the same mistakes, to learn how to stick around for the long haul, and stay instead of running away. But just because I need to take things slow, doesn't mean I don't want us."

I nod, my voice scraping. "I know I'm not who you pictured yourself with. I'm nothing like Anthony. I don't care what people think of me, except for you. Even though we're really different, I won't give up on us. So if you need me to go, to give you space tonight to think—"

"Vale," she cuts me off. "Don't go." She stills, her thumbs resting on the inside of my wrists. "I don't need to think about it anymore. You told me you're not staying in my bedroom until I ask you. Until I'm no longer afraid of what might happen between us."

I wrap my arms around her, tugging her closer. The moment feels full, like any second the glass might overflow.

"This is me asking. Will you stay tonight?" Her hands climb to the back of my neck, stroke the curve of my shoulder. "I want you to hold me. As my husband."

I touch her chin, brush my thumb over her lips before answering, "Anything for my wife."

Sloan

I've never slept so well as last night. Vale holding me all night was tender, satisfying, better than all the dreams I've ever had. And perhaps highly unusual since nothing beyond that happened. But I've never fit in with the usual standards of how to do things, especially not when it comes to love. My life has been a series of missteps, of figuring out what works for me. It's part of my quirkiness, and maybe my superpower, to think outside the box, doing things backward: marriage first, then the real relationship.

But in this case, it's also my guardrail. Taking things slow will give me time to figure things out, to finally prove to myself I'm not who everyone says. *Not the impulsive one who runs off to the next thing.* Not the one making hasty decisions, then regretting them. The only reason I stayed with Anthony is I thought I could be different. What he needed me to be. I never had feelings for him the way I do for Vale.

I hadn't seen it before, but Anthony leaving me was a small mercy. Because it's what led me to Vale.

Back then, I was broken in so many ways, but that didn't stop Vale from seeing past the mess. It's madness, really, but love can be like that—it makes no sense in the moment.

If we're taking things slow, then rushing into a physical relationship before we've even defined our relationship would be like diving off a cliff before checking the depth of the water below.

Insanity.

I've already made a mess of things. I rushed into marriage to solve one problem, only to create a dozen more.

Even knowing that, I wouldn't hesitate to do it again. I still want to dive right into Vale's arms. But behind this feeling of *nothing could go wrong now* is a tiny niggling doubt that I can't put my finger on. Maybe it's because I've been hit by too many hard things, like waves battering the shore: Mom dying, Dad remarrying and then divorcing, a car accident and brain injury, the breakup with Anthony, and then a relapse.

Life has taught me that love doesn't protect you from hard things. It doesn't shelter you from the storm. Instead, the torrents will come, pummeling you in a thousand small ways, and it's love that buoys you, keeps you from going under, gives you reason to hold on.

I roll over in bed, stretching my arm across the silky smooth cotton, reaching for Vale. My hand lands on an empty pillow.

"Vale?" I call sleepily.

I prop myself on my elbows, rub my eyes, and take a deep breath. The dark nutty smell of coffee hits me like the first light of morning.

There's a soft knock at the door before Vale peeks his head in. "I hope I didn't wake you," he says with a lazy morning grin and mussed waves that make me want to thread my fingers through his hair. I love being the only one privy to this part of his life, the side that isn't polished and PR ready.

Vale sets the coffee on a small table next to my bed before opening the curtains. "Have you seen the view outside?" he asks, opening the blackout shades. The light is nearly blinding. The sky is a blue ribbon, the ocean a wavy blanket.

I take a sip of coffee, drink in the dark bitter bite, the touch of cream. Neither of us brings up last night, like the dream of it might disappear, a soap bubble mid-air.

I just drink in the goodness in front of me. His dark silhouette outlined in the bedroom window as he puts one hand on the sill.

Vale is my husband. *Mine.*

That thought thrills me and terrifies me in equal measure.

What if I can't be the wife he needs? What if I mess this up? What then?

It feels like a weight on my chest, pressing the air from my lungs like a slow leak. I want so badly to talk to Jaz about last night, how everything shifted from *I* and *me*, to *us* and *we.*

The best thing about having a sister is telling her everything, the deepest secrets of my heart, knowing she'll carry them too.

But this is the one thing I can't tell her. My most life-changing secret will stay buried under half-truths. She can't ever know we weren't really together, that our relationship was a fraud and we married so I could get Vale's insurance.

If that ever comes out, it could wreck our relationship.

Because if there's one thing Jaz hates, it's lying. All because of Dad, who broke our family apart over a lie. After that mistake, every promise felt like one he couldn't keep. *I'll be at your recital. I won't forget your birthday party. I'll make it up to you.*

The promises piled up like bad excuses. They're the only thing he left behind.

"What do you want to do today?" Vale says, watching me as I stretch my arms in the air.

"I'm looking forward to being thoroughly lazy," I say with a yawn.

"And I support you being thoroughly lazy," Vale says with a grin that shows he approves. "Is that thoroughly lazy by the pool or thoroughly lazy in the bedroom?"

"Most definitely poolside," I say. "I'm planning on reading a book and ordering pink lemonade from the tiki bar." I shift my legs over the edge of the bed. "Care to join me?"

"I will, as soon as I take a run with Brax. We can't let this trip make us soft." He crosses the room to kiss the top of my head before he leaves. My pulse stutters. "When I finish, I'm back on duty as your personal cabana boy."

"You mean *husband*," I clarify. I don't want him to ever feel like our relationship is a joke again.

"I like that even better." He leaves with a wink, and my heart spins like a top. *If this is happiness, please don't let it ever end.*

I know that eventually we'll have to return to real life and figure out what we'll do about us. But for now, I'd like to sink my toes deep into this dream world, the one where Vale and I are together forever. If I'm being honest, this could go on forever. Because I'm not sure I ever want to return to reality after last night.

The rest of the day is a hazy blur of pool time with Jaz as we read and dip our feet in the water. The boys join us after their morning run and then decide to do some paddleboarding. I'm still sore from snorkeling, so Jaz and I stay behind while the boys dash off for a day of fun. This feels downright irresponsible, taking a day of doing nothing but lounging around in paradise. In fact, this entire honeymoon feels like a much-needed break after a long stretch of relentless change. And I'm dying to tell Jaz what's happened between Vale and me, if only to confide in someone how deliriously happy I am. How, for once, I'm sticking to what I promised.

"I have to tell you something," I say, closing my book, leaving one finger tucked inside the flap in case I chicken out. I take a deep breath. "It's about Vale and me."

For so long I've wanted to tell her, but I don't want her to look at me the way she does our father. Now that Vale and I are finally a couple, how we came together seems less significant, and somehow, more forgivable.

Jaz looks up from her magazine, her big sunglasses hiding her eyes, a floppy hat shading her face. "What's that?"

"I need to tell you about something that happened in Vegas."

"With Vale?"

I bite my lip. "Yes . . . and Anthony."

"Anthony?" She leaves her magazine open in her lap. "What does he have to do with Vegas?"

"He was there. At the gala," I start slowly.

"Was his little girlfriend there too?" Jaz is still furious at Anthony for dropping me and running straight into the arms of one of his skaters. "I would've loved to have seen his face when he saw you with Vale. Anthony and Vale couldn't be more different."

"He was shocked to find out we were a couple," I say. *Even though Vale made it up.* Our relationship started out as a ruse, then continued that way into our marriage. Saying it out loud sounds ludicrous, but I try.

"It's how everything began," I say, fumbling for words. "They were engaged. And Vale suggested we one-up them."

"By getting married?" Her eyebrows fly up.

"No, engaged." It's hard to explain the sequence of events now. It all happened so fast. Pretending we were engaged, then deciding to elope. In hindsight, it seemed like the answer to my problems—the breakup, the relapse—all solved with a quick trip to the altar. "It wasn't because of Anthony that we married. There's more to it." That part is true at least.

"Love, right?" Her response is so automatic, it pains me.

I hesitate. Right now, I wish I could go back to Vegas, rewind the clock and call Jaz before I made this enormous, life-changing decision. But part of me was afraid she'd talk me out of going through with it, explaining all the ways it could go off the rails, like a checklist of how to ruin your life by eloping with your best friend. *You're not good at sticking with things. Can you really be different now?*

Yes, I can. I know that now.

But I also feel a pinch of regret: I should've told Jaz and not waited. I should've braced myself for her pushing back on my insecurities. In the end, I still would've married Vale. That was the right thing to do because underneath the excuses, I love him.

But I can't undo what's already done. I can only choose to tell her the truth now. "Well, about that . . ."

Jaz's phone buzzes from her beach bag. She glances at the screen, her brow furrowing.

"Something wrong?" I ask.

"It's Dad. Wondering where I am."

"Dad? Why would he ask where you are, unless . . ."

She stares at his message. "He's in Sully's Beach. At our house. And Leo just answered the door."

"Uh-oh. Why is he there?"

She shrugs. "Because he couldn't find anyone better to hang out with would be my guess. I'm telling him we're on vacation." She types a text, then laughs. "I bet Leo gave him a warm welcome."

"More like growled at him to get off our property," I add.

I blink and wonder if I should let her resolve this with Dad first. *Why didn't Dad text me?*

Probably because he knows how much Jaz holds against him. How she's always hated his lies and never forgiven him for walking away from our family after the truth came out.

Her phone beeps. She studies the text, then shakes her head. "He says he wants to get together when we get back." She tosses her phone back in her bag.

"Aren't you going to answer him?"

"No. You know he hides the truth. Makes promises he can't keep. I can't stand when people lie to me. Especially family."

Something twists inside me, wrenching me.

Before Mom died, Dad promised he'd always put us first. That he'd be there for us. For a long time, he was. He remarried, and things were good for years, until that one day, when we found out Dad was cheating. When Jaz walked in on him kissing someone who wasn't our stepmom, it broke something in her. She couldn't trust Dad after that, and it altered her ability to forgive anyone who lied to her, no matter the reason. After that, whenever Dad made a promise, then didn't show up, it felt like he was reopening a scab.

"What if he's there when we get back?" I ask.

"That's not like Dad," she says, turning back to her magazine. "He'll be gone. Some people never change." She flips a page, her knee propping up the magazine, her eyes flicking over the stylized images of a stranger's home remodel. A family poses on a porch—a picture of joy in the perfect home. It's so uncomplicated, and at the same time so out of reach, it's laughable.

"What was it you were saying about you and Vale?" she asks, never looking away from the page.

"Nothing," I murmur, the guilt clawing at my throat. I can't have her look at me the way she does when she talks about Dad.

Some people never change.

I shake my head, let my book fall open in my lap. "Nothing at all."

TWENTY-FOUR

Sloan

The rest of the week feels like speed dating on *The Bachelor*. Every day is an endless stretch of outrageously romantic settings: long walks on the beach as the sun sets, dazzling views in high-end oceanfront restaurants, and so much kissing my lips turn raw and tender.

I don't want to leave whatever this is: an idyllic beach vacation where we figure out our new future together. Everything feels like a dream here. But I also know that when we return to the life we left in Sully's Beach, things won't be easier for us. If anything, life will only get harder.

We have our wedding renewal and a full reception Jaz is planning—and the fact that a major publication will cover it only ramps up my anxiety. I can't make vows in front of God and everyone without telling Vale how I feel and why I'm nervous about marrying him in a public ceremony, even though I absolutely want to. But this time, I want things to be different. No more charades. No more lies. This time, I want to marry for real.

And that means I have to tell my sister everything. Because if I don't, I might gain Vale as a forever partner, but I'll lose my sister, and I can't stand for that to happen.

The truth needs to come out, no matter how much it hurts.

On our last night in Cancun, I know Vale and I need to have "the talk" about what happens when we get home. But I can also see from the look in Vale's eyes that talking is the last thing he wants to do.

He takes me to the most beautiful date location yet—another hidden gem from his Facebook group: a waterfall in a stunning hidden lagoon.

I stay on one side of the lagoon while he stays on the other. You couldn't charge the air between us more if we were struck by lightning. I keep my distance, just so I can think instead of completely crumbling from his touch.

With his eyes fixed on me, one side of his mouth curls up. "What are you thinking about, Sloan?"

You. Touching you. Being close to you. Kissing you. All the things involving you.

Instead, I slick back my wet hair, and calculate my next move so that I don't forget the elephant in the lagoon. "I'm thinking about going home. What happens next."

"I don't want to think about that tonight." He smiles and something prickles under my skin, electrical impulses zipping from me to him in a never-ending circuit.

His eyes land on me, linger too long, and I know I'm in trouble. One look from him causes my brain cells to spontaneously combust so I can't think straight, can't even form a coherent sentence. Every time he touches me, I completely lose my train of thought.

He swims toward me, his eyes trailing from my head, to my neck, to my shoulders, like a shark deciding which part to devour first.

And the thing is, I want him to.

"Vale, I want . . ." My voice falters as he rises from the water like some sort of exotic creature from an underwater kingdom.

"What is it you want?" he asks, smirking.

My mouth gapes at the sight of him, and I totally forget what I wanted. He's unearthly. All stacked muscle, totally ripped compared to me, except that I know how hard he works for it. I'm not mad. Just speechless.

"You know what I want?" he says with a glint in his eyes. "To kiss you under the waterfall."

He sweeps his hands under me and carries me to the waterfall, which resembles something from a movie set. Even if I'd wanted to stop him, I'm powerless. My body succumbs like limp spaghetti in his arms.

As we draw close to the falls, water droplets splatter our shoulders, softening the air like a heavenly mist. He sets me down, but not before leaving a line of kisses across my collarbone. Soft, sweet, unspoken promises that there's more to come.

My eyes flutter closed and I want so desperately to drift off to the land of waterfall bliss. But I can't let myself fall into a Vale-trance, no matter how much I want my husband now.

"Vale, I need to talk to you," I say, more urgently.

He steps back, studying me, brows furrowed. "You want to talk—*now*?" It's obvious that talking is the last thing on his mind.

"I know it's our last night here. But I think we have some unanswered questions between us. Important ones."

He rubs the back of his neck and sighs. "Okay." He didn't take me to an exotic waterfall so we could discuss our taxes. This was his attempt at wooing his wife, and I'm spoiling our adventure. "But can we make this fun?"

"I guess?" I'm not sure how to make this as fun as kissing him under a waterfall. They are not even in the same ballpark. More like different galaxies. But before I can give him all of me, I need to know *everything*—to know if this feeling that things could work is just a mirage, or if we have a chance together.

"Let's make it a game," he suggests, his competitive streak coming out. "Since we failed at the question game at the hockey team party, why don't we try again? Except this time, if you pause before you answer, then you have to kiss the other person."

"Wait—it's a *speed* question game?"

"Don't the best games test your ability to act on reflexes?" He knows he's got an advantage honed from years on the ice. And this added twist will only work if I answer without thinking. Otherwise, I'm going down like an airplane with engine failure.

"Seems fair enough." I nod, crossing my arms. "But I'm adding one more rule. No touching while I answer."

He lifts an eyebrow. "You think I'll distract you?"

"You most definitely will distract me. So keep your distance, MacPherson."

He raises his hands. "You can tie my hands behind my back if you want."

"You would like that way too much," I say with a smirk.

"Are all questions legit?"

I shrug. "I don't see why not." If I keep my options open, that means I get to ask him whatever I want. Seems totally fair to me. "You want to go first?"

He nods, then gives me a look that says he's up to something. "Sloan, why did you say no when I asked you out the first time?"

I was definitely not expecting that one. I bite my lip. "You couldn't take things easy on me?"

"Never," he says, his eyes glinting. "The stakes are too high. And I want to *win*." His voice rumbles on the last word.

If I answer honestly, then I'm confessing my secret—how long I've wanted him. But I'm too competitive to give up on the first try, and I refuse to lose this game.

"Are you stalling for time?" he asks with an amused grin.

"No. Absolutely not," I fire back. "When you asked me out the first time, we barely knew each other. You had just moved in, and I wasn't in a good head space. I was still recovering from the accident, fighting headaches and in a mild depression. I wasn't *me*. The girl who likes to throw parties and cook Italian dinners and *go, go go*. I was afraid that if you dated that version of me, the one who was sad and struggling, you'd run the opposite direction and never give me a chance. You'd only see the parts of me that were broken and never the real me underneath. It seemed too risky, like I might lose your friendship. If I'm honest, I was embarrassed that I'd never be enough. So I pretended I wasn't interested because I wanted to save one scrap of my dignity, even if it meant pushing you away."

His eyes soften as he brushes his knuckles over my cheek. "You have always been enough, Sloan. Why do you think I wanted to marry you?"

"Because you felt sorry for me?"

"Maybe it was selfish of me, but I wanted to be with you however and whenever I could. Even if it meant convincing you to marry me for practical reasons."

My heart thunders in my chest. I feel like I could faint. Is it possible Vale MacPherson feels more than raw attraction for me? That he might even love me? I can't think about the possibility or I might fold right on the spot.

"Which brings me to my question," I say, straightening my shoulders. "You confessed to me that you've never told a woman before that you love her. So why is that?"

His studies me for a beat, then takes my hands in his. "For two reasons. One, because I didn't want to be my father. I didn't want to tell someone I loved them and then change my mind. Love isn't just based on feelings. It's a choice we make. We choose to stay. And I decided to save it for someone I'd never change my mind about."

"You said there were two reasons," I remind him. "What's the other one?"

His jaw flexes. "Because I never fell in love with anyone before." He hesitates a beat. "Until now."

My heart drops out of my chest. I don't believe it's possible. He can't love me.

"Then why . . .?" Maybe it's selfish to ask, but I want to know. I need to hear him say it.

He gives me that trademark grin that makes him America's hottest athlete. "Wait your turn, you impatient woman." His eyes are dancing. He knows he has me in the palm of his hand—waiting for something that I need from him. I have to know *now*.

I scoff. "But how could you drop that kind of bomb on me without an explanation?"

He levels his gaze and shakes his head. "I'm not answering you because it's my turn to ask." Then he gives me a look that disarms me. "How can I convince you to stop asking me for an end date to this marriage?"

I cross my arms. "Unfair question. We already agreed there have to be rules."

He touches my lips to silence me. "All questions are legit. You said so at the beginning."

I suck air though my teeth. "Fine. You want an answer on why I keep pressuring you to set a date? We went into this arrangement with the understanding that we would end it. *Eventually.* This gives you an out if things aren't working."

"Who says I want out?" he challenges, narrowing his eyes.

Is he reneging on our agreement? Changing the terms? "I thought it would be better if we both believed it would be temporary."

"Sloan," he says. "I never wanted this to be temporary."

The words feel like a grenade to my heart. "Never? Not even when you married me?"

"Never." His voice is a low rasp.

The scene around me swims in my vision, my legs feel like spaghetti, and the only thing I can focus on are the dark pupils of his eyes, pulling me under. "But you can't change the rules in the middle of our agreement. I know we're trying to make this relationship work. That we're doing everything backward by dating now, after we're married. But I never want you to feel tied down. Pressured to stay with me when things aren't working and you want . . ."

"An out?" he finishes. He shakes his head, his eyes never leaving mine. "Sloan. I don't need an out. Not when it comes to you. I've already decided: I'm staying with you for the long haul, if you'll have me. If you need more proof, then look at how I've behaved in our marriage so far. I've followed all the rules. *For you.*

And I've tried to honor you in every way possible, waiting on you to decide you don't need an escape clause from this marriage. I'm trying to be an honorable man until you finally accept that this marriage is real. At some point you need to decide you won't run when things get hard. And you'll stick around long enough for me to prove to you that I will always be there for you."

"Wait—what?" I say, feeling like Vale just knocked the wind out of me.

He cups my face in his hands. "I love you, Sloan. You just have to decide for yourself if you want this marriage. Because there is no end date in my book."

He's waiting on me to decide? It doesn't make sense, unless he knows me all too well. Which of course he does. He knows my temptation is to run away when life gets too hard. When it comes down to it, I'm the one who always gives up first. This is his game. To convince me that I need to see myself the way he does.

"Vale, I don't know if I can be different," I say, shaking my head. "Every time I think I can, I end up failing miserably. And then I prove to myself that I'm not capable of changing. I'm so afraid that I'll disappoint you like my dad did to us. Losing my mom wrecked him, and he never got over it. It's like he was always looking for something to make that part of him better and nothing ever could. And I'm afraid I'll just disappoint you like I've already disappointed my sister by not telling her the truth about us." I look down at the water swirling around me, because I can't meet his eyes. "I want to be with you more than anything. But I'm too afraid of failing you to try. And you mean too much to me to let you down."

"Then give us a chance," he says, his voice hoarse, hands sliding to my jaw. "I think when you look in the mirror, you see someone who's already failed. You're afraid of getting hurt, of reopening the scars left over from your father. But I'm not him. Leaving will never be an option. When it comes to you and me, there is no end date."

I blink back tears. I don't know why I ever thought that Vale would turn out like my father, or that in the end, he'd fail me too.

Tears slip down my cheeks. "But how do you know you'll still want me?"

"I will *never stop* wanting you," he says, kissing the tears away. "And I'm yours if you'll have me, Sloan. I'm on my knees for you. Because I love you. I love every part of you. And I always will." He pauses, holding my gaze.

He's never said I love you before today. Those words feel like the sun, warming my back, filling me with indescribable happiness.

His thumb strokes my cheekbone. "The only question is *will you?*"

I gaze into his eyes and willingly decide to lose the game.

I reach up on my toes and crash into his lips with a kiss that says everything he needs to know. *Without question, I love you.*

TWENTY-FIVE

Vale

I'm still floating from last night. That last kiss by the waterfall —along with everything that was said and left unsaid—made me never want to leave paradise. But our obscenely early morning alarm clock for the airport ripped away that dream like a cruel joke.

No more waterfall kisses or snorkeling adventures. Time to head back to reality, one that feels more like whiplash than a gentle reentry to life together.

Not only do we have a wedding ceremony and reception to finish planning, we also have to prepare for *The Star Report*'s full coverage of the event. And because things have been so busy, I haven't even mentioned my hockey contract and the no-movement clause—something I was waiting to tell Sloan once things had settled down.

Even now, I can tell Sloan's already nervous about the wedding, because her leg keeps bouncing up and down the entire plane trip home.

I lay a hand on her knee. She looks down at it and gives me an apologetic wince. "Sorry."

"Tell me what's bothering you," I say, keeping my hand there.

"Nothing's bothering me," she says, her smile tense.

I don't buy it. "Is it all the wedding prep when we get back? Is it *The Star Report*'s coverage of our big day?"

"Neither," she says. Then she looks down the aisle at Brax and Jaz in the back of the plane. "Except for the part about the whole world seeing our pictures after *The Star Report* publishes it. I could do without that part."

"Sloan, we can cancel the contract with them if it bothers you."

"No!" she says. "If we don't go through with it, you know the reporters will show up on our doorstep. This limits who gets in. It's the better option."

She bites a nail.

"What else are you nervous about?"

She lets out a sigh, glances over her shoulder again. "Dad texted Jaz when we were in Cancun. Apparently, he tried to stop by. Which means he could still be there."

I narrow my eyes. "Why is that a problem?"

"I was hoping we'd have some time before everyone arrived for our wedding. Time to get used to *us*. I don't need my dad getting in the way of our big day. Because wherever he goes, he brings the stress level up a thousand notches."

"Hey," I say, turning her face to mine. "That's not going to happen. I will keep things under control. There will be plenty of time for us. And if you feel pressure, I'm here to help you. Just tell me what you need."

She shakes her head. "It's not just that. My dad and Jaz have never gotten along. He lied to us a long time ago, and she's never forgiven him. It's tense between them."

"How does that involve you?"

"Because she hates lying." Then she lowers her voice. "And I kept the truth from her. About us."

"Do you want me to talk to her?" I say. "I'll take the blame for it. I'm the one who suggested it."

"I won't let you," she warns. "Even if we tried that, she'd see right through it. I need to do it. Before our wedding."

I get the feeling this is some sisterly thing between Sloan and Jaz that I can't fix for her. Sloan is notorious for feeling incredibly guilty for hiding anything. She's got a terrible poker face, which is why pretending to be married to me was so hard for her. She's one of those people who couldn't lie to save her life.

"Sloan, if you tell her what happened and how we're in love with each other now, how could she hold it against you?"

"Because I wasn't honest with her when I should've been," she says. "I could've told her in Vegas. I had the chance to. I was just afraid . . ."

"Of what?"

"Of her talking me out of it." Sloan closes her eyes and rests her head on the back of her seat. "I was rash. Just like I always am. She would've told me that."

"For what it's worth, you actually said no to me at first. If anyone was rash, it was me. I was the one who pressured you." I wait a beat. "There's always another option, you know."

She opens her eyes. "What's that?"

"Not telling her. What she doesn't know can't hurt her."

"That's what I did in Vegas, and look where I am now." She shakes her head. "Lying is the one thing she won't tolerate. When she talks about our father, she gets this look of disgust on her face. And I feel so guilty because I know I'm no better than him."

I take her hand in mine and squeeze it.

"You are better than him," I remind her. "Because you're choosing to stay."

———

As soon as we walk in the front door, Leo and Tate crowd around us, their faces hiding something.

"Welcome home!" Tate says.

"Why are you blocking our way?" Brax asks, looking between them.

"We have company," Leo says.

My sister jumps out from the living room. "Surprise!"

"Mia?" I step toward her, giving her a hug. "What are you doing here?"

"I'm here for the wedding prep."

"Alone?"

"No, I brought Mom too."

Mom walks out from the living room. "You're looking tan and happy," she says, giving me a hug before she wraps an arm around Sloan too.

"This is unexpected," I say, looking between them. "And early. Like, two weeks early."

"This is my last child's wedding," she says, pinching my cheek like I'm five. It's almost like she forgets I tower over her now. "And I know Sloan and Jaz don't have their mom around to help. So I'm glad to fill in, in any way I can."

"I thought you were kidding when you said you might stop by to help me with the wedding prep," Jaz says.

Mia hooks an arm around her friend's shoulders. "You know how I like to plan big events. And I couldn't stay away."

"Where's Jace?" I ask, looking around the corner for my sister's famous country music star husband.

"He's using the time to write new songs. Says the peace and quiet will force him to work. Don't worry, he'll be here for the big day."

"Mom, are you sure you're up for this?" I ask, taking her arm and walking her to the dining room. "I thought you weren't feeling well." Mom's back pain has gotten worse over the last year, and I was worried she might not be able to stand the plane ride here for the wedding. But even more concerning is how she's going to get along now that Brax and I aren't close by. Mia is the only one who lives in Vermont and part of me feels guilty for moving so far away for my career.

"Stop fussing over me." She waves me off. "Now that I finally retired, I have so much time on my hands. I might have missed your wedding in Vegas, but I will *not* miss this one."

"Tate offered us your old bedroom," Mia says. "Hope that's okay?"

"You're staying here?" Sloan asks, her eyebrows flying up.

"Yeah. Is that a problem?" Mia asks.

"Not at all," I say, grabbing Sloan's hand. I know what she's thinking. She was hoping we'd have time together before everyone arrived for the wedding. Now we're going to adjust our plans to include having guests in the house, which won't make it easy to talk to Jaz about what really happened in Vegas.

"No one else is here to surprise us, right?" Sloan asks, her eyes flicking from the living room to the dining room. She's probably expecting her dad to jump out next, but the rest of the house is strangely quiet.

"Your dad left yesterday when Vale's family showed up," Tate says. "I think he realized we had a full house."

Sloan looks at her sister and a look passes between them.

"He said he might be back sometime," Tate adds. "He wasn't specific."

"He never is," Jaz mutters. "It's his usual excuse. *I'll be back. Yada, yada, yada.* Then he shows up two years too late." She pulls her computer from her carry-on, ready to forget everything related to her father. "Why don't we start working through wedding prep tonight? I even have color-coded spreadsheets!"

"Perfect!" Mia says. "You know how I love my rainbow-colored spreadsheets."

"Those two are way too similar," Sloan whispers to me.

"Be glad they're doing everything for you," I remind her. "They want your wedding to be spectacular. Just like you." I wrap my arm around her waist and kiss the side of her head.

"You're all too good to me," she murmurs. "I suppose I should pay them in brownies."

"I won't say no to brownies," I say.

She looks at my mom, who's sitting at the dining room table. "Does he ever stop eating?"

Mom shakes her head. "Never."

The women settle at the dining room table as Sloan opens a brownie mix and gets out the eggs.

"You don't want to be in there helping them make plans for your wedding?" I ask with a frown.

"It's just a wedding renewal ceremony," she says, cracking eggs into a bowl.

"For me it's not a renewal," I say, wrapping my arms around her waist. I move my lips close to her ear. "I'm considering this the real deal, Sloan. Not what we had in Vegas."

She shakes her head. "But I don't need all *this.*"

I know what she's thinking because I can see the doubt in her eyes. She hasn't told the truth about our first wedding, so she doesn't deserve this big celebration.

"That's not the way it works," I say, clamping my hand on hers to stop her from avoiding this conversation.

"What do you want, Vale?" She spins to look at me, and I can see the fear in her eyes, the doubts swirling there. She's afraid the other shoe will drop. Something will go wrong. Someone will find out about us. Everything will fall apart.

I take her hands in mine and bring them to my lips. "Sloan, we are getting married, no matter what happens. Just because we did things backward doesn't mean you don't deserve a fancy party and all the extras. And even though you're afraid it doesn't mean that anything is going to go wrong. If I'm marrying you in front of God and everyone, we're going to do it right this time."

"Sloan, are you coming?" her sister calls from the other room. "We need your opinion on the entertainment."

"See what I have to put up with," she says. "So bossy."

"Kind of like another girl I know," I say with a smirk.

She hides a grin. "You're not going to let me get out of this, are you?"

"Absolutely not," I say. "So let me put the brownies in the oven for you, and you go plan your dream wedding."

Sloan heads to the dining room as I slide the brownies into the oven and set a timer.

"I don't need any entertainment," Sloan announces as soon as she sits down.

Jaz scoffs. "You have to. *The Star Report* expects you and Vale to have a first dance for their photography list. They've already requested it."

"Photography list?" Sloan asks. She rubs her forehead. I can tell she's not pleased by this at all.

Mia nods. "You definitely need a DJ because I want to dance. And Vale needs to dance with Mom. Right, Mom?"

"I would love that," Mom says, looking up at me as I stand next to Sloan's chair.

"I thought we were keeping this small," Sloan says, looking over Jaz's shoulder at her list.

"*The Star Report* expects this event to be a big deal. And you said you wanted your dream wedding."

"I didn't say my dream wedding would be a ridiculously over-the-top affair," she says.

She is already nervous about the wedding. Having *The Star Report* there only adds to the stress. I get why Jaz wants them there—it's great press for me and the team and will restrict other media outlets from crashing our wedding.

"How about food?" Jaz presses. "I'm thinking something really bougie. Elaborate charcuterie boards, a full buffet, a lavish dessert bar."

"I love that idea," Mia agrees before turning to Sloan. "What are you wearing for the wedding?"

Sloan looks at me. "I guess the gown from my gala. It's what I wore in Vegas."

Jaz leans over to Mia and whispers something, and Mia nods.

"What are you two talking about?" Sloan asks.

"You need a wedding dress," Jaz says. "We're taking you shopping tomorrow."

Sloan looks almost panicked now. "Definitely not." She wheels around toward the kitchen, not wanting to have this conversation.

"You can't say no," Jaz says. "Because I've already decided. Tomorrow you will say yes to the dress."

Sloan looks at me. "This is all your fault."

I laugh. "I told you before. My wife deserves the best."

TWENTY-SIX

Vale

"What were you thinking about?" Leo says on the ice at practice the next day.

"What?" I say, spinning toward him. I glance around the ice for the puck we were passing. It's nowhere in sight.

"Look behind you, idiot," Leo says with his trademark smirk, pointing his stick to where Tate's picked up the puck that I totally missed.

Lucian skates over and flicks the puck my way. "So unlike you, MacPherson. You're totally checked out."

"So I'm a little rough around the edges on my first day back," I say. "Cut me some slack."

I'm not going to tell them the truth. I was thinking about my upcoming wedding, and more specifically, the wedding night. They'd laugh me off the ice if they knew we still hadn't made this marriage official in the old-fashioned way.

Ever since Sloan agreed to go through with another ceremony —finally making our relationship more than a marriage of convenience—my thoughts are anywhere but here.

Leo skates backward, studying me. "Maybe you should take the job as water boy for the team instead." He whips another shot toward me, slightly off mark, forcing me to scramble to chase it down.

Unfortunately, I don't see Rourke behind me and crash into his brick wall of a chest.

"Somebody's distracted," he mutters.

"Not distracted," I say. "Leo set that one up."

"Don't blame me," Leo defends. "You're the one who missed it."

"I know what the problem is," Rourke says, circling back to me while doing some quick stick work. He stops in front of me. "You can't wait to give your little wifey a kiss."

The others snicker.

"I think you're just jealous," I fire back. "Because you don't have anyone to kiss." I pucker up and make kissing sounds with my lips.

"The only thing you can kiss is this." Rourke turns around and smacks his backside.

"Guys, are we twelve?" Leo asks, rolling his eyes.

"Wait until you find someone, Leo," Tate says. "You're gonna be twice as distracted as Brax and Vale."

"What are you saying about me?" Brax asks from the other side of the ice.

"Nothing!" I answer, trying to end this conversation.

"Just discussing Vale's marital problems," Lucian adds.

I shake my head. "We are definitely *not* discussing my marital problems."

"What problems?" Brax skates over, his brow creased.

"He can't concentrate," Rourke says.

"We think it's Sloan's fault," Tate says.

"His shots are off," Lucian adds.

"I've heard most problems start in the bedroom," Leo says, like he's the expert. "You need a marriage counselor?"

"No!" I say, the irritation rising in my chest. "This has nothing to do with my marriage!" I skate away from the guys.

Leo frowns. "Why are you so touchy? We're trying to help you."

"Oh, is that why you're making up problems for me? You're trying to make me feel better about myself?"

Leo frowns. "No, why would I do that?"

"Ignore them," Brax says. "I'm sure whatever it is can be solved by hitting the weight room."

"Can't," I say. "Sloan asked me to come home right away and finalize some of the wedding plans with Jaz."

Leo grimaces. "I thought you lucked out not having to go through the misery of wedding planning?"

"Well, somebody's wife was pretty ticked she didn't get to go to our Vegas wedding." I give my brother a pointed look.

"Don't look at me! It's not my fault the woman loves weddings," Brax mutters. "Plus, Mom was fully in support of the idea."

"She won't admit it, but I think Sloan needs the full wedding experience," I say, heading off the ice. "If we don't have it, she'll always regret not having a real wedding. It's one of those things girls dream about from the time they're little, starting with the proposal."

"Where did you propose?" Tate asks as all the guys circle around me on the bench.

"We went to the gala, and it sort of happened," I say, unlacing a skate.

Leo stops. "Wait—what do you mean it *sort of happened?*"

"I said, *'Let's get married in Vegas'* and then we did." I glance up and notice all the guys are staring at me. "What?"

Brax's eyebrows rise. "You skipped proposing?" He shakes his head. "Dude, that's bad."

"Not on purpose," I say. But I realize the mistake I've made. I once read an article about babies who go straight to walking and bypass the crawling stage. Sometimes they have to loop back to the part they skipped, just to connect all the dots in their brains. And I wonder if this is Sloan's issue too. We've done everything backward and have skipped parts, without her realizing how much she needs it. That's why it's hard for her to trust me, to believe this is it between us and I'm not leaving.

"You said you want her to have the full experience," Leo says. "And girls get into proposals."

I frown. "But she already has the ring. How am I going to propose without it?"

"Does she ever take it off?" Tate asks.

"I don't know," I say. "Maybe?" Now that I think about it, I can't remember if she's *ever* taken off the ring. This could be a problem.

"Just wait for her to remove it, then steal it," Rourke says. "It's that simple."

"I don't know about this," I say, running my hands through my hair. "Seems risky."

"Then let us help. Team effort," Lucian the captain says, then puts his hand in the middle for a team huddle. "We'll make sure she gets a proposal to remember."

The guys join him, hands stacked on top of each other.

I look around and my stomach flip-flops. Then I add my hand to the pile.

This could go very right. Or very wrong.

I'm about to find out which one it is.

———

I'm calling it Operation Proposal. Tonight, it's Sloan's night to wash dishes, and hopefully, she'll take off her ring. Once she does, I'm counting on the fact it won't be hard to distract her, and Brax will slip in and steal the ring.

Tate gives an overdramatic yawn as he takes his plate to the sink after dinner. "Think I'll head to bed early tonight."

"You never go to bed early." Sloan frowns, studying Tate like he must be coming down with the plague. "You feel okay?"

"Yep, just tired." He bounces up the steps, taking two at a time.

"I'm heading to the store. Need anything?" Leo asks no one in particular.

"Can you pick up some glazed donuts? I have an early morning practice," Sloan says.

"You're giving your skaters donuts and not sharing them with us?" Leo looks almost offended by this.

Sloan squeezes dish soap into the water before sliding her ring off and setting it on the lip of the sink. "I never said you couldn't have any, Leo."

"I'll pick up extras." Leo grabs his keys and heads out the back door. I make eye contact with Brax, who's already noticed the ring.

He stands and heads to the living room couch, turning on the TV just like we planned.

Sloan plunges her hands into the soapy bubbles. I wrap my arms around her waist, hugging her from behind.

"Well, hello, *you*," she says with a grin. Her head turns slightly, and I kiss the soft hollow of her cheek, then her earlobe.

"Looks like we're alone, finally."

"It appears that way," she murmurs. She seems reluctant, or maybe just has a lot on her mind, I can't tell which.

"I was hoping we could spend some time together." Which is code for kissing her as long as possible.

"And by time together, you mean doing the laundry, right?"

"Not exactly," I laugh.

"Well, let me finish these dishes first, and then I'd be happy to."

"Dishes can wait," I say, taking a dripping plate from her hands. I need to get her away from the sink now before she finishes and slides on her ring. I slowly turn her so she's facing me. "Why don't we go for a walk? If we leave now, we'll see the sunset." I grab her hand and lead her toward the door.

She tilts her head. "Why are you in such a hurry?"

"No reason," I say. "Other than I don't want to miss the sunset."

She frowns. "You're up to something, Vale MacPherson."

I straighten my face. "I'm not." *Except I am and now she's onto me.*

The sound of a car engine in the driveway turns her attention toward the window that faces the drive. "The girls are home." She opens the front door. "Any luck?"

Jaz crawls out of the car with my mom beside her. "We got a wedding haul for you."

Mia unloads several bags from the back seat as Sloan meets them at the car to see what they bought.

I spin around and catch Brax sneaking toward the kitchen. "Now?" he whispers.

I wave him toward the sink and mouth the word, *"Hurry."* Brax disappears into the kitchen, and a few seconds later, he mutters, "Uh-oh."

When I run into the kitchen, Brax has his hand down the garbage disposal.

"What are you doing?" I ask, hoping that the sinking feeling in my gut is not correct.

"What does it look like I'm doing?" he grumbles.

"It looks like you're risking a limb."

"Yes, for you, in fact. When I picked up the ring, it fell down the drain."

"You dropped the ring in the garbage disposal?" I whisper-shout. This is horrifically bad timing. Especially since Sloan isn't finished with the dishes.

"Is there any other reason I'd stick my hand down this filthy hole?"

I glance out the window and see Sloan and the girls are making their way up the steps. I point at Brax. "You have exactly five seconds to find that ring, or I'm going to turn on the garbage disposal."

His eyes bulge. "You should be thanking me right now."

"Right now, I'm furious at you. You had one job," I say holding up my finger to his face. "One. Job."

Just then Leo enters from the back, mysteriously empty-handed. "Where are the donuts?" I ask.

"Donut shop was closed," he says before he looks at Brax. "Did you get it?"

"The ring fell down the drain," Brax mutters. "And my fat fingers can't seem to grab the slippery sucker."

"Let me try." Leo elbows him out of the way as the front door opens and laughter spills into the house. Leo shakes his head. "The things I do for you."

"Vale, come see what the girls found!"

"Be there in a second," I singsong, before I mutter through gritted teeth, "We're gonna be busted in two seconds."

In one swift movement, Leo jams his hand into the disposal and fishes out the ring just as the girls enter the kitchen. He shoves his hand in his pocket as we all wheel around.

"Look at these adorable . . ." Sloan stops as she notices our guilty-looking faces. "What's up with you guys?"

"Nothing," Brax says, shaking his head quickly.

Sloan frowns. "Why are you standing in a line at the sink unless . . ." She pauses and walks toward us. *We're so busted.* She stops and peeks over my shoulder. "Are you doing the dishes for me?"

Leo nudges me in the side.

"Um, okay, it was supposed to be a surprise, but you caught us." I spin around and start washing a dish and then hand it to a confused Brax. Leo hands him a dish towel.

"Take the night off," I say. "We've got this." I have no idea how we'll hide the fact that her ring is gone.

She blinks. "I thought we were taking a walk?"

I wash another dish and hand it to Leo, who passes it to Brax. "Another night? I know you're busy with wedding planning, and we only have a week."

Her face melts into a smile. "Thank you for understanding,

Vale. That's really sweet." She leaves a kiss on my cheek before returning to the piles of bags in the hallway.

It's only going to be a matter of time before she realizes her ring is gone, but at least that gives me a chance to come up with an excuse.

And since Brax actually did drop it down the sink, he just gave me the best excuse in the world.

I hand Leo a dish rag. "Trade?"

He sinks his hand into his pocket and plucks out the ring. "I have to do dishes too? I never agreed to this."

I pocket the ring. "Anything for love, right?"

He shakes his head and plunges his hands into the sink.

Part one of Operation Proposal is a success.

Now I just need to get her to say yes . . . and pull off a few more secrets up my sleeve.

TWENTY-SEVEN

Sloan

On the night of Vale's first game, I can tell something is up. Right after he left the house, I discovered a new jersey on our bed, one he had custom made for me by Jaz. It's wedding-white with teal letters and sparkly gold edging. The same colors as both his team and our wedding. Maybe he's trying to make up for the fact that I still haven't found my ring after losing it the other night. Vale promised he'd get me another one but that doesn't make me feel better. I want the one I picked out in Vegas, the antique one with the diamonds in the shape of a flower.

I unfold the jersey and a note falls out: "Hoping you'll wear this to tonight's game as my bride. After the wedding, I want to see you in nothing but this."

My knees buckle when I read it and heat soars through my body. We haven't slept together yet, other than sawing logs together in Cancun. But since we arrived home, Vale's back on the floor.

And this time, it's *his* choice. He says it's because I'm too tempting, but I get the feeling it's because he's trying to rewind time and wait until our wedding night. And I know he's not doing it for himself, but me.

But something else has changed too. In the past, when we

joked about us being a couple, it had to do with the act we were putting on. But now things are real. Any reference to our wedding night is only a reminder that we're about to break the last rule we set up for our marriage.

I slide on the jersey with a cute pair of joggers. If this doesn't give Vale MacPherson a taste of our wedding night, I don't know what will.

As soon as I arrive at the arena, I can tell something's different.

The team introductions don't begin with their usual music number. Instead, it's the song we danced to on the dinner cruise in Cancun. The team begins skating out for the introductions and Vale isn't at his usual spot in the lineup.

Instead, he's last. And when he bursts out of the tunnel, he doesn't stop on center ice, but heads straight toward me in the first row. Last season, I sat with Jaz in the staff box, but tonight she insisted I sit down front with all the other wives and girlfriends.

"You belong there now," she told me, walking me to my front-row seat.

Vale stops right next to the plexiglass and puts his hands against it, almost like he's reaching for me. He's not wearing his usual gloves, which seems strange. Then he mouths the words, "Hello, *beautiful*," before his eyes graze over my body. "*Nice jersey.*"

Warmth zings through me, and I spin around so he can see his name on my back.

Jaz added "Mrs." to the "MacPherson" and I couldn't love it more.

His eyes spark and I know he's just as pleased because he waves me toward him. "Come here, Sloan."

I stand, matching my hands to his on the other side of the plexiglass. "I can't come any closer," I say with a laugh. "But I wish I could kiss you." I don't care who hears me now. He's going to be my official husband, and I want the world to know.

"Then do," he says. Someone unlatches a door nearby that leads to the rink, and an usher for the game whisks me through it.

Suddenly I'm stepping onto the ice and Vale is there, throwing off his helmet, looking into my eyes with that unfairly sexy smirk he reserves for me. This will be my undoing. I reach for his face, cup his jaw in my hands and give him a tame but mesmerizing kiss in front of everyone. He threads his fingers through my hair and I moan just a little. The taste of his lips makes me want to devour him right here. I'm vaguely aware of the cheers and catcalls as our faces are projected onto the Jumbotron above us.

Never thought I'd be doing a closeup kiss for the camera, but here we are. And there's no one I rather do it with than Vale.

Vale pulls away just enough for me to catch my breath and leans his forehead against mine. The lights suddenly dim in the arena, and special moving lights that look like stars frame the ice around us. We're standing in our own galaxy.

"What is going on?" I whisper. I glance, noticing the crowd has been plunged into darkness. When I finally look back at Vale, he's on his knees with a ring in his hands. *My ring.*

"You found it?" I cry.

"I found you *first*," he says. "And I want to do things the right way this time. I want to start over and give you the ring the way you always dreamed of—with an official proposal. So will you marry me, Sloan?"

I blink, the room spins. I don't even care how he found my ring. All I care about is him. "Aren't we already married?"

"By law, yes. But we've done everything backward. And I never asked you to marry me officially, and that was wrong. You deserve the full experience. You deserve everything, Sloan. Thank you for trusting me enough to marry me in Vegas. I just hope this time, you'll say yes, even if I'm a little late."

"Yes," I say enthusiastically, while blinking back a flood in my eyes. "I'll say yes a thousand times more if you want me to. Thank you for being there for me, even though I didn't deserve your love."

I throw myself into his arms as they wrap around my body. The crowd erupts into cheers, longer and louder than any game-winning goal.

Finally, a hand taps Vale's shoulder, breaking up our moment.

He spins around and sees Leo impatiently waiting behind him.

"You gonna kiss all night?" Leo asks.

"You're gonna pay for this, Ego," Vale says, shaking his head.

"Shut up, *Romeo*," he says, skating away. "We've got a game to win."

Vale

"I want to sign the contract," I tell my agent the next day over the phone. I scored two goals in last night's game, more than any player, which gives me leverage for renegotiating my contract. Adding the no-movement clause will allow me to be home with Sloan as much as possible. The sooner I can provide the stability Sloan needs, the better.

"Unfortunately, Mr. Marco has a full schedule and can't join us, but the operating manager can be there," Jimmy says. "You wanna wait?"

It would be nice to have another person in the room who's on my side, but I can't delay this any longer.

"No, I'm ready to sign," I decide.

If I'm staying with the Crushers, I want to finalize the no-movement clause before our wedding ceremony. There's no question—I want to be with my wife as much as possible. Adding this clause keeps me in Sully's Beach. I'll still have to travel for away games, but I won't get moved to another city. I can't wait to see Sloan's face when I reveal this surprise.

"How's your wife?" Jimmy asks when he arrives at the Crushers' office.

"Feeling better than ever," I say. "Thanks to this new medication."

"That's what I want to hear," Jimmy says with a pleased smile. He knows that gives us leverage for our negotiations today. Forget Zach's allegations that I wouldn't be able to fulfill my obligations to the team. This proves I'm unlikely to miss a game due to Sloan's health.

"Are you sure you want to do this?" Jimmy studies me when we sit down at the conference table in the Crushers' office. "You know Tampa has been hounding me ever since we talked last. They really want you on their team and are willing to make a very nice offer."

I swallow the lump in my throat. "I'm not taking an offer from Tampa right now. Only reason I'm here is to add the no-movement clause."

Jimmy lets out a disappointed sigh. "I understand, even if I think you should reconsider. I have the feeling that Tampa's contract would have blown away what the Crushers are going to offer you today."

"It's not about the money, Jimmy," I say, leaning my elbows on my knees. "I'd rather have my wife than an NHL career."

This time, I'm not just saying it. I mean it. Hockey has always been my focus, until Sloan walked into my life and flipped every-thing I thought I wanted on its head.

Jimmy nods once. "I'm glad it was a straightforward decision for you. How about this? I'll tell Tampa you're not interested for the next few months. We'll reevaluate later."

"I won't need to," I reply. "I'm staying here."

"Vale, this is just smart business. Keep your opportunities open. You don't know how things could change down the road."

"What if I've already decided?" I say, more determined than ever.

Jimmy shakes his head. "You're not my first player who's said that and then changed his mind. I've asked for the new contract to only include half the season. If the Crushers give you a lowball offer, you can always renegotiate later in the year. This is in your best interest."

"Then I'll want the same contract drawn up later," I insist. Does Jimmy think my marriage might not work out? That I'll wish I hadn't added the clause? Because he's wrong. I'm staying in Sully's Beach with the Crushers, even if it means I might let the opportunity of a lifetime slip away.

Zach enters the room in a frenzy, barely even offering a nod as a greeting.

"Sorry I'm late. We've got a situation that's blown up today," he says, frazzled. "We're headed into a meeting with everyone next."

"About?" I ask, sensing this isn't good news.

He avoids looking directly at me as he sorts through a pile of papers. "I've been told to keep it strictly confidential."

He opens a folder and takes out two identical contracts and slides them toward us. "As we discussed previously, we've offered the no-movement clause in your contract. But like your agent warned you, it doesn't give us flexibility, so we've made adjustments to your salary and given you some performance bonuses instead. They don't make up for your previous contract, but it's the best we can do."

I look over the numbers. They're definitely much lower than I'd expected. But I'm doing this for Sloan, not for the money. Isn't that just what I told my agent?

Jimmy furrows his brow as he looks over the contract. "Seems like a big difference from his last one. Especially since Tampa would love to have him."

Zach leans back in his chair. "If he wants to stay, this is the offer." Then he glances at me. "Of course, he's free to turn it down and move to the NHL."

He's got me in a chokehold, and he knows it. It's not that he's exploiting the situation. I'm the one asking for the no-movement clause—an exception to our original deal. If this is the price I have to pay to get it, then I'll sign.

"Where's a pen?" I say.

Jimmy's eyes widen. "Maybe you should discuss it with Sloan. It's a big decision, Vale."

I shake my head. "I've already decided."

Jimmy doesn't know that Sloan hasn't heard about the no-movement clause yet. I planned on telling her after I signed the contract. Maybe it's because I'm afraid she'll try to talk me out of it, but this is my decision alone. My way of proving I'm willing to sacrifice anything for her. If I never make it to the NHL, I'll accept that—just to stay close to her.

Zach hands me a pen and I sign my name at the bottom.

"Just for the record, I'm planning on obliterating those performance bonuses."

Zach smirks. "I'm sure you will."

There's a knock at the door as Jaz pokes her head inside. "Mr. Marco said that he needs everyone in the conference room now."

When we arrive, Mr. Marco is sitting at the head of the table, along with the rest of the administrative staff. Everyone is quietly waiting for whatever announcement is about to shake things up.

I find a chair in the back, alongside Brax.

"Where have you been?" he asks. "We've been waiting on you."

"In a meeting with Jimmy and Zach."

Brax frowns. "What's Jimmy doing here?" He knows that when an agent shows up, there's only one explanation.

"Later," I mouth to him.

Mr. Marco clears his throat. "If you're wondering why I called this meeting—don't worry, the team is not in financial trouble. We're still playing hockey."

A few of the guys visibly relax. Mr. Marco nods to Libby, who immediately starts handing out a stack of papers.

"When I bought this team, it was like pouring money through a bucket with a hole. We've managed to keep our heads above water, but we have to roll with the changes," Mr. Marco explains. "Unfortunately, the plan we had with our last insurance company is no longer an option, so we're discontinuing our contract with them."

In the past, whenever insurance came up, I'd tune it out. But now that I'm married to Sloan, every detail matters. I sift through the papers in front of me, find the new insurance website and get on my phone to look up details.

"We were as surprised as you when this happened," he says. "And we apologize for the last-minute change."

Most of the guys nod and accept whatever Rafael Marco says, but that's not good enough for me. As soon as the meeting ends, I'm on the phone with the insurance company. After a long wait, a customer service agent tells me the prescription medication Sloan is on isn't covered. It's too new and there aren't enough studies to prove it works.

"Are you sure there isn't another way we can get this medicine covered?" I ask.

On the other end, the man taps his keyboard. "Her doctor can try to appeal the denial but there are no guarantees." He doesn't sound hopeful.

"And if that doesn't work?"

"There is one more thing," he says slowly. "An organization that provides financial assistance for new drugs. You could check into that."

He gives me the information, but it seems like a long shot.

"Thanks for trying," I mutter, feeling sick over this new development.

Even if I use my savings account to pay for the drug, how long will that last? A few months to a year, at most. Not long enough for Sloan. She needs that medicine. It's the only thing that's made her feel like herself again.

I glance at the newly signed contract in my hand. I've already given up my chance to move to another team—one with better benefits or more money. I was so focused on being away from Sloan that I never stopped to think about what would happen if her medicine wasn't covered.

I rub my forehead before sliding off my hoodie. No one else is in the locker room when Brax comes in. He sits next to me. "Why's Jimmy here?"

I don't look at him. "I asked for a no-movement clause in my contract."

"For Sloan." It's not a question—he already knows the answer. "You took Jimmy's advice, right?"

I shake my head. "Jimmy wanted me to think it over, but I didn't want to wait. I signed before I knew about the insurance." I finally meet my brother's eyes. "Sloan's medicine isn't covered. I know we'll figure it out, but it's terrible timing." I wad up the hoodie and throw it in my locker. Even though our relationship has changed since Vegas, I'm worried how she'll react when she finds out I kept this from her.

"At least you won't get moved around during the season," Brax says, trying to make me feel better. "That's what she wanted."

"I haven't told her."

Brax stares at me. "You didn't talk about it first?"

I drag my hand through my hair. "She would've felt guilty. Told me no. Blamed herself for me giving up the NHL, even though this is my decision."

"She's your wife. She'll understand," Brax says.

But will she?

I bang my fist against the locker.

"You're a MacPherson. You'll figure this out. It's not like she married you for your insurance."

Except she did. And that's what I can't reveal to my brother.

TWENTY-NINE

Sloan

"Hold it right there," the photographer says, motioning for me to freeze in my wedding gown.

I smile as he takes what feels like a million shots from different angles. "A few more in case you blink," he explains, clicking the button. "Okay, you can relax."

I can't decide what I'm more nervous about—this ridiculously over-the-top photoshoot before the wedding ceremony or my wedding night with Vale. There's no doubt which one I'm more excited for. Ever since the honeymoon, I've been waiting for tonight. Honestly, it feels like a waste of time not to skip this whole shindig and head straight to the honeymoon. But we owe our family and friends this wedding. After all, they missed our first one, and we can't just bail on them now.

Our family and friends have insisted on celebrating the MacPherson Wedding 2.0. We're making up for everything Vegas lacked—no white dress, no loved ones to cheer us on, no after-party to celebrate the biggest decision of our lives. Even the vows we exchanged at the Little Pink Chapel of Love felt more like going through the motions than real promises.

Yes, we're married by law, but what is marriage if there's no commitment, no agreement to love someone through all the wonderful and horrible things life throws at you? Today, we're making that kind of promise.

In the meantime, we agreed to let *The Star Report* do separate photoshoots with each of us right before the wedding ceremony. We'll have final approval of all photos and demanded only two conditions from them: Vale won't get to see me until I walk down the aisle—something we both wanted for our wedding day—and Jaz gets to be here instead, making sure I don't end up with lipstick on my teeth or tripping over my dress in front of the camera.

As a last-minute request, a journalist tagging along with the photographer asked if they could interview us beforehand—something I wasn't thrilled about, but Jaz encouraged us to agree to.

"The more information you control, the better," she told us. "Otherwise, they'll be asking your guests questions about you. Do you really want Leo or Rourke to comment on your marriage?"

"No," we both answered in unison.

Jaz may not be our official PR person, but after marrying Brax, she quickly figured out how to work the press to her advantage, one of her many useful skills.

While I endure my photoshoot, Vale is being interviewed privately. It must be going well, because he sends a quick message.

VALE

There's something we need to talk about. A surprise for our wedding today.

Jaz glances over my gown and gives me a smile of approval. "I was right," she says as she approaches me. "Vale won't be able to concentrate on anything but you when he sees you in that dress."

She and Mia picked it out—or in my case, *insisted* I buy the formfitting silk gown that shows off my shoulders and my curves.

"I wish Vale were here for this part," I say. "I don't know why they need to interview us alone. It feels like a crime interrogation."

She fixes my hair, brushing it over my shoulders with her fingers. "They want your perspective. And I'll be there."

Although the photographer has been perfectly pleasant during the shoot, the journalist gives off a cagey vibe that makes me uncomfortable. He waves Jaz and me over to a private outdoor tent set up away from the ceremony. Even though we're having the wedding in our backyard, *The Star Report* insisted on setting up their own headquarters for their equipment. I sit across from the journalist as he pulls out his laptop and opens a list of questions. His phone buzzes, and he glances at the message, his brow wrinkling slightly before turning back to his laptop. "Let's go back to the beginning—in Vegas."

"You want to talk about our first wedding?" I keep my expression neutral, though I'm surprised they want to rehash it again. We've told this story more times than I can count.

"Yes," he says. "Just to confirm some new developments in your story."

New developments? I don't know what he's talking about unless Vale mentioned something. This is the downside of not getting interviewed at the same time.

I fiddle with my fingers, afraid of saying too much about our elopement. "Since we'd been friends for a couple of years, we already knew each other well. Maybe it looked like insta-love, but really it was a slow-burn romance."

"Romance?" he questions. "You didn't consider it a convenient solution?"

I frown as something prickles up my spine. "A convenient solution for what?"

"For your insurance problem. You couldn't get coverage for your medicine, and Vale had what you needed—a good plan that covered the drugs. Is that correct?" He makes it sound like I had some devious, gold-digging scheme.

My stomach feels like a bag that someone just dumped over. I don't look at my sister, but I hear her body shift, feel her leaning in. If she sees the fear behind my eyes, she'll know that it's true.

"I'm sorry, but that's none of your business," I say. "Just because Vale had insurance to cover my medicine doesn't mean you can make assumptions about why we married."

It's not that I care about my reputation. They can trash my reputation if they want to. But I care about Vale, especially how the press treats him and what this could mean for his career. I know he wants to make it to the NHL someday, and I don't want to be the obstacle in his way.

The journalist clicks a few buttons, then looks at his screen, which, of course, I conveniently can't see. "We interviewed a source who gave us the complete story."

Who told him this? It had to be someone who overheard us. I might not ever find out who, but right now, my job is damage control—no matter the cost to my reputation. I can't let Vale get dragged down with me.

"So you have one person who made an assumption about us," I argue. "Probably a stranger wanting to make a quick buck. You're going to take their word as truth?"

His lips quirk, like he knows a secret I don't. "We just interviewed your husband. Don't you think he would confirm it?"

My stomach twists. He would never admit to this. He knows how my sister feels about lying, how this would ruin our relationship if she found out, crushing me in the process.

"I don't believe you," I fire back. And then I remember Vale's text, something urgent he wanted to talk about.

I glance over at my sister, whose face has turned ashen. I can't let her think this idiot reporter knows the truth before she does. I have to make her believe me, even if the rest of the world doubts the legitimacy of our relationship. If she doubts me, she'll see me as no better than our father.

I clench my fists in my lap and level my gaze. "I love my husband, and I have zero doubts he feels the same about me. Anyone who questions our marriage will have to answer to us. Insurance or not, I'd marry him again. Which is why we're here today."

"If that's the case, how do you feel about the fact that you no longer have coverage for your new medicine?"

"What?" I frown, wondering where he got this information. "I think you're mistaken."

Jaz clears her throat, glancing between me and the reporter nervously. "He didn't tell you? There was a last-minute announcement about an insurance change. I'm surprised he didn't mention it."

Unless he was scared to, afraid this was one of the reasons I stayed with him. He should know by now that insurance has nothing to do with how I feel about him.

I jut my chin out. "It doesn't matter whether our insurance changes or whether he switches teams or even moves to a new league. I'm with him forever. And that includes going to the NHL someday."

The man lifts an eyebrow. "Then why did Vale sign a new contract that doesn't allow him to move, even though the NHL was interested in a deal?"

I frown. "He didn't sign anything . . ." I begin, but the man wordlessly hands me his phone. My eyes fall on the screen, an article glaring back at me with the headline: *Vale MacPherson Signs New Contract to Stay with the Crushers, Delays NHL Dreams.*

My stomach plummets as I skim over the story. By asking for the no-movement clause, Vale gave up his best shot at the NHL— right when he was on the verge of making it. All because of me.

My whole body goes numb. Even if he feels bound to his promise, this is too much. *I'm too much.* What was I thinking, dragging Vale into my mess? My life has always been a train wreck, and he took it on willingly, thinking he could help. But someday, he'll look at me the way my sister looks at our father—like I'm the one who messed up his life.

I drop his phone on the table. "This interview is over."

When I wheel around to Jaz, her seat is empty. Gone before I can even explain.

If she doesn't understand why I did this, I don't know how I'll live with myself.

There's only one choice left. One way to stop everyone from getting hurt because of me.

THIRTY

Vale

There's panic on Jaz's face when she tracks me down during my photoshoot. She's running across the lawn in her bridesmaid's gown, her face flushed from the heat. "You need to come now."

The deep crease in her brow tells me something bad has happened.

My stomach sinks. "Is Sloan okay? Did she faint?" I try to remember whether she had her medicine or drank any water today. I've been so busy, I didn't even stop to check on how she was feeling.

"It's not that," Jaz says, shaking her head. "The interview didn't go well. The journalist told her about your new contract. He claims you got married so she could get your insurance. You know how she is when she panics. You need to talk to her now before she gets in her head and makes a rash decision."

I know exactly how Sloan is. When she gets scared, she runs. "I'll find her."

She's told me this from the beginning, how everyone thinks she can't stick with things, that it's a character flaw, rather than a self-fulfilling prophecy.

I glance around, searching for any sign of where Sloan might have gone, before my gaze returns to Jaz. "Are you okay?" I ask, suddenly worried about how she's taking this news.

"I'll be fine. Just find Sloan." She gives me a push toward the house.

I sprint through the yard in search of my bride. I'd assumed that when I told Sloan the truth, she'd forgive me for keeping it from her. I had good reason—I wanted to marry her first, so she'd know my commitment was real, without any second-guessing. But the plan was to tell her myself, not have her find out this way. If I'd told her before today, she would've tried to talk me out of sacrificing my shot at the NHL. But the strange thing is, I feel a sense of freedom I haven't had before. I don't have anything to prove anymore. If I play well for the Crushers, that's enough for me—not who I play for.

I run into the house and search both floors. There's no sign of Sloan anywhere.

That's when I hear the front door shut.

"Sloan?" I call, racing down the stairs.

It's Brax, coming to find me. "A neighbor just reported they saw a woman in a wedding dress hop into the limo you rented for the reception."

"Call the driver," I say. "Do you have his number?"

"That's the problem," Brax says. "The driver is out back. Sloan stole the limo."

———

It's not every day you ask the police to look for a bride driving a limo she stole from her own wedding. But right now, I'm desperate for help, worried Sloan will leave town before I get to her. Lucky for me, the local police must be having a slow day, because they jump at the chance to find a runaway bride. After I explain the situation to Brax, he rushes into action by calling the hockey team to track down Sloan. Since Jaz heard everything from the interview, she briefed Brax on the rest. Which means I'm going to get an earful when I return.

After searching downtown Sully's Beach, I try to call Sloan's phone again. It goes straight to voice mail for the fifth time. She doesn't want me to find her, even turning off her location service, which means I can't track her.

This isn't a good sign. If she's not picking up, it means she's in a full-blown doom spiral. She thinks she's saving me from a career-altering decision and is convinced running away is the best option—even though it's the absolute worst thing she could do.

Even if the press spins the story to make us look bad, we can prove them wrong by showing them the truth—that our relationship has always been about love, even if we did it all backward. But that's only if I can reach Sloan in time. If I don't, her disappearance will only confirm what they believe—that our Vegas wedding was a sham.

My phone rings, and the police station's number appears on the screen. "Any news?"

"We found your bride," a police officer cheerily reports.

"Where is she?"

"The airport, trying to book a flight out of here. Do you want us to stop her?"

"No, leave it to me." If I hurry, the airport is only a few minutes away, and I'm the only one who can talk her out of this— if I can reach her in time.

"Best of luck," the officer says.

"I'm gonna need it," I shoot back while doing a U-turn in the middle of the road and then pressing hard on the gas pedal. At least the cops are too busy tracking down Sloan to give me a speeding ticket.

"Yeah, go get your wife," the police officer says with a grin in his voice. "And while you're at it, deal with your other issue."

"What other problem?"

"She parked the limo in a no-parking zone."

I mutter under my breath. "Let me guess—I'm getting a ticket."

"Think of it as a wedding present—from the local police."

"Wow, thanks! Just what we wanted," I say, chuckling. "Well, I guess that makes us even."

I text Brax a message that I've got a lead on Sloan at the airport. When I arrive, it takes me less than two seconds to find her. My eyes immediately land on the breathtaking woman in a stunning gown. She's standing in a long line at the ticket counter, trying to pretend that everyone's *not* staring at a runaway bride who's booking it out of town.

She doesn't notice me striding toward her, doesn't even turn around when I fall into line right behind her. I glance at the departure board for the next flight out of town, then lean in close, my lips just inches from her ear. "I hear Vegas is nice this time of year."

She wheels around, her eyes blinking once as shock passes over her face. "How did you . . . ?"

I shake my head. "You can't speed out of town in a stolen limo and expect no one will notice."

She doesn't answer, just spins away from me. "I can't believe the next flight out is to Vegas. Of all places."

"Seems like a sign, don't you think?" I shove my hands in my pockets. "The place where it all started and you became my wife."

"You probably came here to talk me out of this, but I've already ruined things. Your NHL career. Your reputation. I need some time to think about how to fix this."

I gently place a finger on her lips to stop her from panicking. "First off, you haven't ruined anything. And second, I'm not talking you out of it."

"You aren't?"

"No." I step next to her in line. "Because I'm going with you."

Her head snaps toward me, eyes wide. "You can't just leave. You've got a game this week. We need to let everything cool down after this story comes out."

I turn to her. "So you think leaving will help?"

She looks at me with a stubborn glint in her eyes. "It might."

"It won't," I say firmly. Then I take her left hand and run my thumb over the gold band, the sharp edges of the diamond. "Leaving doesn't solve our problems. Unless you want to confirm what *The Star Report* thinks is true—that you don't love me."

Remarkably, she doesn't pull away. Instead, she looks down at the ring, my thumb stroking her finger gently. Her brows knit together. "Did you tell them our secret about why we married?"

"I told them the truth."

Her head jerks up.

My thumb stills, but I don't let go of her hand. "That I loved you then—and I've always loved you."

She tilts her head, studying me. "Then why didn't you tell me about the contract and insurance?"

I sigh. This is where it gets harder. "I should've told you about the insurance, but part of me hesitated, wondering if that was gone, would you still want me?" I glance away, shame twisting in my chest. "I know it's stupid. But it made me feel like I'm not good enough to give you what you need—and that one's on me— for not trusting you enough. For not believing you loved me for more than what I can offer you."

She stares at me. "You believed I loved you for what you could give me?"

I rub the back of my neck. "I'm not proud that I doubted you. I thought if I could sort out the insurance before you found out, then I could make it all right. So I called your doctor to push for an appeal, but I haven't heard back. Then I reached out to another place the insurance company mentioned that helps cover new drugs. But so far, I've got nothing—and that's what's eating at me. I didn't want you to stress over this on your wedding day."

Her face softens. "You didn't have to do all this alone."

"I know," I admit, dropping my gaze. This has been my MO ever since Dad left Mom. I fix things. I take care of people. I'm not the guy who asks for help—I'm the one who's supposed to give it. When I can't, then I'm a failure.

She places her hand on my chest, like she knows I need her touch more than anything right now. "Vale, you didn't fail me."

"Then why does it feel that way?" I confess.

"Because you're human," she says. "Feeling like a failure doesn't mean you are one, Vale. You've done everything you can, and that's all I've ever needed from you. But giving up the NHL deal without talking to me first? How could you?" She looks more devastated by this news than I expected.

I touch her face, my thumb tracing the curve of her cheekbone. "Because I wanted you more than the NHL. I wanted to make a life with you, to show you I was willing to give up the one thing that meant the most to me."

"Vale," she says, placing both hands on my chest. "You never had to prove your love to me. I already knew what you'd give up for me. You married me in Vegas. You refused to sleep in our bed until I asked. You kissed me to make Anthony jealous."

"Actually, that was just the excuse. I kissed you because I was dying to."

A smile curves her lips.

I place my hands over hers across my chest. "I just hoped you could forgive me for not telling you first, but that's the risk I was willing to take."

"Then why didn't you?" she asks.

"Because I knew if I did, that you'd believe the lies your past has taught you, instead of the truth right in front of you." I need her to understand that her past doesn't define her. In my family's case, I'll never get a chance to ask my father why he chose to leave our family. But I won't repeat the mistake he made. That's the difference between me and Sloan—how we've chosen to carry the same wound in different ways.

"If I left, it would make your life immensely easier," she says, like she's already convinced herself it's the only option.

My hands move to her waist, pulling her closer. "No," I say, resolute. "If you left, it would destroy me."

She stares at me for a long moment, then slowly shakes her head, like she's trying to figure out why I'm even bothering to fight for this. "Why do you make me feel like you would be worse off without me, when we both know I'm the one holding you back?"

My thumb gently strokes her hip, a silent reminder that *I'm here, I'm not leaving*. "When my father left our family, Mom soldiered on, but I could see the hole my dad left, and I decided I'd never cause that same pain for someone. We might share DNA with our families, but that doesn't mean we can't make different choices, that we can't be better people. We don't have to accept that we're destined to become what people believe about us. You're *not* someone who runs when things get hard. What you've shown is that you've already made a different choice. You stay when things get hard. You stick it out, even if it costs you something. You're so present with the people you love, coming through for them even when they don't deserve it. That's what I love about you. Until you came along, I hadn't told any woman I loved her. You were the first. And as my wife, the *last*."

Her mouth opens, like she wants to say something, but can't.

The agent at the ticket counter clears her throat. "You're next, ma'am."

Sloan doesn't move. Just looks at me, torn.

"Please don't go," I say, my voice ragged. "This is not who you are. It never was."

Her gaze flicks to the ticket counter, the departure sign for Vegas, and then to me.

"Do you need a ticket?" the woman asks again.

"I'm sorry," she whispers, holding my gaze. For a split second, my stomach bottoms out. She's apologizing to me, choosing to leave, to give up everything we've worked so hard for.

Then she squeezes my hand once, before dropping it. The feel of her ring, imprinted on my thumb, still pulses from the pressure.

She turns toward the ticket counter, and everything in me wants to push myself in front of her, to stop her from leaving.

And then I remember Mom standing in the doorway after Dad left. It cost her so much to hold love open-fisted, to let love go, but she couldn't stop him any more than she could stop the wind.

Sloan steps toward the woman at the counter. "I don't need a ticket after all."

My heart, still in free fall, feels like it's been swooped up. "You're staying?" I ask.

"Unless you want to go to Vegas with me?" she says, her mouth curving mischievously.

"I want to go *everywhere* with you," I reply, pulling her close, the ache inside more intense than before.

We step away from the line into the crush of travelers, some saying goodbye, others sprinting to make a plane that will take them to a new destination. We're standing in the middle of a crossroads and I want to kiss her more than anything. But she puts up a hand to stop me.

"There's one thing we need to discuss first. I know you signed the contract for me, but I can't let you give up everything for this marriage. If we're going to make promises today—vows I mean with my whole heart—I need you to understand something. I don't need protecting from the truth, Vale. I need a partner. A teammate. Someone who comes to me when there's a problem. When your contract is up, we talk. I'm okay with you moving to the NHL, but we decide together. As long as Sully's Beach remains our home base, I won't be the one who holds you back. As your wife, I'll always be the one cheering you on, no matter who you play for. I'm your number one fan, the only woman who'll obnoxiously kiss you in front of an entire hockey crowd."

I rest my forehead against hers, sliding my hands up her back, hitching her flush against my body. "I would love to be your partner . . ." My hands slide over the curve of her waist as my lips brush hers. "Your teammate . . ." I trail my mouth along her cheekbone, leaving three kisses. "And your lover." My hands graze her neck where I tease the corner of her jaw with kisses. "But first, we have a wedding to go to."

She looks up at me, tangles a hand in my hair, and the whole world falls away. "Can we lock the hockey team out of the house afterwards?"

I laugh. "We'll send them to Brendan's."

She smiles. "I can't wait to start the rest of my life with you—for all the unexpected surprises and every night in bed with you."

"I'm never sleeping on the floor again. Unless you're there with me." I kiss her forehead.

"And I'm never sleeping in bed without you again," she murmurs. "We've waited long enough."

"Is that a promise?" I ask.

She tips her mouth to mine, her lips an invitation I can't resist. "Yes, starting tonight."

I crush her body to mine with a kiss that's a mixture of joy and need and a promise to never leave. I don't care if the limo is illegally parked or the press leaks all our secrets. I don't care what the future throws at us. Right now, all I want is us. Her hips press against mine, my hands slide down her spine. Our bodies locked into an embrace where you can't tell where one of us ends and the other begins.

All that matters is the promise to be together, to stay through the happiness and the pain, the mundane and the fullness of life.

We pull apart, foreheads together, as people openly stare at us. Whistling and cheering erupts behind us. We turn to see the rest of the hockey team standing in a half-circle, smiling like proud parents. More than a few phones have captured the moment.

"Forget what *The Star Report* has to say," Brax says. "Once everyone sees this kiss, there will be no doubt about why you got married." We still have some explaining to do, but these guys already have the answer they need.

"Hey, don't we have a wedding to get to?" Tate asks, checking his watch.

"Yes, we do," I say, my arm still hooked around my bride's waist. "So why are you standing around? Let's go."

As the guys disperse, a man stops behind us, his features vaguely familiar. The same eyes, the same sharp cut of cheekbones.

"Sloan, is that you?" he asks.

Sloan turns around, her mouth falling open. "Dad?" she gasps. "What are you doing here?"

"I came for your wedding," he says.

She glances at me. "Do you know anything about this?"

I knit my fingers through hers. "Remember my text earlier— the surprise I wanted to tell you about?" I nod at her father. "You're looking at him."

THIRTY-ONE

Sloan

When we return to the limo, there's a ticket tucked under the wiper, flapping in the wind. Apparently, I abandoned the limousine on a full yellow line with a "No Parking" sign next to it—a tiny detail my brain missed in the chaos of running away.

Vale plucks it from the windshield. "A wedding gift from the local police department."

He holds it up for me, showing me the handwritten message at the bottom: *No ticket today, only a warning. Now go kiss your wife.*

I laugh, feeling the relief lift off my shoulders. After everything that's happened, this is the least of my worries. A feat that shows growth on my part.

Old Sloan from one year ago would have despaired over this ticket, cried pathetic little tears, even. But New Sloan, who's weathered a breakup, a brain injury, and an impromptu Vegas wedding, just smiles. Because honestly, what's a ticket compared to all that? It's nothing to cry over. Not when I've survived so much and come out stronger.

Vale grins, waving the ticket like a victory flag. "Well, at least the police are rooting for us. Maybe we should invite them to the wedding."

"Or have them escort the reporter from our property," I say. "That would be convenient."

"That's what the hockey team is for," Vale tells me as he opens the door for my dad and me to crawl into the back of the limo.

Dad and I find our spots across from each other on the long bench seats, while Vale handles the driving and Brax sees to his brother's car. There's an awkwardness in our eye contact, probably because it's been so long since we last talked. His skin is darker, more weathered than before. But his eyes are the same—tender, open, sad.

He's the same man who's been wandering like a nomad the last few years, always waiting for something—or someone—better to show up. Some people bury their grief, others run from it. My dad fled. At first, this infuriated me. *How could he just leave us?*

But over time, I've come to understand that grief isn't linear or logical. It doesn't make sense, at least not from the outside. Though I wish my father had made a different choice, at least he's still here. Unlike Vale, who never got answers because his dad passed before he had the chance. That's something I've never been able to stop thinking about—the questions left behind, the ache of words unsaid. And while I don't always understand my dad, at least I still have the chance to try.

"How did this even happen?" I ask Vale as he pulls away from the curb. As uncomfortable as this conversation is, Vale is pushing me to face the one thing I would've gladly avoided forever—starting over with my father.

"When I said we were doing things the right way this time around, I meant it," Vale says, looking at me in the rearview mirror. "It took me forever to track him down. When I did, I called and asked for your hand in marriage."

"You asked for permission?"

Vale shakes his head. "Since we were already married, it wasn't permission exactly. More like an honorable gesture, out of respect."

The fact that Vale recognizes this, even if Dad hasn't lived up to his responsibility, means something. As complicated as family is, he's still my father.

Dad folds his hands together. "I'll admit, the phone call caught me off guard. I haven't been around the last few years, and you're on your own now. When he asked my permission to marry you, it reminded me of when I asked for your mother's hand. Granny was fiercely protective of her daughter, and I had to hide my hands to keep her from seeing them shake. Before she said yes, she asked me one question, 'Are you going to be there for her through thick and thin? Because that's what you're asking to do. It's not a marriage unless you stay.'"

His eyes grow soft and distant, reliving the memory. The emotion makes his voice catch. "I haven't always done that for you." He nods, like he knows how hard this is, how I've waited for him to pull the splinter out. "Vale called me on it. Said you deserved a dad who showed up in your life, that I didn't deserve a daughter as good as you. He was right, even though it hurt to hear it. You and Jaz were always so steady. So willing to give everything. Even willing to love your lousy excuse for a father." He looks down, unable to meet my eyes.

I reach across the aisle and take my father's hands in mine, closing the space between us. Until now, I've never considered myself the steady one. Maybe this is what Vale has wanted me to understand from the beginning. That the way I've measured myself—and come up short—is only through a flawed perspective of my own making. Maybe if I'd been kinder to myself and seen my shortcomings with a little more compassion, I wouldn't have considered myself unworthy of love. I wouldn't have been so quick to run away from my fears and seen that when you let love in, it's a sacrifice *and* a kindness. None of us deserves it.

"You were not a lousy father," I tell him. "You were hurting. And I didn't know what to do with that kind of pain."

"You probably think I didn't care, but I did—too much," he admits. "Part of me thought you could never forgive me for the mistakes I made. I told myself it would be easier to love you from a distance. Then I couldn't risk feeling the pain of losing you, like I lost your mother."

The pieces of the past shuffle into place like a deck of cards. Not perfectly, of course, but with more compassion than Old Sloan might have been able to show. It's not that I can dismiss the hard questions. There's still so much to uncover, complicated truths I may not want to face. But with time, maybe I can begin to understand that my father didn't leave because he stopped loving us. He left because love was too risky for him.

Dad scrapes his hand over his beard. "When Vale invited me to your wedding, he begged me to come. Said this was my shot at starting over with you and Jaz." He looks at Vale in the rearview mirror. "Remember what I said?"

"You told me no," Vale says with a laugh. "And that's when I called your dad a coward."

Dad grins, not offended by Vale's remark. "I didn't want to face your sister. She caught me in a mistake I still haven't forgiven myself for. But Vale told me if I ever wanted to make things right, I should come today." He pauses for a beat. "That is, if you'll have me there for the wedding."

I squeeze his hand and hope my eyes don't start leaking all over my wedding dress. The words come out, barely more than a whisper. "It would mean the world to have you stay."

Vale doesn't say anything when he stops the car so I can lean across the aisle to hug my father. He just looks on in the rearview mirror with a silent smile, knowing this is the best gift he could've given me on our wedding day.

———

I tell my dad to wait outside the house until I find Jaz. The guests are already starting to file in to our backyard where we have wooden folding seats on the lawn, facing a beautifully decorated pergola covered with flowers. It's all I ever wanted, really—to marry in Granny's backyard, near the rose gardens. Though *The Star Report's* payment for exclusive coverage could have easily covered any dream wedding venue, I opted for tradition, for a connection to Granny and home and all the things I love.

When I locate Jaz, she's inside taking a phone call, her brow knitted. "It's Scarlett," she whispers to me. "Her car died. Brendan is running over to pick her up. I offered to help."

She turns her attention back to the call. "We'll hold the ceremony until you get here. It's no problem, seriously! See you soon."

My sister, wanting to save the day. She's always been like this—her need to help everyone trumps any of her needs. Right now, she just wants to make sure my wedding is the most amazing one ever and that all the people I love are there.

"Sorry if I just delayed your big day," she says with an apologetic smile.

"I'm not worried about the delay," I say, quietly. "I think we need to talk about what happened earlier. What you heard in the interview."

She looks at me, before her eyes slide to her checklist. "You know I believe you. I've already scheduled a meeting with some lawyers next week. They had no right to blindside you during that interview. We might be able to settle this in court."

I step closer. "I can't place the full blame on them," I say, then wait a beat. "They were only questioning me about what was true."

My sister's head snaps up. "What do you mean?"

"I wasn't prepared for their questions. I didn't know that Vale had turned down the NHL or the insurance problem." I hesitate. "But their accusations about our elopement . . . were not entirely *untrue.*"

She looks behind me, her face panicked. "Where's Vale?" She frowns. "You're not pulling out, are you?"

"No!" I assure her. "He's waiting outside. I wanted to talk to you alone. To make something right before I get married today."

I don't want this to come out rushed or fumble this moment between us. This isn't just about confessing a secret—it's about making our relationship right—something Dad hasn't done until today. I'm choosing to do the best thing for us, even if it hurts. My sister deserves to know what happened, and if I keep it from her, the guilt will eat me alive. For once, I'm being brave enough to face my fears instead of turning and running.

"When Vale and I eloped in Vegas, it wasn't because we had admitted our love for each other. That came later." I fiddle with my fingers.

She narrows her eyes. "What they said . . . was accurate, then?"

I nod. "When Vale found out that I couldn't afford my medicine, he wanted me to have insurance to cover it. He offered to marry me so he could put me on his insurance plan. It was complicated and wrong and I'm so sorry." I dig my palms into my eyes and shake my head. "I made a rash decision, and I should've told you, but when I saw how excited you were, I felt like I couldn't go back."

"So you're not in love?" she asks, clearly confused.

I uncover my eyes, finally meeting her gaze. "No, I *am* in love with Vale. That's the part I couldn't admit back then. When we married the first time, we had feelings for each other—we just didn't want to tell the other person for fear of ruining our friendship. That was the surprise for us—finding out we were both in love. We've had our share of obstacles, but never about how we feel. I'm really sorry, Jaz."

"So you were in love the whole time?" Her face brightens. "I knew it was true."

I shake my head, not understanding. "Didn't I just say that?"

Jaz goes on, "When *The Star Report* claimed you only married for Vale's insurance, I knew it couldn't be right. I could see it in your eyes every time you looked at him."

I blink. "Did you hear me? I apologized for lying to you," I remind her in case she missed it the first time.

"I know."

"And you're okay with it?"

"Sloan, you married your best friend, the guy you fell in love with. If you had to tell yourself you were doing it for the insurance in order to go through with it, how can I blame you? I would've done the same."

My mouth falls open, but I can't get any words out. This isn't what I expected from the woman who's held a very long grudge against our dad. "But what about the fact that Dad lied to us? You said yourself you hate it when people don't tell you the truth."

"I did," she admits. "But there's a difference between your situation and Dad's—and the motivation behind it. Dad lied to cover up something heinous. I couldn't accept that he betrayed our stepmom. But in your case, you did it out of survival."

"I'm not sure that's any better," I say.

"You didn't betray me by standing up for yourself or choosing your health. I'm proud you were brave enough to put yourself first. If you'd asked me before all this whether you should go through with it, I would've said yes, *no question*. Not just because of the insurance, but because you need Vale. You were meant to be together."

I arch an eyebrow. "You would?" Ever since we got married, I've been trying to convince myself of Jaz's arguments against this marriage, when all along, she was for us.

She takes my hands in hers. "He's a good man who loves you. I knew that from the beginning."

I shake my head, the emotion welling up in my eyes. All this time I was terrified about her reaction, sure that she'd lump me together with my father as someone she couldn't forgive. But the truth of the matter is never that simple. Real family will always love you, even when your decisions make no sense to them.

For now, I'm learning how to do that for my father, whose decision to leave was unfathomable to me at the time. I might not have understood why he had to go, or the complications of grief that drove him away, but now I realize he still loved us, in his own way.

I glance out the window and see my father still waiting, leaning against the limo. I rest a hand on my stomach, which is churning from my nerves. I want things to go right for him but I'm not even sure that's possible. "Jaz, there's something I need to tell you."

She glances down at my hand, then back at me. "Wait a minute, are you . . . *pregnant*?"

I blink for a second, then burst out laughing, because that's not even a possibility. "Oh, *definitely* not. And this time, I'm not hiding anything from you."

"For a second I thought . . ." She stops, her face betraying everything. Her hand mirrors mine, resting where the dress stretches tightly over her belly.

"Wait, are you . . .?" I can't even say the words.

She blinks and then slowly nods, a smile spreading across her face. "I found out on our Cancun trip. I was going to tell you, but I hadn't gone to the doctor yet and I wanted to make sure."

"You're having a baby?!" I nearly scream, pulling her into my arms.

"Keep it down. It's still a secret."

"Who knows about this?" I whisper.

"Other than Brax? Nobody. I hated not telling you sooner. This whole time I felt like I was keeping a secret from you."

I shake my head. "But you weren't. It's just like you said before—you didn't betray me by keeping this secret or choosing your health. You just couldn't tell me until it was the right time."

"Are you sure you're not mad?" she asks, her eyes filling with happy tears. "I was so worried I'd steal your thunder today. Like, the ultimate sister fail—totally outshining you on your big day."

"Stop." I put my hand up. "You didn't steal anything. Besides, if anyone's going to outshine me, I'd want it to be you."

She wipes the corners of her eyes, and her makeup smears, so I hand her a tissue. This is what sisters do. We fix each other's mistakes. We keep trying even when we fail. We'll never do it perfectly, but if we show up when the other person needs us, that fixes ninety-nine percent of the mistakes we make.

She crumples the tissue I gave her and tucks it into her bra.

I snort-laugh.

She shrugs. "In case I get teary during the ceremony. My hormones are raging with this baby!" she says with a laugh. "Now what's the other surprise you wanted to tell me?"

I glance out the window where Dad paces the sidewalk. This can't wait, or Dad will lose his nerve. I'm like him that way—or at least, I was. *But people change, if you let them.*

"How much time do we have?" I ask. "There's someone you need to talk to."

She looks at me, wide-eyed. "But the wedding . . .?"

"It can wait a few more minutes," I say, grabbing her hand and pulling her toward the door. "There's someone else who definitely needs to hear this news."

———

By the time I'm ready to walk down the aisle, I've already cried twice, belly laughed a half-dozen times, and hugged my family and the entire hockey team. But it was all worth it, especially after witnessing what just happened between Dad and Jaz. One conversation hasn't fixed everything—far from it—but it cracked open a door. A door that could possibly lead to something better.

Dad apologized for what happened, for his shortcomings as a father, and the way he left things. He's been rehearsing this speech since we arrived in the limo, but my guess is that he's been thinking about it for far longer. When he finished, he hugged her, and she let him. Maybe it's the new reality of her becoming a parent herself, and realizing just how much that changes things. Sharing that news with him became an unexpected way to try again. As long as we can believe we're not defined by our mistakes, there's hope for all of us. Maybe, just maybe, we can still be a family.

Which is why, just before the ceremony begins, I ask my father to walk me down the aisle. Not out of obligation, but because this is how you start over again.

I smooth my skirt, and hook my arm through my father's as Jaz scrubs the streaks off my face with her tissue.

"Are you sure this is necessary?" I ask. "*The Star Report* might like the scary-bride look." Brax and Leo already kicked out the journalist after Jaz told him what happened. We can't stop him from leaking the news now, but I also know it will blow over in time. Especially after people see the video of us kissing at the airport.

"My job is to make you look good. That's what sisters do." She wipes my cheek one final time. "Vegas has nothing on today's party. I want this to be the best wedding you've ever had."

I look at her and smile. "It already is."

THIRTY-TWO

Vale

"It's only our third try at a honeymoon if you count Vegas," I say as we get out of the limo—the same one Sloan stole earlier—and head toward the log cabin buried deep in the Carolina woods. After the wedding, I surprised Sloan with an Airbnb tucked just outside Sully's Beach in a remote spot where the hockey team won't be able to track us down—at least not if I can help it. Tonight's our wedding night, and I've waited a long time for this moment. After everything we've been through, I don't want *any* interruptions.

When we open the door, the soft glow of the cabin welcomes us, and the big picture window frames a gorgeous view of the woods. But honestly, the only thing I want to stare at tonight is my wife. Who needs a view when I've got the most beautiful distraction right here?

I turn to Sloan and slip my hands around her waist—just as my phone rings in my pocket.

My stomach flips when I see the name on the screen. "It's Dr. Phillips." Why would he be calling on the weekend? "Should I answer it?"

"If you don't, I will," Sloan says, trying to steal the phone from me.

Guess that's my cue to answer. "What's up, Doc?" I say, dropping our bags in the living room. "Don't tell me you're working on a Saturday."

"Not if I can help it, but this was too important. I didn't interrupt anything, did I?"

I chuckle. "Well, only our wedding night." Sloan stifles a laugh as I turn on the speakerphone.

"Oh, I'm so sorry!" he says, clearly embarrassed. "This is NOT that urgent!"

"As long as it's good news, you've got exactly one minute," I half joke. I'm counting down the seconds until I can finally have this woman all to myself.

"I thought you'd want to know right away. I just got news that the insurance company approved our appeal. Sloan's medicine will be fully covered."

"Are you serious?" I burst out as Sloan claps her hands over her mouth and silently screams.

"Hopefully that was worth the interruption," he adds.

"We're both thrilled," I say with a laugh, throwing my arms around Sloan and lifting her off the ground.

"I'll let you get to more important matters. Enjoy the rest of your night—and don't worry, no more calls from me."

I hang up and turn to Sloan, who's watching me with a knowing grin.

"I think you were more worried about this than I was," she says.

I let out a long exhale and rub the back of my neck. "All I've ever wanted was for you to be happy and healthy. I could do something about the first, but the second was harder."

"Nothing makes me happier than being with you," she says, wrapping her arms around my shoulders.

"Now, where were we?" I say, nuzzling my nose into the curve of her neck. My lips trail over her skin, leaving a line of kisses across her collarbone.

My phone rings again. "You've gotta be kidding me," I growl, pulling my phone from my pocket. "It's Brax. We're ignoring it."

"No!" Sloan shouts. "What if it's about my sister? Or the baby?"

I sigh. "Okay, fine. I'll give him five minutes, but that's it." I turn on the video call, and Brax's face fills the screen. "This better be important."

"Don't blame me," Brax says. "I was overruled."

The phone is yanked away, and suddenly Jaz, Tate, and Leo are all there, battling for screen time. "Turn the phone around so I can see your place," Jaz asks.

Sloan takes the phone and shows off our quaint, one-bedroom cabin, complete with a fireplace and hot tub.

The screen jerks, and Tate's big mug fills the frame. "I just want to state, for the record, I told them crashing your honeymoon was a terrible idea. But hey, what kind of honeymoon would it be without us barging in?"

"It would be the best day of my life," I deadpan. "Now, if you'll excuse us . . ."

"Hang on a second, I didn't get my time." Leo elbows Tate out of the way, giving us an unfortunate close-up of his nose. "I just wanted to give you some wedding night advice."

"Oh, great," I mutter. Sloan coughs out a laugh.

"For dudes who need help in the romance department," Leo says.

"I think I'm fine in that department, thanks," I reply.

Leo ignores me and goes on, "Some women have told me I'm a magnet for the opposite sex."

"You know magnets work two ways," Tate interrupts. "They attract *and* repel."

"Shut up, Tate," Leo snaps. "As I was saying, women need romance. The emotional connection . . ."

"Go on, this is highly amusing," Brax says, folding his arms.

Leo frowns. "You might be surprised, but underneath this

scowl, I'm quite the romantic. I just don't show you clowns that side of me."

"Are you going to use your moves on Victoria?" Sloan asks with a mischievous smile.

"I'm not dating Victoria," he shoots back. "Just helping her out for the next few months."

"As her new skating partner," Jaz adds.

"Figure skating?" I burst out laughing. "Oh man, I cannot wait to see you in a sparkly jumpsuit."

Leo rolls his eyes. "I'm not competing with her. It's just for practice. Coach said Victoria needs a temporary skating partner, and I'd be perfect for the job."

"I thought Coach called it your community service after you lost your temper in a game?" Brax clarifies.

Leo huffs. "Details, details."

"It doesn't hurt that she's hot," Tate remarks.

Leo gives Tate a death glare. "I can't help it if she happens to be pretty."

"What a noble sacrifice," I mutter.

Leo holds up a finger. "Listen, I knew her back in college. We even dated for a while. She's the bossiest woman I've ever met."

"Kind of like a female version of you," Brax says, and we all laugh except for Leo, who's scowling.

Apparently Leo has met his match in the form of an attractive female figure skater.

"Well, guys, I hate to cut this short . . ." I stop, then rephrase. "Actually, I don't hate it at all. I'm quite looking forward to cutting you off."

Brax laughs. "Yeah, yeah, get back to your wedding night. We'll see you when the honeymoon's over."

"*If* we come back," I add just before turning off the phone. Finally, no more interruptions.

Sloan smiles up at me. "You think you can survive a whole night without your team calling?"

I grin. "I think I'll manage." Then I pull her closer, my voice low. "Besides, according to our marriage rules, I think there's one more thing we haven't done."

"I wonder what that is?" Sloan asks with an innocent smile that tells me she knows *exactly* what it is.

She wraps her arms around my neck and starts to trail kisses along my jaw, which makes my whole body practically melt.

"As good as that feels," I say, pulling away slightly, "I don't want to rush tonight. I've waited so long for this."

A smile tugs at the corners of her lips. "So you're saying you want to watch a movie first?"

A low laugh rumbles out of me. "I definitely do *not* want to watch a movie." I trace the outline of her lips with my thumb. "I want to watch you. Memorize every part of you. Starting with this."

I leave a soft kiss on her collarbone as I trace the curve of her neck with my knuckles.

"And this."

Then I move to the side of her neck, sliding my fingers into her hair.

"And this."

I tease her earlobe with my lips before whispering, "But first, I have another surprise."

She looks unconvinced. "If any more surprise guests interrupt, I'm going to kick them out . . . *personally*."

I laugh. "No surprise guests tonight. I promise." Then I take her hand and lead her to the bedroom. "You'll see."

Her gaze lands on the bed. Rose petals cover the entire bed, just like in our Cancun honeymoon suite.

Her mouth falls open. "Did you do this?"

"I always remembered that night in Cancun," I say. "It wasn't the right time, and we weren't ready for that step. You had to learn to trust me first."

"Which was so aggravating and sexy, I could hardly stand it."

"It was worth it, if it means I get to have you now," I say.

Her eyes hold mine. "I've replayed the moment in my head more times than I can count."

I pull her body close to me, feel my heart thrumming against my chest. "So have I."

She reaches up to kiss me, and I place a finger on her lips, stopping her. "Before we move on, I have one request."

She looks at me, puzzled. "What is it?"

I take her wrist in my hand, my thumb circling it lightly. "The question game."

She frowns. "The game we played at the waterfall?"

"We never finished," I say, my lips kissing each of her wrists.

Her eyes spark. "I think it's because you were too busy kissing me."

"Well, you were highly distracting in that swimsuit. I totally lost my train of thought." I trace my finger across her arm as goose bumps flood her skin. Just thinking about it makes me want to toss these cards aside and skip to the good part. But I'm taking it slow tonight, letting Sloan lead.

Her eyelids flutter as she inches closer to me. "If you do that again, we're never going to start—let alone finish—this game." She pulls away gently, giving me a look that says I'm dangerous.

"One final round of the question game. You either answer or lose a point. Whoever gets the most points gets to initiate our first kiss tonight."

She looks me over skeptically. "What's your game, MacPherson? You could just kiss me now. I won't stop you."

I lift an eyebrow. "Impatient, are we?"

Her cheeks flush lightly. "Maybe a little."

"Sloan, I want to savor tonight with you—for as long as possible." I pull out three cards from my pocket, handing her a card. She skims over the question. "You can't ask this." She turns the card around. *"What did Jaz's note from the honeymoon say—the one you kept hidden?"*

I lift an eyebrow. "I figured if you couldn't tell me then, it must be important."

She bites her lip. "You really want to know?"

"I wouldn't have asked otherwise." A slow grin spreads across my face. "But if you want to lose the game, I wouldn't hate that either."

"You sneaky thing," she says with a smirk. "Jaz's advice was something I needed to hear, even if I didn't realize it at the time. The first part of her note said to always say yes when you asked me to do something, even if it scared me . . . or involved putting on a swimsuit. That's why I agreed to all those dates on our honeymoon." She pauses for a beat. "But the second part was harder. She told me not to be afraid to tell you the truth, even if it was something difficult. That night in the hot tub, when I finally said you're the one I wanted to be with, was me admitting the truth I'd been avoiding for too long. I'd learned that trust is earned, not given easily. And you were incredibly patient, helping me say yes to things I wouldn't have otherwise."

I lean in closer. "Being patient—waiting for you—may have been the hardest thing I've ever done."

Sloan smirks. "Now who's the impatient one?"

I hold up my card. "It wouldn't be fair if I didn't answer a question." Then I turn the card around so she can see it. "*What is the one rule we haven't broken?*"

"You already know the answer," she protests.

"I do, but where's the fun if we don't make it official? The only rule we haven't broken is the one we're about to *shatter* tonight—like an Olympic record."

She steps closer, her eyes saying *yes* as my body feels that pull, but I hold up a hand. "Not until we've finished the game."

Her eyes ask—no, *beg* me to kiss her, but I don't give in, even though I want to. "Last question is yours." I nod toward the lone card.

"I have a feeling you've got something up your sleeve," she

says, eyeing me warily. She reads it, then looks up at me, puzzled. "You're letting me win?"

I smirk. "You forgot. In this game, everyone wins."

She reads the card slowly. *"Is there anything Vale wouldn't do for Sloan?"* Then she shakes her head. "I already know the answer. You'd do anything for me. The fact that you married me in Vegas—and risked your reputation. You even delayed your NHL dreams for me."

"I'd do it all over again in a heartbeat," I say softly. "You were always worth whatever I was giving up." I cup her face with my hands, tip her chin toward me.

"Then I win?" she asks with a gleeful smile, wrapping her arms around my neck.

"Not quite," I say, watching her closely. "There's one thing I wouldn't do for you—and I need to tell you now."

"Now?" She frowns. "You couldn't say it later, at a more convenient time?"

"Absolutely not," I say with a grin, sitting on the bed so I can have her full attention. "The one thing I won't do—the one thing I'll never consider—is setting an end date for our marriage. The first time you asked, I was *livid* that you'd even think I'd agree to it. Because even back then, I already knew what I know now: I want you, I've always wanted you. I've waited my whole life to make you mine. That's the one thing you can't ask, the one thing I'll refuse—every single time."

She takes it in, pressing her body closer to mine. "Does this mean the game is over and we can finally move things along? Because in case you didn't notice, I'm okay with losing this game."

Something sparks in my chest. The way she's looking at me from under her dark lashes makes me want to surrender everything to her. I'm at her feet now, completely hers.

I wrap my arms around her waist and tip my face to hers. "As long as you answer one question for me: Are you ready to be my wife? Because tonight, you lead. I'm yours, if you'll have me."

Even though I won the game, I'm letting her make the first move, because that's what marriage is. Giving more than you take, making life glorious and beautiful in the most unexpected ways.

She doesn't answer. She leaps without looking back. She launches herself into my arms, an unspoken *yes, I love you. Again and again.*

THIRTY-THREE

Epilogue

SLOAN

Our First New Year's Eve as Husband and Wife

"Why does it look like Santa dropped off his luggage to stay for a week?" Leo barks when he spies three suitcases and a giant box stacked in the back hall.

The leftover decorations are still twinkling from Christmas as we gear up for tonight's festivities. Since the team spends Christmas with their families, we always celebrate the holidays together on New Year's Eve.

"Not Santa. Someone cuter," I say, as the chime of the oven timer cuts through the rowdy crowd playing holiday charades in the dining room. I flip on the interior oven light to check that the Christmas bread knots are puffy and golden, the white glaze melting over them like snow on a mountaintop. I pull them out of the oven, eyeing the clock. Not long until midnight and barely enough time to prepare Leo for our mystery houseguest.

The fresh rolls are heavy on the cinnamon and vanilla and fill the house with the glorious scent of home. Lights twinkle around the windows and a fat, slightly misshapen Christmas tree fills the corner of the living room, its branches weighed down by teal, red, and gold balls, the Crushers' colors. The fire crackles in the fireplace as overcrowded stockings line the mantel. This year, Jaz decided to gift the entire team Crushers' stockings, decorated with the logo and each player's number.

When we first bought the house and rented out rooms to a few hockey players, we hosted a New Year's Eve party, complete with ridiculous holiday games and toasts at midnight. It's become an annual tradition now, along with most of the team, a few friends, and some staff crammed into the dining room, picking the buffet clean like vultures. They're tossing out outlandish guesses for charades—things like "Santa stuck in a chimney" and "Mrs. Claus wrestling a reindeer." And, in true Crushers' fashion, the competitiveness makes it feel like we're one big, dysfunctional family.

In the background, Elvis bemoans his "Blue Christmas," and Dad nurses a Christmas mule drink next to the fire, discussing the best Christmas movies with Tate.

"I like *It's a Wonderful Life* and *A Christmas Story*," Dad says.

"*Die Hard* is the best Christmas movie ever!" Leo shouts from the hallway where he's trying to figure out who our mystery guest is.

"*Die Hard* is not a Christmas movie," Tate fires back.

"It has Christmas in it—that makes it a Christmas movie," Leo argues.

Dad chuckles, then looks at me, and I offer him a smile that says I'm glad he's here. I'm working on feeling excited about having him in my life again, rather than being nervous about what the future might hold. This is only his second visit since the wedding, and we're still figuring out how to be a family again. He's not a completely different person, but it seems like he's trying. We all are.

There's a thud in the hallway as Leo shouts a muffled "What in the . . ." before I realize what's happened.

"Drop a suitcase on your foot?" I ask, lining one of Granny's Christmas trays with the fresh bread knots.

Vale laughs, then wraps an arm around my waist, tugging me closer. "He deserves it for being a Grinch during our holiday party."

Leo limps into the kitchen, his brow knitted in frustration. "Who's responsible for the pink suitcases? I'm pretty sure the small one is packed with bricks."

I hand Vale the tray before turning to Leo. "I'll give you three hints. She's prettier than you, skates well, and her apartment has water everywhere."

Leo huffs out a frustrated growl, his eyes pure fire. "It's Victoria's stuff, isn't it? Please tell me she's making a donation to the needy and not staying here."

"Oh she's staying," I confirm. "And not just for one night."

"You can't let her stay here," he argues.

"Why not?" Vale asks, still holding the tray of Christmas rolls while wearing Granny's Christmas apron that looks adorably out of place on his stellar body.

"Because she's . . ." Leo searches for the word.

"Annoyingly pretty?" I ask.

"Inconveniently immune to your charms?" Vale adds.

"I was going to say unpleasant," Leo corrects us.

"Maybe you should try being nice to her," Vale suggests, as he steals one of the Christmas knots, inhaling it before I can swat his hand away.

"I have tried, but she's impossible."

"And you're so easy to live with?" I arch an eyebrow.

He doesn't deny this, but he can't stand that he's met his match—fire colliding with fire.

"You'll survive," I tell Leo unsympathetically. "Her pipes burst in her apartment due to the cold snap. She got the water turned off, but it's a disaster. And with it being the holidays, she has to wait for someone to fix the damage. In this weather, I'm not turning down someone who needs our help over the holidays."

He drags a hand through his hair and exhales loudly. "Well, she's not staying upstairs . . . or using my bathroom. The last thing I need is her bath gel hoarding space in my shower."

"You don't want to smell like Japanese cherry blossoms?" I ask with a smirk.

Vale leans against the counter. "My old room is the only one we have, unless you want to volunteer yours?"

He scoffs. "I'd rather sleep next to Tate before I give that woman anything of mine. As long as she's here, I'm going to lock myself in my room. Pretend she doesn't exist."

"Let me know how that works out for you," Vale says with a wink. "By the way, she's coming to the party any minute."

His eyebrows fly up. "Tonight?"

"Rourke invited her." I point my spatula at him. "Which means you need to be nice."

Leo smirks. "During the holidays, there are only two choices —naughty or nice. And I think we both know which one I'm leaning toward."

"It's only for a few days," Vale says, taking another Christmas knot. This time I pull it away before he stuffs it in his mouth.

Leo crosses his arms. "Then I'll gladly pay for a hotel room. But she can't stay here."

"Who can't be here?" Tate asks, suddenly appearing in the kitchen with an empty bowl. "By the way, we're out of the holiday pretzel mix."

"Again?" I ask, even though I secretly love that the guys inhale whatever I put in front of them.

I pass him another bowl of the chocolate-covered peanuts-caramel corn-and-pretzel mix. "By the way, Victoria's moving in temporarily." Then I nod toward Leo, who's rubbing his sore foot. "Scrooge here wants to put her up in a hotel when the weather is terrible."

"It's already snowing," Tate says, glancing out the window. "And it *never* snows here."

"Perfect for the ice queen," Leo mutters.

"Oh come on, Leo, where's your holiday spirit?" I tweak his cheek as the doorbell rings. Since it only rings every fourth time or so, this is a minor Christmas miracle.

"Hello?" Victoria's voice calls from the hall.

Leo scowls.

I bat his arm. "You look like you swallowed a grumpy elf." Then I give him a warning look before I leave to welcome Victoria.

Victoria stands in the front hall, admiring the small Christmas tree on a table as she shrugs off her red wool coat dusted in snowflakes. "It's like a snow globe out there—even the roads are turning into a skating rink."

She's holding a dozen snowman cookies on a plate, wearing a cute white stocking cap with a furry ball on top. It matches the soft white sweater that slips off one shoulder.

Rourke appears in the hall behind me, grinning like he's up to something. "Here, let me help," he says, taking her cookies. "Sounds like the roads are too bad to drive home tonight. I call first dibs on the couch!"

Given the way he's suddenly turned on the charm, he's clearly staking his claim on our pretty guest.

"No, you can't," Leo barks, standing in the corner of the dining room with arms crossed, looking surly.

"Why do you care? You already have a bed here," Rourke argues.

"I don't care about *you*," Leo argues as his jaw tightens. "But you're not staying here. You can skate home if it's that bad." He shoots Rourke a dark look.

I clear my throat, and give Victoria an apologetic smile. "Maybe you can join Jaz in the dining room for charades. They're just starting another round."

Jaz waves from the dining room, her adorable baby bump peeking from under her shirt.

"She can be on my team," Rourke volunteers.

Leo hangs back, his eyes following Victoria and Rourke to their seats. He looks like he's about to shoot flaming darts from his eyes and pin Rourke to the ground.

I grab Vale in the kitchen. "You need to play referee."

He frowns. "But I thought I was helping you in the kitchen tonight. I'm not risking your health on those two idiots." He wraps his arms around me and pulls me closer, kissing my nose.

"Vale, I've never felt better, and I haven't fainted since our honeymoon. But I'm afraid of a hockey brawl breaking out over a certain figure skater. Here . . ." I grab a tray of holiday cheesecake, drizzled in strawberry and chocolate sauce, and shove it into Vale's hands. "Distract them with dessert."

For the next hour, Vale passes out cheesecake and keeps our holiday charades civil, until the game ends in a tie. When I finally join the party in the living room, Victoria is chatting with Jaz by the fireplace, while Leo moves to sit with Lauren, our PR director. Victoria takes a sip of her drink, her eyes flicking to Leo who's laughing at something Lauren says. Jaz and I exchange a knowing look.

"So, Victoria, how was your Christmas?" I ask, trying to lighten the mood.

She shrugs. "The usual. Tense and awkward," she says, giving me a weary smile. "I was so relieved when Rourke invited me tonight. It gave me a legitimate excuse for not attending my parents' party."

Rourke perks up across the room at the sound of his name and makes his way over, his gaze pinned on Victoria. It's not that I care if Rourke flirts with our guest. The real problem is that Leo cares . . . a little too much.

"Hey, Rourke," Victoria says. "Do you have some kind of superhuman hearing? We were literally just talking about you."

Rourke raises an eyebrow, clearly amused. "Well, I wouldn't

want to brag, but I have a lot of superpowers." He grins and flexes slightly. "Might have something to do with these guns."

Victoria laughs, then lightly touches his arm. "Is that the secret?"

Across the room, Leo's attention snaps toward us. His jaw clenches as he watches Victoria, her laugh a little too forced, her hand lingering on Rourke's arm. Lauren says something to him, but he doesn't respond—his focus is locked on Victoria.

"Hey, Rourke," Leo calls out, his voice louder than necessary as he strides over, a fake smile plastered on his face. "Didn't know you were taking tips from me."

Rourke nearly chokes on his eggnog. "You? Everyone knows I'm the team's heartthrob."

A strained laugh comes out of Leo's mouth, and I can tell Rourke's grating on his nerves. "I seriously question that."

The problem with *Leo the Ego* is that he won't back down. Even if he doesn't actually want to date Victoria, he's not about to let Rourke win.

"Let Victoria decide," Rourke says, turning to her. "Who's the bigger heartthrob?"

Victoria glances between the two hockey players, her lips quirking before she locks eyes with Leo. "At least Rourke knows how to charm a lady."

"Does he?" Leo says cooly. There's no anger in his eyes—just a spark, like he's enjoying the challenge.

I spin around to find Vale, but he's nowhere in sight. "Do you know where Vale went?" I whisper to Jaz.

"I saw him step outside to take a call," she says. "He told Brax it was important."

Jaz hurries off to track down the brothers while I step into the middle of the living room, raising my glass. "Alright, since it's almost the new year, has anyone made a resolution they actually plan on sticking to this time?"

Tate sits on the arm of the couch. "I'm going to stop

pretending I like kale smoothies. It's basically grass, and I'm done pretending it's not."

Everyone laughs, their high spirits fueled by eggnog and Christmas mules. I sneak a glance toward the door, waiting for Vale to come back in. He's been outside for a few minutes now, and it's either his mom wishing him a happy New Year, or something big is happening.

"Well, Jaz and I have an announcement for the team," I say. "We're starting a new social media account and this will be unlike anything we've ever done."

"How's that news?" Jaxon asks.

"Because the account is a fan account, called *Crushin' on Crushers*. It's for people who want to submit their fan love for a player. They fill out an anonymous form and we post it."

"You mean a place they can troll us?" Leo asks.

Jaz suddenly comes inside, her cheeks pink from the cold, jumping right into the conversation. "No, it's a place where they can give an anonymous shoutout to their favorite players. We want to encourage more women to attend hockey games and shift your reputations from macho men to sweethearts."

"Who said we want to be sweethearts?" Leo asks, crossing his arms. "I'm okay with our image."

Okay, so maybe this is going to be a harder sell with the team than I thought. But the women we've talked to love the idea. If it boosts interest in the team—and our attendance numbers—we'll consider it a win.

"Funny thing, Leo," I say with a smile. "You were the first person who got a shoutout."

"Really?" He sits up a little straighter. "What's it say?"

I lift a shoulder. "I thought you weren't interested?"

"I'm not . . ." he backpedals.

"Then you'll have to wait and see," I say. "We'll officially start posting them after the New Year and continue to the end of the season."

Suddenly, the door swings open, and Vale steps back inside

with his brother, his face lit up with the biggest smile I've ever seen. His cheeks are red from the cold as he strides toward me, his eyes locking with mine.

"What happened?" I ask.

Vale pulls me close and whispers in my ear, "That was my agent. I got it. The NHL contract with Tampa."

My breath catches, and I pull back to look at him, and see the joy on his face.

"Vale, that's amazing!" I shriek, but my voice is lost in the swell of laughter and Christmas music. "How did this happen?"

"After my agent said the short-term contract was up at the end of the year, you told me to take the offer with the best contract. Jimmy went straight to Tampa. Apparently, they didn't want to wait until after the New Year. They sent the contract tonight." He pauses to study me. "Are you sure you're okay with this?"

"I couldn't be happier," I murmur. "As long as this is home for you."

"*You* are home for me." He slips his arms around my waist, the smell of cinnamon and fresh snow wrapping around me. My heart kicks up as he leans closer. Vale kisses the side of my neck, reminding me all the ways he loves me. I snuggle into his warmth, leaning into his chest, and when his lips find mine, I drink him in. It's the best feeling in the world to be loved by my husband, and though I'd like to kiss him more, I have to keep this PG-rated in front of my dad.

"Hey, everyone, it's time for the countdown to midnight!" Jaz announces. A few people group up, ready to hug whoever is close by when the clock strikes the hour.

"Ten, nine, eight . . ." We count down together before the clock hits midnight and the room erupts with cheers, confetti, and the clink of glasses. Everyone is hugging, kissing, and celebrating, but I can't stop staring at Vale, feeling like this moment is ours. He leans down and kisses me, slow and tender this time, his hands cradling my face. The world seems to pause, just for us, as if this moment will never end. So many things have changed, but this will be the one thing that lasts—*us together, always.*

I glance over Vale's shoulder and catch sight of Leo and Victoria standing awkwardly near the back of the room. Leo shifts his weight and tips a drink to his lips, while Victoria crosses her arms, looking anywhere but at him.

"Look at them," I whisper to Vale. "It's like they're trying to pretend the other person doesn't exist."

"He's got it bad," Vale remarks.

"You think?" I feel my eyebrows lift.

"It's so obvious it hurts to watch him."

Suddenly, Victoria turns to Leo and says something. He freezes for a beat, before he steps forward, and pulls her in for a kiss. Then he pulls back and walks away, like it never happened.

I cover my mouth to stifle a laugh. "It's about time."

Vale wraps his arm around my waist, pulling me closer. "New Year's magic," he murmurs against my ear.

Everyone is loading up on food and drinks again as my dad turns to us. "How did you guys end up married in Vegas again? I haven't heard the full story."

The room quiets and everyone shifts toward us.

"Vale pretended to be her fiancé to make her ex-boyfriend jealous," Brax puts in.

"Why haven't I heard this before?" Victoria asks.

"Leo didn't tell you?" Jaz asks.

Victoria shakes her head.

"It's our perfect wedding story." Vale grins, his hand stroking my back lightly. "Never planned to elope in Vegas."

Victoria claps her hands together. "I adore surprise Vegas weddings. Go on."

I look at Vale, who's watching me with a smile that invites me to tell the story. His grin unlocks my heart, like a tiny key opening a diary, as sunlight falls across the pages of our story.

He squeezes my hand and waits for me to begin. He knows I

love this story. "It all started when I woke up to an impossibly good dream."

————

If you enjoyed this book, be sure to check out the next book featuring Leo and Victoria's story: *Perfectly Faked.*

BONUS SCENE
Want to see Vale and Sloan's wedding day?
Get the bonus scene here or find it at graceworthington.com.

The Next Book: Perfectly Faked

Book Two in a Hockey Spinoff Series about the Carolina Crushers

He's a hot-headed hockey star. A grump with broody glare. Hater of playing by the rules. Bigger hater of figure skaters like me. And now . . . my new skating partner.

I've spent my entire life working for a shot at Nationals, but when my figure skating partner gets an injury right before the biggest season of my career, my chances of making a comeback vanish overnight.

Until my dad—the Carolina Crushers hockey coach—forces me to pair up with the last person I'd ever choose as my partner: Leo Anderson. Sure, he's got the whole brooding, bad-boy thing down, but he's also got anger issues that land him in trouble with my dad's team.

He's on probation, forced to serve his community service hours with me, and my dad thinks I'm the perfect way to kill two birds with one hockey stick.

Leo needs to fulfill his hours to get back in the game. I need to revive my skating career with a new partner, and we both need this partnership to work so we can rebuild our flailing careers.

The only hitch? Leo also happens to be my ridiculously hot ex-boyfriend. You know, the guy I never quite got over.

When I accidentally confess my lingering feelings to a stranger, the news spreads like wildfire. Overnight, Leo and I become America's hottest "it" couple, and sponsorships start rolling in. So, what's the harm if we pretend we really are together? A fake relationship might be exactly what we need.

Except the more time we spend together, the harder it gets to tell what's real and what's fake. His touch feels like more than just an act, and the way he looks at me? Let's just say I'm in serious danger of losing my heart over a guy I can't have.

Because I learned my lesson before: hockey players and figure skaters don't stand a chance at love.

But when our fake dating breaks the rules and sparks start to fly, I'm going to have to decide whether to save my career—or risk everything for a second chance at love.

Get it on Amazon.

Author Note and Acknowledgments

Originally, I'd only planned to write Brax and Jaz's story in *The Roommate Remodel* and wrap up my journey with hockey romances there. But readers kept asking when the next hockey book was coming, and, truthfully, I loved the idea. This fictional team of hockey players, who felt like family, had taken root in my mind, and I couldn't just leave them hanging.

What I didn't anticipate was how challenging it would be to write a marriage-of-convenience story that felt real and meaningful.

I wanted to create a story where marriage was taken seriously, where my characters grappled with the promises they made and asked themselves tough questions: Am I ready to commit to this person for the long haul? Can I be the person I want to be in this marriage? What does it truly mean to make a promise? Those aren't easy questions, even under perfect circumstances. And given the trauma these characters carried from past experiences, every challenge they faced became that much more complex.

In the end, I wanted this book to show that people can overcome their past traumas. They can change. They can make a promise and stand by it. Marriage can be an incredibly hard thing and, at the same time, an exceptionally beautiful one. But in exploring these questions, I came to understand the heart of their journey—and, ultimately, that's thanks to you, my readers, who pushed me to write this book.

To everyone who helped bring this story to life—thank you from the bottom of my heart.

To my readers who give me the most loving feedback and encouragement ever: Heidi, Joy and Wendy, I owe you so much. Thank you for your support and encouragement and for reading my early drafts.

Thanks to my editor Emily Poole who continues to shape my work and keep it polished, and my proofreader, Judy Zweifel. Thanks to Melissa at Alt 19 Creative for the character designs.

To the ARC readers, bookstagrammers, and booktok community: You're rockstars and I wish I could hug each one of you for so generously sharing Vale and Sloan's story. It means so much to see the love you give these characters. I only wish I wrote faster so I could give you more stories to devour. What you do for the book community is huge and you're inspiring so many people to discover new books.

Thanks to those author friends who've offered me the pep talks I've needed in my moments of doubt.

To my family, I love you and am so grateful to be your mom.

For Sam, there's a piece of you in every book I write, but being married to you is so much better. You're the real deal. My first reader. And the best thing that's ever happened to me.

—Grace

Carolina Crushers Hockey Roster

Brax MacPherson: Center. "Big Mac." Married to Jaz. Featured in *The Roommate Remodel*. Twin to Vale.

Vale MacPherson: Right winger. "Phersonator." Married to Sloan. Twin to Brax.

Leo Anderson: Left winger. "Ego." Cocky and competitive. Love interest is Victoria, who is also the coach's daughter.

Dawson Hayes: Goalie. Cinnamon roll. Featured in *The Friend Face Off*. Moves from the Carolina Crushers to the Ice Breakers. Love interest is Emmy.

Tate Foster: Defenseman. "Sheriff." Book-reading grump who likes rules.

Lucian Lowe: Captain of the team. Defenseman. "Ice Man."

Rourke Riley: Defenseman. Rival to Leo.

Jaxon: Defenseman. Friend to Rourke.

Coach Jenkins: New coach for the Crushers after the previous coach retired. His daughter, Victoria, is Leo's love interest.

Brendan: Part of the main friend group from the *Renovation Romance* series and a good friend to Jaz. He's the conditioning coach for the Crushers.

Rafael Marco: New owner of the Carolina Crushers. Brendan's uncle.

Also by Grace Worthington

**All books are standalone novels with interconnected characters.
You can read these in any order that makes you happy!**

PERFECT CRUSH HOCKEY ROMANCE

Perfectly Wedded

Perfectly Faked

Perfectly Grumpy

Perfectly Complicated Christmas Romance

Perfectly Pretend

THE RENOVATION ROMANCE ROMCOMS

The Neighbor Renovation

The Second Chance Fixer Upper

The Mistletoe Makeover

The Roommate Remodel (Start here for hockey romance!)

THE WILD HARBOR BEACH SERIES

Love at Wild Harbor

Summer Nights in Wild Harbor

Christmas Wishes in Wild Harbor

The Inn at Wild Harbor

A Wedding in Wild Harbor

The Wild Harbor Beach Collection

LOVE ON THIN ICE

The Friend Face Off

The Icing on the Cake

Check out Grace's entire backlist here.

Romcom Novella

THE DATING HYPOTHESIS

What happens when you're forced to team up with the MOST infuriating man alive for a research experiment on dating?

You make sure you don't fall for him. Easy, right?
Not when it's the guy known as Dr. Romeo.

The Dating Hypothesis is a free prequel novella when you join Grace Worthington's newsletter at graceworthington.com.

Grace Worthington is a three-time award-winning author who lives and breathes sweet romcoms.

A former musical theatre gal and playwright, she brings that same energy, heart, and comedic timing to her stories, crafting witty banter and lovable characters you can't help but root for.

She holds a master's degree in psychology and human development and has also completed graduate studies in creative writing. Her inspiration comes from classic romcoms from the '80s and '90s.

When she's not writing, she enjoys spending time with her husband and two kids.

Follow Grace on Amazon to be notified of future releases or follow Grace on Instagram.

FREE ROMCOM NOVELLA

Get a free novella or a bonus epilogue for *Perfectly Faked* at
graceworthington.com